D0629811

IMPOSTOR

SUSANNE
WINNACKER

razOr bill

An Imprint of
Penguin Group (USA) Inc.

Published by the Penguin Group
Penguin Group (USA) Inc., 375 Hudson Street, New York, New York 10014, USA
Penguin Group (Canada), 90 Eglinton Avenue East, Suite 700, Toronto, Ontario M4P
2Y3, Canada (a division of Pearson Penguin Canada Inc.)
Penguin Books Ltd, 80 Strand, London WC2R 0RL, England
Penguin Ireland, 25 St Stephen's Green, Dublin 2, Ireland (a division of Penguin Books Ltd)
Penguin Group (Australia), 707 Collins St., Melbourne, Victoria 3008, Australia
(a division of Pearson Australia Group Pty Ltd)
Penguin Books India Pvt Ltd, 11 Community Centre, Panchsheel Park,
New Delhi–110 017, India
Penguin Group (NZ), 67 Apollo Drive, Rosedale, Auckland 0632, New Zealand
(a division of Pearson New Zealand Ltd)
Penguin Books, Rosebank Office Park, 181 Jan Smuts Avenue, Parktown North 2193,
South Africa
Penguin China, B7 Jaiming Center, 27 East Third Ring Road North, Chaoyang District,
Beijing 100020, China

Penguin Books Ltd, Registered Offices: 80 Strand, London WC2R 0RL, England

ISBN: 978-1-59514-654-0

Published simultaneously in Canada

Library of Congress Cataloging-in-Publication Data is available

Printed in the United States of America

10 9 8 7 6 5 4 3 2 1

This is a work of fiction. Names, characters, places, and incidents either are the product
of the author's imagination or are used fictitiously, and any resemblance to actual
persons, living or dead, businesses, companies, events, or locales is entirely coincidental.

CHAPTER 1

The straitjacket corseted my body so tightly my arms tingled and my fingers turned numb. I sank beneath the water's surface, the weights on the jacket dragging me down. I gasped, and a spurt of liquid spilled into my mouth. Chlorine burned my eyes as I watched the distance between me and the surface growing. Blurry shapes moved above. They were watching me.

Panic clutched at my chest when my feet hit the ground. Ten feet separated me from desperately needed oxygen. If I didn't move quickly, I was going to drown. I tore at the fabric, pressing my arms against my sides, thrashing and kicking, letting my instinct take over.

It's just a test, I reminded myself. Summers would never have let me do this if it was too dangerous. She'd been a Variation trainer for years—she knew what we were capable of.

And Alec wouldn't let anything happen to me.

I stopped struggling and settled at the bottom of the pool, resting my knees on the blue concrete floor. Closing my eyes, I tried my best to ignore the steady pressure building in my chest. I needed air. I'd already wasted too much time panicking.

Focus.

I coaxed the memory of a little girl I'd bumped in the mall. I pictured her delicate features, her narrow shoulders, her slender limbs. I imagined looking through her eyes, inhabiting her body. Immediately, the familiar rippling sensation started in my toes and crept up my calves. Once it reached my chest, the pressure of the jacket loosened. It was several sizes too big now. I wiggled out of my restraints, opened my eyes, and pushed off the ground. With a gasp, I burst through the water's surface, gulping down air. I felt my limbs lengthening, my body returning to its own form. As soon as my vision was clear, I noticed Alec perched on the edge of the pool, ready to jump in. His dark brows were still knitted, his gray eyes full of worry.

Summers, Tanner, and Holly had gathered around to watch. Tanner winked at me and gestured at the pile of towels in the corner; one of them lifted off and floated toward his outstretched hand.

"Show-off," I mouthed with a smile and swam toward the ladder.

I took Alec's hand and let him pull me out of the pool. He wrapped a towel around my shoulders, and I snuggled into the fluffy material, wishing it were Alec's chest instead. I sank down on the bench, my back against the wall. My teeth chattered as I released a shaky breath. I could feel the panic slowly ebbing away, but my heart kept up its erratic rhythm.

Holly wrapped an arm around me. "Shit. I can't believe how long it took you to resurface. Are you okay?"

I shrugged and leaned my head against her shoulder. I could feel everyone's eyes on me.

"Morphing into a little girl—that's quite a party trick, Tessa. But there's nothing like a near-death experience to get your blood pumping, right?" Tanner said with a grin. His teeth flashed white in his dark face. His red mohawk defied gravity the way it always did—one of the perks of having a telekinetic Variation.

"It's *not* funny. Tessa could've gotten hurt," Alec snapped. He pressed his balled fists against the wall; the muscles in his back quivered as if he was trying to stop himself from driving his hands through the wall—which he could have easily done with his own Variation. He was stronger and faster than normal human beings—and other Variants, for that matter.

"Everyone needs to learn how to use their Variations in extreme situations. We can't coddle students and then expect them to survive a mission," Summers said, running an impatient hand over her messy ponytail. Summers had been an agent for the FEA—Forces with Extraordinary Abilities—since before we were born and had complete authority during our Variation training. But that didn't stop Alec from challenging her on a regular basis.

"Don't turn this into a bigger deal than it is, Alec," she warned, pivoting on one heel and exiting the pool area.

Tanner clapped Alec's shoulder. "She's right. You've got to chill." He sat down on the bench beside Holly and me and leaned back against the wall. "Have you guys heard the news?"

"What news?" Holly asked.

"Kate and Major left headquarters before sunrise. They're on their way to Livingston, some hick town out in Oregon."

So that was why I hadn't seen Kate all day. Usually she never left Alec's side. "Isn't that the place where that awful murder happened?" I asked.

Tanner nodded. "Yep. And I heard there was another incident."

Water trickled over my face, but I didn't bother wiping it off. "Why are they even interested, though? It's just a small town. And it's not like every killer is FEA business."

The FEA was officially a section of the FBI, and the majority of our cases came assigned by them—though we were also involved in larger counterterrorism and espionage efforts. But apart from having the FBI motto FIDELITY, BRAVERY, INTEGRITY engraved above the entrance to FEA headquarters, our organization was pretty much autonomous. Whenever a crime reeked of Variant involvement, FEA agents were sent to investigate. Otherwise the FBI left us to our own devices as long as we didn't draw any attention to our existence. Major wouldn't have had it any other way.

Tanner shrugged. "Who knows what's going on in Major's head. Maybe there's more to the case that we're not aware of."

"Maybe the FBI suspects a Variant," Holly added.

"If the FEA does get involved, I wonder who they'll pick for the mission," I said. We would find out soon enough.

The intercom hissed.

Holly groaned, bleached-blond hair falling over her face as she sat up. "Ugh. What do they want now?"

I didn't move. I was beat from my morning in the pool, followed closely by our afternoon run, and wanted to catch a few blissful minutes of rest before Holly and I had ballistics training.

"Tessa. Meeting in my office ASAP," Major Sanchez bellowed, his voice warped by the old speakers. One would think the FEA could afford up-to-date hardware.

In Major's world, *ASAP* meant "right this second or you'll run three laps." With my legs still burning from my daily run, I wasn't keen on being late.

Holly grinned. "Good luck."

I jumped out of bed and hurried out of the room. When had Kate and Major returned from Livingston, anyway?

Major Sanchez's closed door greeted me, the DO NOT INTERRUPT sign taunting me with its fat black letters. I knocked, and without waiting for an invitation—which would never come—I gingerly opened the door. Major stood behind his desk, his thick arms crossed. His black hair was slicked back with enough pomade to grease the hinges in the entire complex. His dark eyes glared at me, but I'd been on the receiving end of that look so often that I barely flinched.

"Get your butt into the chair, Tessa."

I stumbled toward the free chair and sank down onto it. It was the kind of chair that made you want to get the hell out of it as soon as possible: high-gloss black hardwood—unyielding and impeccable, like the man who'd chosen it. Not that such a chair was even necessary, as a few minutes in Major's company had the same effect on most people.

Alec and Kate were already seated, holding hands. Or rather, Kate was clutching Alec's hand like she was afraid he'd run away. He wore one of the white button-down shirts Kate had bought for him, his hair still wet from his post-run shower. Kate's narrowed eyes came into my focus: amber with a weird coppery tint—if my turquoise eyes were uncommon, hers were outright unsettling.

I whipped my head around and turned my attention back to Major. If Kate got a direct look into my eyes, she'd use her Variation to read exactly what was on my mind, and that could get awkward.

Major didn't sit down; instead he stood behind his desk chair, hands gripping the backrest so tightly his knuckles were turning white. Not an easy feat with skin as tanned as his.

I shifted in the chair. My eyes were drawn to the pinboard behind Major's desk. It had been a while since I had been in his office, and the board had changed since then. Back then, the disturbing photos hadn't been there.

The first showed a woman splayed on her stomach, a wire coiled tightly around her throat. My own breath hitched at the thought of being strangled, of looking into the eyes of my murderer as I struggled for breath, of dying with a killer's cruel face as my last glimpse of the world. My eyes drifted over to the second photo, of another female—it was hard to tell her age, as her body had grown bloated and taken on a greenish hue. Floaters were the most horrid corpses of all. I'd never seen one in real life—or any other dead body, for that matter. But I'd seen plenty of pictures during Basic Forensic Pathology, and those were disturbing enough.

"There's been a new development in the serial killer case in Livingston."

I sat up, startled by the topic. Major had never spoken directly to me about that case—or any case. Kate and Alec nodded in unison.

"His fourth victim." Major continued.

"Fourth? Who was the third victim?" I'd only heard of two. Apparently, the gossip channels in the FEA didn't work as well as I'd hoped.

"A Mr. Chen. He was a janitor in Livingston's high school," Major said.

"A man?"

Major sighed. "That gave our profiling team quite a stir. Their analysis up until then had suggested a misogynist."

Four murders. That must have been a shock for a town as small as Livingston. "Why do we even think it's a serial killer? What seems to be the connection?"

Major released his grip on the chair. "Two victims were killed with a wire around their necks. Two were found in or near the lake—we can't say for sure how they were killed. But they all had one thing in common: the killer had cut an *A* into the skin over their rib cages. We don't yet know why."

"Did he do it postmortem?" I asked as all kinds of horrible images flooded my head.

"Yes. But that's not why I ordered you into my office; you'll become familiar with the cases soon enough."

The thought was enough to make my pulse speed up.

"Yesterday the killer tried to strike again," Major said.

"Tried?"

Major's glower made me add a hasty "sir," but it didn't change his expression.

"Yes, tried. He strangled a girl and threw her into the lake afterward, but she washed onto the shore, where a jogger found her. He called an ambulance. She sustained severe brain damage and was placed in an artificial coma. That's where it gets interesting."

Interesting? I glanced at Alec and Kate, my stomach knotting into a tight ball, but they just listened, straight-faced.

"The doctors give her a few days to live, at most. Once she's dead, Tessa, you'll take her place."

CHAPTER 2

My fingers gripped the sleek wooden armrest. I felt as if a hole had suddenly opened into the earth and threatened to swallow me. "You can't be serious." He wanted me to pose as a dead girl to chase a serial killer?

Major straightened, eyes narrowed.

I took a deep breath. "I'll take her place?" My voice shook, despite my best attempts to appear strong. I knew I should be grateful for the opportunity, but this was more than the usual entry-level missions, like reconnaissance or conducting background investigations. This was me at the front.

"Yes, that is what I said. Once she's dead, you'll pretend to be her."

He said it like it was nothing, like posing as a murder victim was a perfectly normal occurrence.

"But everybody will already know she's dead, won't they? I can't pretend to be a corpse."

"No, they won't. Everyone will think there's been a miracle and she recovered."

"But what about her parents?" I asked.

Major traced a finger over the photos on the wall. "They won't know, either. They'll simply think that you're her."

"Don't you think they'll get suspicious if I don't act exactly like their daughter? They know her better than anyone. I'll never be just like her, no matter how hard I try."

"Yes, but *think*, Tessa. Why would they suspect anything? For them there'll be no other explanation for their daughter's recovery than a miracle. And any small changes in her behavior will be attributed to the trauma. They could never imagine that Variants exist. An average human's imagination doesn't reach that far."

Average human—only Major was able to make it sound like an insult. He looked at me like I was precious, his most prized possession. His trophy Variant.

Alec sprang out of his seat and began to pace the room, stalking past Major's glass case of tin soldiers and awards, past the filing cabinet, before he finally stopped in front of the picture window.

"Don't you think the mission is too dangerous? The murderer will obviously try to get rid of the only person who might be able to identify him. Tessa will be his prime target."

A tight knot of unease gathered in my stomach, but I tried to ignore it. If I let it gain momentum, I'd dissolve into a puddle of anxiety.

Major smirked, as though Alec's words had been a joke. "Alec, Tessa will be facing much worse once her training is over. All of you will be."

Our training was ultimately geared toward one goal: to prepare us for more important future missions all over the world. Tanner's brother Ty had recently completed training and was immediately sent on a covert assignment abroad. We didn't know where he was, but rumors said Iran or China. Only ten percent of all agents were currently stationed at headquarters; the rest were out in the field.

"This case will look like a piece of cake compared to what's ahead. Do you think it'll be safe to impersonate the leader of a terrorist group or the president of a country that's spiraling out of control? That's what awaits Tessa in the future, because she's the only one who could do it. I don't have to tell you that some people in the Department of Defense and the CIA are licking their fingers at the prospect of having Tessa's talent at their disposal. She is the perfect spy—the ultimate weapon. So far I've been successful at keeping them at bay, but it's time to prepare for the future. This mission is the perfect test run."

Ultimate weapon. The words echoed in my head. I pressed my arm against my stomach. Even with my Variation, I was still just a girl, not some extraordinary spy. Alec's eyes met mine, his jaw locked tight.

"Regarding this case, Tessa's attracting the killer's attention is exactly what we're hoping for. He's killed three people, and the fourth is as good as dead. We must find him before he strikes again."

Alec's dark eyebrows drew together in a V. "So Tessa will be bait?" His voice sounded calm as river water moments before a flash flood.

"She'll also try to find out more about the girl's friends, about her school, about every single inhabitant of Livingston." With a sigh, Major lowered himself into his chair.

"I don't like it. Tessa isn't bait," Alec said, stalking around the desk to face Major.

Kate pursed her lips, rose from her chair, and hit me with a withering glare before she placed a hand on Alec's shoulder. "Alec, honey, Major knows what he's doing. Tessa doesn't need your protection."

This mission probably had Kate secretly elated. If it were up to her, she'd lock me in a room with the killer and throw away the key.

Alec braced his hands on the desk. "No. I won't allow it."

Defying Major was unheard of. As head of the FEA, Major's opinion was the only one that counted. Even the FBI and the deputy director respected that. But Alec wanted to protect *me*. Warmth spread through my body at the very thought of it.

"I don't need your permission. Remember your place," Major snapped.

Kate's fingers bored into Alec's upper arm. "Stop it. This is bigger than you. This is about the FEA, not your own worries."

Alec's hands dug harder into the wood of the desk, his strength causing it to crack. I darted out of my chair and rested my hand over one of his. "It's okay. I'll be fine."

The hard lines on his face smoothed. Kate jerked away and sidled over to her chair, dramatically scraping it over the floor as she plopped down.

Alec straightened, and my hand slipped from his. I itched to take hold of it again. He leaned against the wall—away from Major, who was glaring at him with a quiet fury unlike anything I'd ever witnessed before.

The ticking of the clock sounded in the room.

Tick. Tock.

I slinked back to my chair, my rubber soles squeaking on the linoleum floor. The hard wood of the backrest pressed against my spine.

Tick. Tock.

Major folded his hands on the desk and cleared his throat. "We can't begin our mission as long as the last victim's still alive."

We were waiting for someone to die. It felt all kinds of wrong.

"But, sir, I have to see her before she dies," I said, my voice catching on the last word. After all, I could only take the shape of people I'd touched.

Major nodded. "That's all been taken care of. I'll accompany you and Kate to the hospital this afternoon."

Kate's expression fell. What right did she have to be dismayed? She didn't have to pretend to be a dead girl; she didn't have to lie to someone's parents. She just had to secretly search people's brains without their ever being the wiser.

Major leaned back in his chair, his face businesslike. "You'll get a few minutes alone with the victim so your body can gather her data."

He made it sound all clinical and easy, but it wasn't.

He turned to Kate. "And you, Kate, will try to gather more information from the family and the hospital staff. Unfortunately, most of the doctors are men."

I envied boys and men, who were safe from Kate's power. There wasn't much I wouldn't do to permanently avoid her gaze. FEA scientists had searched for an explanation for Kate's selective talent but hadn't come up with one. By definition, Variants deviated from the norm, defied the laws of nature. Analyzing our gifts wasn't exactly easy.

"And Alec, I'll need you to speed up Tessa's training. This mission is potentially very dangerous. I wish we didn't need her so soon, but it's necessary. You're our best fighter. Get her ready." The way Major and Alec looked at each other, I had a feeling there was more to Alec's involvement in this case than just self-defense lessons.

"Sir, I know how to fire a gun, and I've been taking karate since I arrived here," I said.

"Two years of karate and knowing how to fire on an unmoving target aren't enough. In the next few days, Alec will teach you how to fight for your life." Major trained his gaze on Alec. "Teach her how to walk away from a fight as the winner."

The fire in Alec's eyes sent a jolt of electricity through my body.

"Kate, Tessa, get ready. We'll set out in thirty minutes."

Alec smiled encouragingly as he walked past me. I wanted to return the gesture, but the muscles in my face refused to obey. I was going on my first real mission. As bait.

I hurried along the ocher corridor, in the direction of my room. The dismal yellow shade reminded me of the carpet in my old room back at home.

Two years.

Sometimes I forgot how long I'd been living with the agency. The last image I had of my mother was of her back as she'd let Alec and Major take me away. She hadn't even turned around to say good-bye. And now I was supposed to pose as someone else's daughter, become a part of a normal family, which was the last thing I knew how to pretend. Even before I came to the FEA, a family was the one thing I'd never had. I couldn't remember a single thing about my father since he left with my brother when I was only a toddler.

Loud booms greeted me as I stepped into my room. Holly was sprawled out on her bed, reading a book and moving her legs in rhythm with the music. I switched the speakers off, launching the room into a sudden silence. Holly whirled around and sat up. "What did Major want?"

I leaned against our door, trying to take some weight off my trembling legs. Outside the picture windows, dark clouds were gathering in the sky over the forest—harbingers of another snow storm. It was March, but here in Montana, so close to the Canadian border, the winters were long and brutal. In the distance I could make out the mountains of Glacier National Park, their peaks still crowned by snow.

"He wanted to talk about the serial killer case in Livingston. There's been another victim—the fourth. She's still alive, but she doesn't have long, and—" I hesitated a moment before continuing. "I'm supposed to take her place once she dies."

Holly's eyes grew wide. "You're going on a real mission?" She couldn't keep the envy from coloring her voice. Holly and I had started at the agency at the same time and were usually called into training together. I was sure her invisibility had the head of the CIA and the Department of Defense salivating. *If* she ever got a grip on her talent.

"The mission can't start until the girl *is dead.*" Maybe she hadn't absorbed that detail the first time I told her.

Holly still looked enthusiastic. "Wow. I can't believe they're going to let you work on a real murder case. I've always wanted to pretend to be someone else. You must be so excited."

I shot her a withering glance. I was about as far from excited as one could get.

"So wait, you're leaving now? Are you going out in the field already?" Holly twittered close behind me as I gathered my coat and slipped a few essentials into my purse.

I shrugged. "Today's just preparation. The real action doesn't start for a couple of days." The flight to the hospital would take at least two hours, enough time for me to completely and utterly freak out.

"Good luck!" Holly shouted as I left the room.

I would need more than just luck.

The gray facade of St. Elizabeth's Hospital loomed above me, lightning flashing in the sky behind it. If it hadn't been for Kate and Major, I'd have turned on my heel and hidden in the sleek black Mercedes limousine that brought us here from the heliport.

The sliding doors glided open without a sound, giving way to the sterile white reception area. My nose stung from the smell of disinfectants. We breezed ahead without asking for directions. Major knew his way and nobody stopped him; not the nurses who whispered to each other as we passed or the doctor who nodded his head in greeting. The FEA was thorough in absolutely everything.

The corridor looked like an endless tunnel with walls that threatened to close in on me. One identical door followed after the other, concealing an endless succession of patients.

Finally, Major stopped beside a door being guarded by a man in a black suit. FEA, no doubt. He had a hooked nose set within a narrow face and reminded me of a hawk. He was probably one of the many external agents scattered around the country—those unfortunate agents whose Variations weren't useful enough to be part of the more prestigious espionage and counterterrorism missions. The local agents' jobs were considered boring by some, but at that moment I'd have switched places with him in a heartbeat.

"Where are they?" Major's tone took on the condescending edge it always did when he talked to people from the outer circle— everyone who didn't live or work in headquarters. Hawk-Face stood up straighter, and though he was about a head taller than Major, he managed to appear much smaller. "Cafeteria, sir. They won't come back before six."

That gave us twenty minutes. I didn't know why the family had gone to the cafeteria or why Hawk-Face knew when they'd return, but some FEA agents could mess with other people's minds in all kinds of ways.

Mental Variations were the most valued in our world. Major's official Variation was "night-sight," but many people believed he was one of the few Dual Variants whose second mental Variation remained a secret. Apparently most Dual Variants hid their more powerful mental Variation behind the obvious physical one.

"Kate, you know what to do," Major said.

She nodded and set out for the cafeteria, where Mrs. Chambers would soon have her mind raided.

Hawk-Face stepped aside as Major opened the door and gestured for me to enter. As soon as I set foot into the room, I wanted to turn around and bolt. But Major was right behind me, blocking my only way of escape.

My eyes were instantly glued to Madison Chambers, still and silent in her green hospital gown. Her pale skin was almost the exact same shade as the white walls surrounding her. Veins shone through her skin, like blue vines had been painted on her arms. I tried to swallow, but my throat was too dry.

Madison's dull blond hair fanned out on the pillow around her head like a faded halo. Her neck was wrapped with gauze. Was that where the wire had cut into her skin? She appeared so fragile, so tenuous amid all the tubes and beeping machines. I backed away and collided with Major's muscular body.

"What's the matter?"

What *wasn't* the matter? There were so many answers to that question. With Major's presence looming close behind me, I inched closer to the bed. Closer to the girl who needed to die so I could pretend to be her. Major's hand landed on my shoulder, but it wasn't a comforting touch.

"This is your chance to prove yourself, Tessa."

I pulled away from him, shaking myself free of his grip. My hand trembled as I extended it toward Madison.

"I'm sorry," I whispered as my fingertips touched her arm. It didn't feel as warm as I'd expected. I knew her body was still alive, though maybe Major was right when he'd said it was really just an empty shell. Something was missing. Usually when I touched someone, there was a certain kind of energy, a unique presence I could feel; but with Madison I felt nothing. Still, as I stood there among the beeping machines, I could feel my body absorb her "data."

As far as FEA scientists could gather, my DNA incorporated foreign genetic instructions into its own unique strand as dormant

DNA that could be activated when necessary. I felt the familiar tingling starting in my toes, the way it always did when my brain memorized every detail of someone's appearance and my body felt eager to try it on. I suppressed the sensation. I wouldn't change into her now; I would wait until I no longer had a choice. Soon, I'd be able to copy her perfectly despite the fact that I didn't yet know anything about her—not about her worries, her fears, or her dreams. I'd be nothing but a hollow imitation of the girl she used to be.

After a few seconds, I pulled back, but I still couldn't take my eyes off the girl who'd never walk out of this room again. And though her survival would ruin the mission, I wished that she'd prove everyone wrong, that she'd miraculously heal and return to her family and friends.

"You should dry your tears before you leave the room," Major said.

I looked up. He had already turned to talk to Hawk-Face in the doorway. I wiped the moisture from my cheeks and leaned down, close to Madison's face. "You have to live, do you hear me? Please, please live." But a part of me knew there was nothing left in her to listen to my plea.

A few hours later, I tossed in my bed, unable to fall asleep. The image of Madison was stamped into my mind. I shifted uncomfortably. My tablet felt like it had burned a hole into my upper thighs. I'd been watching movie after movie, which usually helped lull me to sleep. But not tonight.

A knock sounded from the door. I pulled my earbuds out and

turned off the screen. Holly had turned her back to me and was breathing evenly. She always dozed off at exactly 11 P.M. You could set a timer by her.

I tiptoed toward the door, shivering as the cold from the tiled floor seeped into my bare feet, and quietly pried it open.

Alec stood waiting in the corridor. He held up a DVD. The jacket showed a warped, scarred face partly covered with an ax. "Want to watch the newest horror shocker?" I glanced at the clock. It was almost midnight. "We haven't done a movie night in weeks," he added.

Yeah, more like *months*.

"That's not my fault," I said, a heavy silence descending on us. Kate had destroyed movie night—what had been Alec's and my tradition since I'd joined the FEA.

He lowered the DVD. "Is that a no?"

I snatched the DVD from his hand and brushed past him into the corridor. "You take care of the snacks. I'll take care of the rest."

Alec caught up with me in two sweeping steps. From the corner of my eye, I saw him smile. His hand brushed against my arm, and I had to stop myself from grabbing hold of it.

A few minutes later, we settled onto the uber-comfy sofa in the common living area. It was deserted, silent except for the hum of the vending machine that sat in the far corner.

Alec put a bowl of gummy bears between us and propped his legs up on the table. He was wearing black jeans and a tight black T-shirt with a picture of Chucky, the killer doll, printed on the front. I'd given it to him shortly after moving in with the FEA. He'd worn it often—until Kate. She preferred him in boring collared button-downs.

Alec kept glancing over at me. "Are you okay?"

"I'm fine."

"You know, if you don't feel ready for the mission, I'm sure Major would understand."

I laughed. "Are we talking about the same person?"

Alec's expression became fierce. "He can't force you to do something you're not ready for. I'll talk to him."

"No." I touched his arm. "It'll be okay. I can do this."

He didn't seem convinced.

I started the movie and a scream ripped through the silence as the ax murderer killed his first victim. Keeping an eye on the screen, I sorted the gummy bears, piling the green and white ones in a heap on my thighs and leaving the others for Alec.

"You always do that, you know," Alec said.

I swallowed a gummy bear. "Do what?"

"Bite their heads off first."

I shrugged. "It's the nice thing to do. If you could choose, would you rather be eaten alive starting at your feet or would you want it to be over quickly?"

"Well, if it was up to me, I'd rather not be eaten at all." Slowly, a grin crept over his face. It was a look I hadn't seen in a while. Lately, he'd been so serious all the time. His moods had almost matched Major's. Ever since he and Kate had been sent out into the field a few months ago—the mission from which they'd returned as a couple—Alec had been changing. Every day I felt him slipping away from me, our friendship crumbling before my eyes. But I had no idea what had transpired between then and now, as neither he nor Kate ever spoke a word about the mission—Major's orders.

"You're weird. You know that, right?" he said.

I poked his chest. The muscles felt like steel under my fingertip. He snagged my hand, his thumb and forefinger curling around my wrist. His other hand shot forward and began tickling my side. A mix of laughter and screeching tumbled from my lips as I tried to wriggle out of his grip, but with his strength it was useless. I pulled my legs up to my chest and tried to push Alec off with them. Suddenly, he leaned over me, his face mere inches from mine. I stopped struggling, for a moment even stopped breathing. He was so close. If I moved my head forward, our lips would touch. His breath fanned over my face, his eyes darting to my mouth, but then he settled back against the cushions, as far from me as possible. My cheeks burned as I returned my attention to the screen, just in time to see someone get beheaded by an ax. *Figures.* That's just how I felt.

For a few minutes, it had been like old times—like the days before Kate became Alec's girlfriend. But those days were over now.

CHAPTER 3

The next morning, my preparations for mission "Be Madison Chambers" began. It was sad how easy it was to summarize the life of an eighteen-year-old girl in eighty neatly typed pages. In uncaring black and white, the report told me everything I needed to know in order to blend in with Madison's friends and family. Or so Major thought.

Kate had done a good job extracting information from the minds of Madison's friends and mother. But the file still lacked any mention of Madison's emotions, her thoughts, her internal life. It was like telling someone to enjoy a beautiful piece of music simply by looking at the notes.

Madison weighed 7 pounds and 2 ounces when she was born. She started playing the piano when she was seven years old. She had a cat named Fluffy that she'd gotten for her ninth birthday and a fraternal twin brother, Devon. She loved peanut butter cookies and was allergic to tuna and capers. She had been a cheerleader until shortly before the attack.

A stack of photos fell out of the file, spreading around my feet. I crouched down to pick them up and began looking through them.

There was Madison as a little girl, dressed in a bunny costume. Madison in the middle of a group of grinning girls, braces flashing in her mouth. Madison hugging her father and brother.

I didn't even want to imagine how the FEA had gotten access to them.

Madison was so full of life in the photos; all shiny blond hair, sparkling blue eyes, and happy smiles. And someone had taken that light from her.

I snapped the file shut as tears prickled the corners of my eyes. I didn't want to get to know Madison, didn't want to learn about her quirks and interests, because it made her too real. This wasn't right.

"Tessa?"

Alec.

I rubbed my hands over my face—silently thankful for water-proof mascara—and rearranged my ponytail. "Come in."

The door opened with a creak.

Alec took up most of the doorway, tall and muscled as ever. He'd never entered my room before, and it didn't look like that would change anytime soon. Sometimes I wondered why he was so reluctant to come in. I often wondered if he didn't trust himself to be alone there with me. But I knew that was probably just wishful thinking.

"You okay?"

I felt my skin flush. "Yeah, I'm fine. Is there something you want?"

For a moment he seemed to look right through me. His eyes were so intense. Did he remember that moment last night? Heat gathered in my stomach, but then he cleared his throat. "Major wants our training to start today."

"Oh, right. Sure." We didn't normally have any classes on the weekends, but our time before the mission was tight. Alec's eyes lingered on me for a moment before he disappeared from view. "In the dojo in ten minutes. Don't be late."

Had I imagined the way he'd just looked at me? I shook my head to get rid of the thought.

I grabbed simple gray sweat pants and a white T-shirt from my drawer. Just as I was about to get dressed, Holly burst in, her hair still damp from her morning swim. Her natural color, a nice light brown, showed at the hairline. "You're leaving already?"

"Yeah, Alec wants me in the dojo in—" I glanced at the clock on the wall. "Nine minutes."

She took my clothes from me and dropped them on the ground. "You're not wearing those."

"Holly, I don't have time for your styling tips right now." And I didn't have the patience either. Looking cute wouldn't get me out of the mission alive.

"Don't be stupid. You're having one-on-one lessons with Alec. Let me spell it out for you: Alone. With Alec. This is your chance."

If she'd seen us last night, she'd know how hopeless it was.

"You know how focused Alec is during training. He wouldn't even notice me if I walked into the dojo naked."

"We'll see."

I slumped down on my bed and watched Holly rummage in her drawer. When she actually set her mind on something, she was a force to be reckoned with, and Alec and I were on top of her to-do list.

She flung an article of clothing at me and it hit me in the face. The scent of peach and vanilla filled my nose as I pulled it over my head. It was a white T-shirt. Without protest, I put it on.

"What's so much better about this shirt?"

Holly pointed at my chest.

"Holly!"

"It's funny."

I groaned. In big red letters, PLEASE TALK TO MY FACE; MY BREASTS CAN'T HEAR YOU was written across my chest. "I'm not wearing this."

"Oh, you are. And here, take these sweatpants. They're not as loose as yours."

I didn't have the energy to argue with her, not with the way my brain had been in turmoil ever since I saw Madison. I wiggled into Holly's sweatpants. At least they were black and happily devoid of any printed sayings.

I glanced at the clock. "Great, now I'm late," I said as I hurried out of our room.

"Your legs look great," Holly called after me.

"No running in the corridors!" Mrs. Finnigan, Major's secretary, shouted. I'd never seen her run in the corridors, but she barely fit through the doorframe so it wasn't really an option for her. I stumbled down the staircase, hurrying as fast as I could to the ground floor.

Within a minute, I arrived in the dojo, breathless from running four floors. I glanced over the green mats, floor-to-ceiling mirrors, and suspended punching bags. Alec was practicing high-kicks on one of the bags. I stopped short in the doorway. He wasn't wearing a shirt, only black training pants. His muscles tensed with every kick, and the artificial light of the halogen lamps made his skin look golden. A large black dragon tattoo covered his right shoulder, hiding the scar he got as a small boy. He'd fallen through a banister, down two floors, after his parents had abandoned him in a crowded mall the day before Christmas. He shouldn't have survived the fall, but his Variation saved him. Alec always said his Variation helped him cheat death but the FEA helped him survive.

Without looking over at me, he said, "You're two minutes late." He did another kick before he turned around.

His eyes immediately dropped to read the words on my chest. Warmth crawled up my neck, and I promised myself I'd thank Holly later.

He tore his gaze away from my breasts and looked at my face, showing not a hint of embarrassment. "Nice shirt," he said dryly. "Oh, and twenty push-ups for being late."

My smile faded. I walked up to him, trying my best not to openly admire the display of muscles on his chest. "Oh come on, Alec. Don't act all high and mighty. You're not Major."

His gray eyes held mine, his expression hard. "Thirty push-ups, Tess." His voice was strained.

Every time he used that nickname I wanted to bury my nose in his neck and let him hold me. Many years ago my mom had called me that. Back when she'd still cared for me, maybe even loved me.

I got down on my knees and supported my weight with my arms. The first few push-ups were okay, the following ones not so much, and by the time I reached number twenty my arms began to quiver.

"You should work out more often. Your arm muscles are almost nonexistent."

What the hell. Was he trying to be funny? My arms weren't that bad. Not everyone could be as strong and muscley as Alec. Actually, nobody was.

"Shut up," I retorted.

I pushed myself up again. Only ten more to go. The mat beneath my body was the same pale green as the hospital gown Madison wore. A vivid image of her frail body flashed before my eyes. My arms gave way and my face hit the mat. The faint smell of feet and sweat crawled into my nose.

"Tess?" Alec put a warm hand on my shoulder. His voice was colored with worry.

He sat down beside me, and silence settled around us. "Do you want to talk about it?" Suddenly, I wanted to talk to him, wanted to tell him everything—much more than my thoughts about Madison. I pulled away. "No. Let's practice."

"You sure? I can tell Holly and Tanner that training is postponed."

I jumped to my feet. "I'm fine."

Alec took it easy on me after that. I could tell. My high-kicks were miserable. There was barely any power behind them. I had horrible aim and was out of breath within a few minutes. But every time I tried to summon my power, I was haunted by thoughts of Madison. Madison, the girl not much older than me who lay dying. The girl who wanted to become a vet. The girl who wanted to spend a year living abroad after high school. The girl who never would.

"Let's see how good you are at getting rid of an attacker."

I nodded, glad for the distraction.

Alec wrapped his arms around my waist and tried to drag me away. My attempts at stomping on his foot or kicking his shin were half-hearted at best. The feel of his naked chest pressed against my back wasn't something I was desperate to get rid of.

"You're not really trying, Tess." His lips brushed my ear as he spoke, and a shiver shot through my body. My muscles went slack, any will to defend myself against him gone. His closeness felt so good, so right. I leaned my head back against his chest. He smelled like a spring morning in the woods, like spearmint and something spicy. Deep down I knew I shouldn't crave his closeness as much as I did. I shouldn't want him at all. He wasn't mine to want.

He stiffened when our eyes met.

I still remembered the first time I'd seen him. He and Major had stood in their prim suits amid the ragged furniture and empty beer bottles littering my mom's living room. Despite my fear and embarrassment, his grey eyes had set me at ease, his smile assuring me I'd be safe with him.

And now, I couldn't stop myself from looking at his lips. Slowly, he leaned down.

"Alec?"

Kate's voice hit me like a wrecking ball. Alec dropped his arms and stepped back. She stood in the doorway, her copper eyes narrowed. I wasn't sure how long she'd been watching us, but it was obvious that she was furious, despite the fact that nothing had happened. A tiny part of me felt bad for wanting Alec. He was with Kate. I shouldn't like someone who had a girlfriend, but I couldn't help it. I'd liked him from the day he'd taken me from my home, long before she'd come into the picture. Sometimes it felt like I'd never stop wanting him.

Kate smirked. "Nice shirt. Pity that you don't have any real breasts to speak of."

I crossed my arms over my chest, avoiding her gaze. I wouldn't give her the satisfaction of reading my thoughts.

"Kate, stop it." Alec's voice held a warning.

He looked at me with an apologetic smile, but I didn't want his pity, especially not after what Kate had just said.

"I thought we were going to watch a movie. Remember?"

I hated how her voice took on a whiny edge whenever she didn't get her way. I wished Alec wouldn't fall for it, wished he wouldn't watch anything with her. Movie night was supposed to be our thing.

He grabbed a towel and wiped his face. "I can't. Tessa and I are training for the mission. Holly and Tanner are going to join us soon." He added the last part as if to placate Kate, whose face looked like she'd tasted something nasty. After a moment, she wrapped her arms around his neck and pulled him down to her. Her lips clung to his like a suction cup. I wanted him to push her away. I wanted him to kiss me like he kissed Kate.

I turned my back to them and took a few swallows from the water fountain, trying to banish the image of Kate's lips on Alec's. The sound of Holly's high-pitched giggling, followed by Tanner's baritone laugh, made me relax, and I finally dared to face the room again. Alec approached me; thankfully, Kate was gone.

Tanner had put in his septum piercing. Summers forbade him to wear it during training or missions. I always pictured a bull charging a red cape when I saw him, though with his skinny frame he looked decidedly more like a walking stick than a bull. Holly looked happy to be part of the preparations, even if she couldn't go on the mission herself.

The two of them stood near the entrance, watching Alec and me until I felt like the awkwardness might crush me. Alec cleared his throat. "Tanner and Holly, thank you for joining us. Major thinks we should prepare for all eventualities and that includes the possibility of Tessa facing off with a Variant."

I took a step back. I'd always known a Variant could be the killer, but somehow I'd never thought it through to the end, never considered the potential of having to fight against someone like me. It opened up so many scary possibilities I didn't even want to think about, much less actually encounter. The killer might be able to manipulate me and make me compliant, could poison or stun me with his touch, could make me trust him against my will, and those were only the options that sprang into my mind; countless others could exist. I'd be heading into a fight without knowing if my opponent was uniquely armed or not, without having any idea how dangerous his weapons were. How could I ever expect to stay safe?

Alec touched my shoulder again, but this time I didn't pull back. My eyes were drawn up to his and I knew he could read the fear and horror written all over my face. His fingers tightened, tension creeping through his body. "We don't know for sure if a Variant is involved. If I thought there was any chance—" he paused for a moment before concluding. "I won't allow anything to happen to you."

I was dimly aware of Holly and Tanner standing beside us, but in that moment there was only Alec and me. And that was when reality really sank in. I'd be all alone, trapped in Madison's home, her body, and her life. I'd meet people I didn't know, people who might lie to me about Madison's past and about their loyalties. I'd be the prime target of a killer who not only had an advantage over me through his local knowledge of Livingston, but possibly through a Variation.

"So what exactly are we supposed to do?" Tanner asked lightly.

The tension suddenly left Alec. "I want you to attack Tessa with your Variation. Holly, you will try to take her by surprise." Holly nodded eagerly.

"It's not likely someone invisible will attack you," Alec said, catching the troubled look on my face. "But it'll heighten your senses and help you focus. Don't trust your eyes; use your ears. Tanner will keep you distracted. Now close your eyes so Holly can have a chance to disappear."

I did as he asked and tried to listen for Holly's steps, but either she wasn't moving or she was a lot more stealthy than I gave her credit for. Alec whispered something, though I couldn't tell what or to whom.

"Ready!" he shouted a second later.

The moment my eyes shot open, a ball was hurtling toward my face. At the last second before impact, I ducked, while scanning the room for Tanner, my still-visible attacker. He stood a few feet to my side, his arms crossed over his chest. Of course, Tanner didn't need to move a muscle to throw things at me; his thoughts alone were enough. With a ripping sound, a jump rope came loose from the wall at the end of the dojo. It shot toward me at knee level, twisting and rotating in the air like a lasso. Sneakers squealed behind me and I whirled around, expecting an attack from Holly, but was greeted with empty air. Something thrust against my calves as pain sliced through my legs. My arms shot out, fighting for balance, when a foot materialized out of nowhere and slammed into my chest. The air shot out of my lungs with a gasp as I fell backward and collided with the ground. Fire slithered up my tailbone and across every inch of my body until I felt sure I was burning alive.

I squeezed my eyes shut, trying to regain my breath. If this had been a real fight for my life, I'd be dead. Defeated by a rope and an invisible girl.

"Are you okay? I'm sorry. I didn't mean to hit you so hard." The feel of Holly's warm hands on my shoulders shook me out of my misery. She, Tanner, and Alec stood over me, watching me with knitted brows.

"No, it was my fault. The rope distracted me and I couldn't shift my focus fast enough. I was just overwhelmed by the situation."

Alec nodded like that was exactly what he'd expected. *Jeez*, I thought, *thanks for the vote of confidence.* "At the beginning of your mission, you'll feel the same way. There are so many facts, so much information you'll have to process all at once. I think this exercise will help you discern the important things from the not-so-important things."

I let him pull me up and dusted myself off, though the mat hadn't left any dirt on my clothes.

"Why didn't you use your Variation?" he asked.

"I—I don't know." It hadn't even crossed my mind. My Variation helped me disguise myself, but I'd never considered it a useful talent in a fight.

"If you want to defeat your opponent, especially if it's another

Variant, you need to use your Variation. It's what gives you an advantage. It's what keeps your moves surprising and what makes you dangerous."

Alec was right. This wasn't the time for holding back.

"Okay, let's try this again," I said, my voice steadier than I'd expected.

Holly became invisible again. I tried to track her movement by sound, but it was useless. Tanner advanced on me, for once unsmiling. He balled his hands into fists as I took a step back from him. Abruptly he stopped, just as a medicine ball hurtled toward me. With a wheeze, I dropped to my knees. The ball had missed my head by mere inches. I looked up in disbelief.

"Maybe you should use objects that won't kill Tessa if they hit her," Alec said, scowling.

I jumped to my feet and charged toward Tanner. A grin flitted across his face, but it quickly disappeared when I thrust my fist into his stomach. He parried my next two punches and I drew back to think of a new tactic. I felt a draft on my back and jumped aside. "Holly?"

She didn't give herself away. Tanner grabbed my arm but I slipped out of his grip. He kicked at my legs, trying to make me stumble. Another medicine ball hurtled toward me at stomach level. That would hurt. I bolted away from it, but the stupid thing continued to follow me.

Use your Variation, I told myself. The rippling tore through my body and I shrank as I stumbled toward Tanner. His face wavered when he saw me—now in the body of the young girl from the mall, no more than five years old. The medicine ball slowed. I darted toward him, fell to my knees, and bit into his calf. He drew back with a yelp and landed on his butt. I grinned as I shifted back to myself. Someone barreled into my back. I fell to the ground beside Tanner, turned around, and saw Holly, who was beginning to slowly materialize.

I groaned. Defeated again.

"This was better," Alec said. "Tanner had qualms about attacking a young child. That's a good way to use your Variation. If you can distract your opponent by eliciting pity for yourself, then you gain an advantage over him—which you used to full capacity."

Tanner rubbed his calf where I'd left the imprint of small teeth. "You wouldn't say that if she'd bitten you."

I stifled a laugh.

"But you let yourself get distracted again, Tess. You forgot about Holly because you were too busy gloating," Alec said.

My cheeks burned, but I didn't try to defend myself. Instead I got to my feet and said, "I want to try it again."

Over the next few days, Alec and I met for training twice a day—in the morning before running practice and again in the afternoon. I was allowed to skip my regular classes so I could focus on the mission—much to Holly's disappointment. As important as they might have been in some cases, forensic pathology, DNA profiling, and criminology wouldn't help me much on the field.

By the end of the week, every inch of my body was bruised and I still hadn't made much progress. At least, that's how I felt. Holly picked up on my worries as usual. She wrapped an arm around me as we walked through the corridor.

"I'm scared, Holly," I said in a small voice.

She squeezed my shoulder.

From the corner of my eye, I spotted Alec entering Kate's room. The sighting felt like the last thing I needed. I wished he'd spend his time with me instead, and distract me from my worries.

"I don't get why he likes her," Holly said, following my gaze.

We stepped into our room, and I flung myself face-down on my bed, breathing in the fresh scent of the pillow.

The mattress dipped as Holly lay down beside me. "Is this about the mission or about Alec?"

I'd whined to her about Alec so often, it wasn't surprising that Holly assumed he was the reason for my outburst. And while a little part of it was because of him, the mission had started consuming every one of my waking thoughts. I wanted to enjoy what little time I had left in headquarters, but the worry and fear seemed attached to me. "What if I fail? What if I don't come back because I get myself killed?" I whispered.

Holly sucked in a breath. "Don't even say such a thing. Major wouldn't send you out there if he thought there was a chance of getting you killed." Her words sounded comforting, but I could still hear the uncertainty in her voice.

"But missions are always dangerous," I countered. "Major wouldn't make an exception for anyone. And how can he make sure the killer doesn't get me? He said it himself. Once I become Madison, I'm bait."

Holly was silent for a moment, her eyes wide and scared.

"I'm sorry," I said. "I didn't mean to worry you."

"Don't be stupid. You can talk about anything with me." She hugged me, and I relaxed against her.

"You know what's kind of pathetic?" I said, hoping to lighten the mood. "If I get myself killed, I'll die without ever having kissed a boy. Pathetic, huh? Bards will sing about the old spinster Tessa."

Holly lifted her head, a flicker of her usual self springing into her eyes. She wiped her hand over her nose. "Well, maybe we can do something about the kissing thing. I mean, you'll totally live, but the never-been-kissed part is pathetic enough to fix anyway." The corners of her lips pulled up and I forced myself to smile back at her.

"Sheesh, thanks! Since when are you so experienced?"

"Since I kissed Tanner."

"Um, that was four months ago and you were both drunk on cough syrup, so it hardly counts."

"Whatever." Holly sat up. "This isn't about me. It's about you losing your kissing virginity."

"Wow, that doesn't make me sound like a loser or anything." Engaging in our usual banter felt so good, even if it was only temporary.

Holly ignored me. "If we're being honest, there's only one person worthy of the job of kissing virginity thief." I cringed, knowing exactly who she'd suggest. "Alec. It's either him or no one. I mean, come on, he's the reason you've been holding off." She shrugged. "That and we're a bit short of guys our age around here."

I bit my lip because it was true. Alec was the reason it had never happened before. I'd wanted him to be my first kiss since the day we met. "I don't know," I wavered.

"You do want to kiss him, right?"

I threw my arms up in the air. "I want to kiss him so badly," I whispered through the palms now covering my face.

"Maybe we can do something about that."

I lowered my hands. "What? Tie him up and force a kiss on him?"

Holly rolled her eyes. "No, but that sounds kind of hot."

I nudged her with my toes.

"How about something more inconspicuous," she ventured. "We could use your talent. Why let it go to waste?"

"It's not going to waste." An unwanted image of Madison's face flashed in my mind, and the fear I'd banished for a moment came rushing back to me with full force. "So what's your plan?"

"You could change into Kate."

"Oh no, not that again."

She clapped her hand over my mouth. "Don't interrupt me."

I glared at her.

"And once you're Kate, you meet with Alec and play sucky-face with him. He won't ever know it's you. Unless you want him to. Maybe your kissing skills are so badass that he dumps the real Kate."

I opened my mouth and she removed her hand.

"Yeah, right. I've never kissed anyone, so it's pretty much a given that I'll suck at it."

She leaned closer, her face hovering above me. She was back to her sunny self and for that reason alone, I was willing to consider her insane plan. "So what do you say?"

"You're crazy, Holly. We've had this talk before. It's not okay to change into someone and kiss their boyfriend."

Holly snorted. "Don't be ridiculous. We're not talking about someone, we're talking about Kate. She treats us like dirt."

Pity that you don't have any real breasts to speak of. The words she'd said to me at my first training session started running a loop in my brain. It was true: Kate didn't mind hurting me. She actually enjoyed it, just like she enjoyed rubbing her relationship with Alec right in my face.

"But still. What about Alec? It's not fair to him either."

"Nobody gets hurt. They won't ever find out and you get what you've always wanted: Your first kiss from Alec."

"But it would be fake."

"Why are you being so difficult? I've been listening to your gushing for two years. It's time we do something about it and you get kissed. Besides, maybe he's a horrible kisser and the kiss will cure you of your crush."

"Yeah, right."

"Oh come on." Holly's whine made me cringe.

"Kate would kill me with her bare hands if she ever found out."

"She won't find out. You're too good for her. She'll never catch you."

"Yeah, unless *you're* not careful and stare into her eyes." I tried to sound light but the words tasted false.

"So will you do it?"

The truth was, I wanted it—wanted Alec to be my first kiss—more than ever. And just as much, I wanted to hold that secret over Kate. I wanted to be able to smile inwardly, knowing something she didn't, whenever she sneered in my direction.

I thought of the rules I'd established for myself a few years ago and the new ones that the agency had imposed on me. We were forbidden to use our Variations against each other. But the thought of getting close to Alec, of being in his arms and kissing him just once, was too enticing.

What could possibly go wrong?

CHAPTER 4

The door burst open, followed by a gust of wind, before it quickly closed again. To a "normal" human it might have appeared as though no one had entered. A giggle revealed Holly's presence. She'd managed to silently sneak up on me once again.

Slowly the edges of her form grew blurry. Her body began to take shape, color bleeding into the fuzzy outline of it until, after a few seconds, Holly stood in front of me, clutching clothes against her chest, her cheeks rosy with excitement. Holly had learned to make the objects she held invisible, and Summers thought she had the potential to hide living things too. So far, though, the training with earthworms hadn't gone well; some of them had disappeared for good.

"It worked and I didn't lose concentration!" She held up the clothes she'd stolen from Kate's room and set them over her chair. "I saw her leave for the pool. She usually spends an hour there." When I didn't get up from my bed, she thrust her arms up. "Hurry!"

"I'm not sure if this is such a good idea."

"Come on, don't be lame. This is your big chance."

There was a knock at the door. Holly shoved Kate's clothes under my pillow as I opened it. Mrs. Finnigan stood in the corridor holding a letter, the corners of her lips drooping in a perpetual frown. I took the envelope as she turned and left without a word.

ADDRESS UNKNOWN glared at me in fat, red letters.

"The letter you sent your mom?" Holly asked.

"Yeah," I whispered. "She moved. She didn't even bother telling me."

"Maybe she just hasn't had the time yet? I'm sure she'll send you a letter soon."

It was doubtful.

One thing I admired about Holly was the way she always tried to see the positive in everyone. But she hadn't met my mom or the many questionable men she'd dated. And Holly couldn't possibly understand. She had caring parents and four younger siblings who loved her despite her Variation, who took her home for Christmas each year and sent her letters and small gifts, though they didn't have much money. She hadn't been abandoned by her father, hadn't been brushed off by her mother like a bothersome pet. Her parents didn't hate her for what she was.

I remembered the first time I shape-shifted; I was five. Mom and I were living in a small, dank one-room apartment in New York with a guy who spent most of his nights screaming and his days passed out on the sofa. There was a playground across from the apartment building, and on that day Mom was nursing a headache like she so often did, so I ventured outside alone. Nobody paid me any attention. Instead of playing with the other kids, I watched the mothers interacting with their children, studying the way they'd hug them and hold their hands. Without realizing what I was doing, I changed into the shape of a girl I'd bumped and went over to her mother, who stood talking to a few other women. I asked her if we could go home and, after a moment of hesitation, she left with me—without noticing that her real daughter was still playing on the other side of the playground.

Holding her hand while we walked home felt wonderful. Unfortunately, I soon shifted back to my own body and the woman immediately realized her mistake. She probably thought she'd gone mental. Maybe that was what kept the woman from asking questions. After she was reunited with her real daughter on the playground, we encountered my mother, who had gone in search of me and witnessed the entire event. I remembered Mom's anger and panic afterward, the way she'd shouted at me for leaving the house and demanded an explanation for what I'd done. Mom hastily packed a suitcase, and we left our apartment two hours later without telling her boyfriend. We never returned. It wasn't our last move. Every time I shifted, Mom feared someone might have seen, and we fled our home once again. I'd lost count of the times it had happened.

"She's probably run off with a new guy." I crumpled the letter before chucking it into the trash can. "Whatever. It doesn't matter."

I turned away from Holly's sympathetic face and concentrated on shifting. The rippling sensation washed over me, making me shudder. Holly kept her eyes on me through the shift, her expression alight with fascination. She'd seen me shift so often, I was amazed she wasn't used to it by now.

"I wish I had your talent. It's so cool."

"Says the invisibility girl."

That raised a smile, but then she shook her head. "It's too hard to be nice to you when you look like that."

Kate's face was staring back at me in the mirror. My own turquoise eyes, auburn hair, and annoyingly freckled nose were gone. Instead I had straight blond hair, strange coppery eyes, and long legs. My T-shirt strained over her bigger chest, and my jeans were too short for her body. That was a reminder of her superior looks that I really didn't need. *She* had breasts to show off. And she, like Holly, had a family who loved her—Variants who were off somewhere in the world working for the FEA. It was frustrating how lucky she was—having parents who were like her, who understood what it meant to be different. Variation usually skipped a generation but, *of course*, even that rule didn't apply to Kate.

"Hey, stop it with the sad-face. Kate never looks like that."

I tried to imitate the slightly bored expression she usually wore.

"Better?" I asked with the perfect imitation of Kate's trademark smirk.

Holly shuddered. "Much better. I want to punch you."

I gave a small bow, but my insides started to do flips. Holly handed me Kate's clothes and I slipped into them. Skinny jeans, half boots, and a silky cream-colored blouse.

"Now go. I'll take a swim to keep an eye on Kate. Don't want her to burst in while you're attached to Alec's lips, right?" She ushered me out of our room, closing the door in my face.

I stared at the wood for a moment before I hurried toward Alec's room at the far end of the corridor. The closer I got to Alec, the stronger the pull seemed to get, and the more uneasy I felt about what I was about to do. I knew there were reasons for the rules of the FEA, meant to strengthen trust and peace among the agents. That kind of unwavering trust was necessary among a group of people who were able to breach the privacy of the mind, change into whoever they liked, and turn invisible. And I was about to risk it all.

I stopped in front of Alec's door. Soft music played behind it.

I raised my hand to knock, the white of the door blurring before my eyes. Did the real Kate knock or would she just barge in? I'd never paid much attention to the way she acted around Alec because the sight of them together made me feel sick.

It wasn't fair; she didn't even like him the way he was. She didn't like the same movies, didn't like the way he dressed, didn't understand how it was to grow up without loving parents the way Alec and I did.

The door swung open and Alec stood in the open space, surprise spreading across his face. I took a step back, almost falling over my too-long legs. "I thought I heard someone out here." I stared at him, unable to move, though every fiber in my body screamed at me to run. "Isn't it time for your swim?"

"Swim?"

Alec's brows furrowed. "Are you all right?"

I nodded. "Yes, sorry. I'm just a bit out of it today."

His eyes made me nervous. *Could he see right through me?*

But he took a step back so I could enter.

My legs shook as I walked past him into his room. I'd never been in here before. Because he was older and had been with the agency longer, he didn't have a roommate. There was nobody to interrupt us. The bed came into my view and heat flooded my body.

"Kate?" Alec's hand on my shoulder made me jump. He turned me around to face him and my eyes were immediately drawn to his lips, and the way his hair was mussed like he'd run his hand through it.

"I . . . I . . ." I trailed off, not sure what to say. I needed to get out of here. This didn't feel right. If I died without ever being kissed, then so be it.

"Are you still angry with me?"

Angry? Did they have a fight?

I hesitated for a beat longer than I should have. His expression turned puzzled.

I was giving myself away. If I acted this confused as Madison, I'd ruin the mission. If I couldn't even pretend to be Kate—whom I knew—how was I supposed to impersonate a girl I'd never actually met?

"Are you sure you're all right? You seem kinda funny."

I took a step back, the urge to flee stronger than ever, and a shudder went through me. Panicked, I tried to suppress the sensation, but the rippling only grew stronger.

Alec froze, his eyes growing wide. "Tess?" His shock morphed into anger. "What the hell are you doing here?"

My hand rose to my hair and I snatched up a strand to inspect it. Auburn. I was so dead. Major would strangle me—if Alec didn't do it first. He drew back as if my closeness burned him. I'd never seen him so furious.

"Tessa, answer me!"

"I . . . I can explain."

Could I?

He folded his arms. "I can't wait to hear it."

Cringing under the vehemence of his gaze, I opened my mouth, hoping the right words would find their way out. Explanation—I needed an explanation.

Just tell him the truth.

"It—" I scanned the room, taking in the white walls with the *Alien* movie posters, the ones we'd ordered on eBay after an *Alien* movie marathon, the desk with the figurine of Freddy Krueger I'd given him last Christmas because we loved to watch *Nightmare on Elm Street* together. *Tell him you're in love with him.* I could feel the words rise into my mouth, but then my eyes landed on the framed photo of him and Kate on the nightstand. "It—it was for practice," I blurted.

"Practice?" Major would have roared, but Alec's voice had become very quiet. If it wasn't for the look in his eyes, I might have thought he was calm. But they were full of emotions I was too scared to understand.

I gripped the edge of the desk. It felt solid, unwavering—everything I was not. "Yes. I thought it would be a good test run to pretend to be someone else before I impersonate Madison."

Doubt flickered across his face. His stance loosened. "That's all?"

I nodded and glanced at the *Alien* poster on his wall.

"But why Kate?"

"I . . . I don't know." My eyes burned. I couldn't stand the disappointment on his face. "I already know her, so it seemed like a good place to start."

His fury gave way to something softer, but just as quickly it was gone, and he turned his back to me. "Why are you making this so difficult?" he murmured. I wasn't sure if the words were meant for me since I barely heard them.

"What?"

"Nothing." He shook his head. A few heartbeats of silence passed between us until I couldn't bear it anymore.

"Alec, I'm so sorry." I took a few steps toward him, hand outstretched. I wasn't sure why I felt the need to bridge the distance between us, why I ached to touch him. But where Alec was concerned, I just *wanted*—wanted to make things better, wanted to take care of him, wanted to be close to him.

He walked to the other side of the room, and I let my arm drop to my side. "Using your Variation to lie to me, even if it's for practice, is inexcusable. It violates our basic premise of trust. Promise me you won't do this ever again."

"I promise," I said in a small voice. "So you won't tell Major?"

He shook his head. "No, I won't tell him. But I think you should go now. I need some time to think."

I left without a word, feeling like I'd been dismissed. I'd betrayed Alec's trust. All because of a stupid kiss.

CHAPTER 5

"Maybe it's not as bad as you think," Holly said. She sat beside me on my bed, worrying her lower lip.

"I lost control of my Variation. That's the worst thing that could have happened. I'm worried that it's a bad sign. That I'm not good enough for this mission."

"Don't say that. Your Variation is as close to perfection as it can get, and it always has been. I've never told you this, but you know, sometimes I really envy you."

I let out a shaky laugh. "I'm the last person anyone should envy. My Variation was the only thing in my life that was consistent, and now? It's like I have nothing that's solid." I shook my head. "Gosh, listen to me. Now I'm being all dramatic, though it's all my fault. I should've never turned into Kate. If Alec tells Major, he'll ban me from the mission." I said it like it was a bad thing, but a small part of me secretly wanted him to. At least then I wouldn't have to face a crazy-ass killer.

"Alec likes you too much to let this get in the way of things. I'm sure he'll forget it ever happened."

"He won't."

I'd broken Alec's trust. I knew this wasn't something he would forget. And if it had been anyone but me, he'd probably tell Major.

"You didn't see Alec's face when he realized it was me." My voice broke. I tried to cover it up with a cough but it was no use. Holly's eyes softened and she wrapped her arms around me. "Everything will be fine. Alec will forgive you and you'll rock the mission."

She nudged me. "Come on. Let's have dinner and pretend nothing ever happened. We'll erase the last two hours from your mind."

I sighed. "I wish you could actually do that."

I was much too busy to curl into a heap of self-pity, though I wanted nothing more. A pile of Madison's yearbooks, her old papers, maps of Livingston, and all sorts of other artifacts sat in a hefty pile on my desk. I picked up the heap, supporting it with my chin to keep it from tipping over, and left the room.

My arms quivered under the weight of the pile. I decided against the staircase for once and let the elevator take me down to the basement floor, where the library and kitchen were situated. Passing the silence of the library doors, I followed the clanking of pots and the sound of singing that drifted from the back of the building. As I stepped through the double swinging doors, I spotted Martha— swaying to the music emanating from an old radio above the sink, her back turned to me, her gray hair bundled in a hairnet. She was a big woman, all softness and curves. Without turning around, she snapped, "Food's upstairs. No sneaking around in my kitchen!" Her words were hardened by her Austrian accent, a remnant from her childhood in Vienna during World War II. Her father, a Variant, had cooperated with the newly founded FEA to help overthrow the

Nazis. But he was captured and killed before the end of the war. The FEA brought Martha and her mother into the U.S. and employed them, though Martha herself didn't have a Variation—like most children of Variants. But Tanner often joked that her otherworldly cooking must be the result of some secret foodie Variation, as it was undeniably superhuman.

Her scowl disappeared when she saw me. "Tessa, *mein Mädchen*." She always called me her girl.

I lowered my stuff onto the kitchen island.

She wiggled her index finger. "Oh oh, Tony won't like that. You'll get grease on your papers!" Martha was the only one who called Major by his first name, Tony, short for Antonio. Most people didn't even dare to address him by his last name, much less a nickname. And the actual chance of getting grease on anything was close to zero. Martha's kitchen was the cleanest room in headquarters.

"He won't find out, will he?" I climbed onto one of the barstools and spread Madison's yearbook and the papers out in front of me. Martha leaned against the sink and watched me.

"Having trouble with your boy?"

"How can you tell?" I asked, not trying to deny it.

"I know that look. All lovelorn. I too was young once, *mein Mädchen*."

Martha was the only person I'd ever heard use the word *lovelorn* in her daily speech. No matter how hard I tried, I couldn't imagine her as a young girl, without a double chin, flappy skin, and wrinkles.

She put a wrinkled hand on mine, her palm rough from baking and washing dishes. "French toast makes everything better. What do you say?"

I smiled. She squeezed my hand and began assembling the ingredients for her famous brioche French toast with fresh raspberries.

I opened the yearbook and skimmed through its pages until I landed on Madison's photo. She looked happy. Right next to it, I found a picture of her best friend, Ana. She had curly brown hair, an oval face, and huge eyes like a girl from a manga. I'd surely recognize her in person. I browsed further, scanning the faces at dances, pep rallies, and school plays, only to stop at a photo of a boy named Phil Faulkner. I was halted by his eyes, which were a translucent, watery blue, like the color had been washed from them. A number of Variants had weird eyes, Kate and I among them. If Phil was a Variant, that might help explain why Major was interested in the case. But strange eyes didn't automatically make him one of us. Still, I told myself, it wouldn't hurt to keep an eye on him just in case.

Martha set a plate down in front of me. It smelled of vanilla, sweetness, and lemon. "Thanks," I said, already bringing a fork to my lips. "Mmm." That was enough validation for Martha. She patted my cheek and returned to scrubbing the counters.

Careful not to drop any food onto the yearbook, I continued to pore over its pages. There were too many names, too many faces with too many histories behind them to remember everything. Moving on to the final pages of the book, I found the superlatives section, where people were awarded titles like Best Artist or Dream Couple.

As I scanned over the photos, I choked on a bite of brioche, my eyes starting to water. Martha looked up from the counter, face tight with disapproval over my ruining a perfectly fine bite of her French toast by coughing. I swallowed, staring at a picture of Madison and Ryan. "The Dream Couple." Holy shit. Why had nobody bothered to tell me this?

So Madison had had a boyfriend, Ryan Wood. Had they been a couple up until her attack?

As I studied the photo, I noticed something was off about their body language. Ryan looked like he couldn't be happier, but Madison's smile was a bit too bright, her expression a bit too devoted, everything about her a bit . . . too much. I wished I could see into her thoughts in that moment, but even Kate wasn't capable of such a thing.

As it was, I'd just have to investigate the old-fashioned way. I slammed the yearbook shut. Martha tsked but didn't say anything.

Next I rummaged through Madison's school papers. There were essays about Tolstoy, Kafka, and even Nabokov's *Lolita*, for which she had earned perfect grades. I hoped no one expected me to write papers about literature, which really wasn't my thing.

I spread the map of Livingston on the kitchen island. Right next to Livingston was Manlow, the neighboring town. Nestled in between them lay the lake where Madison and one of the other victims had been found. Stretches of deep green dominated the map, indicating lots of forest. Livingston had only two main roads, where most of the shops were located. I counted two gas stations, two graveyards, and a drive-in movie theater. Not much of anything really. Madison and her parents lived in one of the newer developments bordering the forest. I folded the map and, after a moment of hesitation, I opened the file about the murders.

The first victim was Dr. Hansen. She'd been a thirty-five-year-old pediatrician at St. Elizabeth's Hospital in Manlow, but she lived in Livingston, close to the lake. She'd been found in her backyard, strangled, with an *A* cut into her rib cage. Soon afterward, Kristen Cynch, a seventeen-year-old high school senior, was found drowned in the lake. She had unusual marks that looked like a snake had wrapped itself around her throat. Her skin was bloated and blue, but the red mark of her killer was impossible to miss. The same signature had been cut into the other two victims, including the janitor, Mr. Chen. Hesitantly, I touched the spot over my ribs where the mark would be. Sickness settled in my stomach.

I hopped off the barstool, deciding to call it a night. "Good night, Martha, and thanks for the food."

She waved me off with a small smile.

The moment I arrived back on the fourth floor, I heard the fighting. The words were hushed, so it took me a moment to recognize the voices: Alec and Kate. I crept closer and peeked around the corner. They stood facing each other by the door to Alec's room.

"I can't read your thoughts but that doesn't mean I don't know what you're thinking!" Kate hissed.

"I don't know why you're so upset," Alec said. There was an edge to his voice, though he was much calmer than Kate.

"Don't play dumb. Everyone notices how you are around her. It's ridiculous."

"This discussion is ridiculous," Alec said. He turned to go into his room but Kate gripped his arm.

"I know you two had movie night last week. You didn't even tell me."

"Kate, I don't have to ask your permission for every little thing I do."

"We're in this together. Remember what Major said." She lowered her voice so I didn't catch her next words, but Alec's face darkened. He stormed into his room with Kate close behind, the door closing behind them.

What had Major said?

No matter what, one thing was clear: they were fighting because of me. I wasn't sure if I should feel elated or worried. Kate was a force to be reckoned with.

The next morning on my way to the dojo, I actually considered breaking my leg so I wouldn't have to face Alec. But I thought better of it, since Major would probably insist I do training with my arms.

I arrived a few minutes early to mentally prepare myself. But when I approached the entrance, Alec was already there, sitting on a bench and staring at his feet. A few strands of black hair fell into his face. For a moment, I was sure he was crying. I froze halfway into the dojo, not sure what to do. I'd never seen Alec cry. He was the epitome of self-control. I inched slowly toward him but he didn't look up, though his body tensed. I touched his shoulder. "What's wrong? Did something happen?"

His muscles shifted under my fingers as though he was bracing himself for his reply, or maybe fighting against it. "I had a talk with Major—about his expectations. He wants me to take more responsibility and—" He stopped midsentence. Anger surged through me. Why was Major pressuring Alec? Sometimes I wondered if he saw Alec as his successor and kept challenging him to determine if he was up for the job.

"Tell him you're not ready for it," I said.

He looked up, his eyes tortured but devoid of tears. "It's not that easy."

I gently kneaded his shoulder, fighting the urge to hug him. "You know I'm there for you if you need me. And you know you can talk to me about anything."

For a moment he looked like he wanted to, like I'd broken through his mask of duty, but then he shook his head. "No. I wish I could, but I can't talk to you about it."

I tried to hide how much that sentence had wounded me. "Then talk to Kate. Maybe she can help you." The words left a bitter taste in my mouth, but I'd rather have Kate take care of Alec than have him suffer alone.

"Kate wouldn't understand. She would just agree with Major. Her first priority has always been the FEA and that won't ever change. I've got to deal with this alone."

How could he be with someone who didn't make him a priority?

"I shouldn't be talking to you about this," he said as he stood, letting my hand slip off his shoulder, bringing a few steps of distance between us.

"I think we need to talk about yesterday," he said.

That was the last thing I wanted to do, especially when he was in such a strange mood. I started wrapping tape around my palms to prepare them for my training, adding one layer after the other. "There's nothing to talk about."

"We have to get this out of the way. We have a job to do. We can't have something—anything—distracting us. Major's worried it'll interfere with the mission."

I dropped the tape. "What's Major got to do with it? Did you tell him about yesterday?"

"No, of course not. He noticed something was . . . going on. Everyone has." He scanned my face, and I had a hard job keeping it in check. "Listen, whatever there is between us, it's got to stop. I'm too old for you and it isn't right."

"You're only three years older than me." Why did I even argue with him? He'd clearly made up his mind, and nothing, certainly nothing I could say, would change that.

"And I'm with Kate."

That was a point I couldn't contradict. They may have fought yesterday and they might be together for reasons I couldn't begin to understand, but they were still a couple. I stared at a spot over his left shoulder. There was a small crack running down the length of the floor-length mirror. It warped my reflection, dividing my face into two distinct halves. I felt a lie slipping out of my mouth. "Don't worry. The mission is the only thing that counts."

I started to stretch my legs and arms, ignoring the tightness in my chest.

Alec came up behind me, but the concern didn't leave his face. "All right. I think you've improved a lot. Someone who doesn't know about your Variation will have trouble beating you."

But for perhaps the first time, I didn't want to hear his praise.

"Ready?" he asked.

"Oh yes."

Alec's arms came around me.

The rippling sensation washed over me. Shrinking, shifting, shaping.

Alec loosened his grip, though he should've been able to predict my move. Now in the body of a small child, I slipped out of his hold and scurried backward. I returned to my own body and aimed a high-kick at his head. He sidestepped my attempt and pushed me back, barely touching my body.

Why was it that he could appear on my doorstep for movie night after months of keeping his distance and then act like nothing happened? Why could he almost kiss me that day but a few days later act like it was all my doing?

"Stop holding back!" I screamed, charging toward him. He only dodged my punches and kicks. It was like he wanted to touch me as little as possible. That thought sent me over the edge. My skin started rippling and I felt myself grow, my skin stretch, my bones tearing and rebuilding.

His eyes widened.

I'd become him. I'd never done that.

My knuckles cracked as they made contact with his abs. I wished the shift would bring the Variant powers of his body with them, but I wasn't any stronger or faster than a normal man. Something changed in Alec's eyes as if a switch had been flicked—a fighter awakened.

I aimed a kick at his head. His hand shot out, grabbed my ankle and twisted. I spun in the air before I collided with the ground. My wrist bent back at an unnatural angle, and I screamed as I shifted back to my own body.

Alec knelt beside me on the mat but I didn't move.

"Tess, shit. Say something."

I pushed myself up into a sitting position and scrambled to

my feet. Cradling my wrist in my other hand, I took a step back as he reached out for me. I didn't want him to touch me if it was out of pity, not when he couldn't stand my closeness for any other reason.

"I don't want to practice with you anymore. Just tell Major I'm ready."

"Tess—"

"Just tell him! I don't want to be near you, Alec."

This . . . *thing* with Alec was messing with my Variation. It was ruining everything I'd worked so hard to achieve.

I didn't wait for his reaction; I left.

The intercom crackled as Major's voice summoned me into his office. I dragged myself out of our room, glad that Holly had criminology and wasn't there to give me a pep talk.

I knocked on Major's open door and stepped inside. He sat behind his desk, a cup of steaming tea in front of him. Worry lined his forehead. He looked up when I entered, and turned on his blank expression.

I lingered in the doorway, pushing my hands into my pockets. If he wanted to shout at me for abusing my Variation, I'd rather be in a position where I could flee as fast as possible. The piercing intensity of his gaze made me squirm. It felt as if he could see right through me. What if he could? What if that was his rumored secret Variation?

His gaze didn't waver. "Sit down."

My skin began to prickle in a way that made me want to scratch it. I perched on the edge of the seat, my hands folded on my lap.

The shiny name plate on Major's desk looked as if it had just been cleaned and polished. It looked odd next to the small crack in the wood Alec had caused the last time I was in there.

"I assume you know the reason for your summoning."

"Yes."

CHAPTER 6

Major nodded. "Good. This is an important matter. We can't afford for you to fail."

This didn't sound like a lecture on the abuse of my powers.

"Sir?"

"It's a pity that Kate's Variation is so limited. I have a feeling that Madison's brother or father might have shed a good deal of light on many aspects of her life." He started tapping the smooth wooden surface of his desk. His nails were short and neat; I'd never seen a speck of dirt on him. He didn't take his eyes off me.

"We talked to her doctors and convinced them it was likely that Madison would suffer from amnesia after she woke from the artificial coma."

"Someone messed with their minds?" The words were out before I could stop them.

Major rose from his chair and loomed over me. "We don't mess with people's minds, Tessa."

I dropped my gaze to my lap. "Of course not, sir."

"This mission is about saving lives. You understand that, don't you?"

"Yes, sir."

"Good. Here are a few pages touching on the typical after-effects of an artificial coma, particularly in a case like Madison's." He pushed a stack of papers over to me. More facts to read and remember, to internalize until there was no room left for anything else.

"Many important figures will be watching you. This mission can be your breakthrough."

There was a knock on the door and Alec walked in. *Fabulous.*

I dropped the stack of papers. The pages scattered across the hardwood floor. My insides clenched as I got to my knees and started picking them up. A pair of strong hands came to my aid. I didn't look up, gingerly taking the papers from him and settling back on my chair.

From the corner of my eye, I watched Alec take his seat beside me. He wasn't looking at me, and he didn't have to. Major's scrutiny was enough to make me jittery.

What was Alec doing here anyway? Our training was supposed to be over.

"Alec and I have spoken, and he will join you on your mission."

"He . . . what?!" I blurted.

Alec turned to me, his forehead furrowed. I avoided his eyes and instead focused on Major, whose expression had turned stern.

"Sir," I added. "Why?" I hated the little part of me that felt elated about the news.

"Alec suggested it would be safer for you if he was around, and I agree. Alec can protect you while conducting his own local investigations."

So it had been his suggestion. Was this his twisted idea of

revenge? He might keep me safe from the killer, but who the hell would protect me from my feelings for him?

"But, sir. How is Alec supposed to fit in?"

Alec's face tightened. "*Alec* plays a new student. He'll be a senior. Also, he's in the room with you."

I glared at him.

"A senior?" I put as much sarcasm into my words as possible. "But he never went to middle school, much less high school."

"Neither did you," Alec snapped.

"I went to middle school."

Major leaned forward in his chair and rested his arms on his desk. "That's enough, you two." Something close to amusement flickered in his dark eyes.

"But, sir, if he pretends to be a student he can't live alone. People will get suspicious."

"He won't be alone. Summers will pretend to be his mother."

Alec leaned back, his legs stretched out on the wood floor in front of him. But behind his mask of relaxation, something was lurking. If I wasn't mistaken, it wasn't even directed at me.

"Agent Summers?"

Major nodded.

Summers. I had to admit, that was clever of Major. There wasn't a better fit to make sure the habitants of Livingston weren't suspicious of Alec and me. Her Variation—diversion—would surely come in handy. Of course, from a practical standpoint, she didn't look one bit like Alec, nor did she possess a single motherly trait. With her underbite and broad shoulders, she looked like someone who enjoyed hanging around in shady bars and fighting scoundrels for money.

And Alec . . . I allowed myself a sideways glance. Alec was Alec. Tall, tan, buff, black-haired, with his gray eyes and his chiseled jaw . . .

"They don't look related."

"Not all children resemble their parents. You, for example, look nothing like your mother."

I shrugged. "Maybe I look like my father." My tone of voice was petulant and one I didn't usually use with Major. But my family was taboo. No one brought them up. Ever. And everyone knew that.

Alec straightened in his seat, his muscles tense.

Major considered my point. "Maybe. But that's not important now. The only thing of importance is that you won't be alone in this mission. Alec will be at your side. And Summers's main job will be to divert the police's attention. We don't want them prying about too much. They don't know what they're doing, and this case is the FEA's business. Especially if there's Variant involvement."

"Has Variant involvement been confirmed, sir?" I ventured.

"No, but I prefer to take all necessary precautions. Two of the victims show extremely atypical pressure marks around their throats. That's our only lead so far." Major scanned my face, then Alec's. What was he looking for? "I hope this arrangement will guarantee the swift success of our mission."

Major started pacing, his arms crossed behind his back. "Let's go over our possible suspects again."

"I thought we didn't know anything conclusive about the murderer, now that he's started killing men," I said.

"That's mostly true. As you may know, the profilers are still trying to narrow down the list of possible suspects. They told me that the killer is almost certainly a man and probably knew all four victims."

That wasn't helpful. Livingston was a small town; everyone knew one another somehow.

"Kate's exploration of Mrs. Chambers showed that she isn't involved, and neither is Madison's aunt Cecilia or Madison's best friend, Ana. As for the rest of her friends and family members, they're all suspects unless proven otherwise—especially the men."

"Why only men? I thought the women didn't show signs of . . ." Alec glanced awkwardly at me. " . . . sexual harassment?"

"No, they didn't. We're not dealing with a sex offender."

"So why only male suspects?"

"Strangling someone requires considerable strength, and serial murderers are typically men. I'm not saying that you shouldn't keep an eye on the women in Madison's life, but I don't want you to waste your energy on unlikely suspects. The killer might have gone to school with Madison or might be involved with the school in some capacity. After all, one of the victims worked in the high school and the other was a senior."

Mr. Chen and Kristen Cynch.

"What about the first victim? Did she have any connection to the high school?" Alec asked.

"No, she was a pediatrician in St. Elizabeth's Hospital. The only possible connection is that she's probably treated most of Livingston's students since they were kids," I said.

It was scary how in the dark we were. Anyone could be the murderer. So far the only connection was the *A* cut into the victims' skin. "Does Madison have the same mark as the other victims?"

"Yes, above her rib cage just like the others." Major cleared his throat and stopped behind his desk chair, hands gripping the backrest. "I think you should keep a close eye on Madison's boy-friend, Tessa. He might be the only one who knew what was really going on in the last few months of her life."

"A boyfriend?" Alec asked, incredulous. "You can't expect Tessa to continue someone else's romantic relationship."

I glanced at him. Was he jealous?

"She won't have to. As it turns out, Madison broke up with him a few weeks before the attack. That puts him very high on our list of suspects."

"But what motive might he have for the other murders?"

"We're not sure about that. But maybe he killed them without reason, and when Madison broke up with him he chose her as his next victim."

"But why the *A*?" I asked.

"That's for you to find out. The mission starts in two hours. Prepare yourself."

My eyes snapped up to Major's. "So soon?"

"Madison died half an hour ago. The doctors and the machines will keep the Chamberses believing that she's alive. But we only have so much time until the first signs of death begin to show."

I gave a numb nod. Why hadn't I felt anything? Shouldn't I have known when she died? After all, her DNA was part of me now. It was all that was left of her.

"Read the papers and be ready in an hour, Tessa," Major said before he zeroed in on Alec. "I'd like to have a word with you."

What did they want to discuss without me?

My feet carried me out of the room but my body felt like it was encased in a bubble. I barely heard the outside chatter, the laughter from the common room, and the music blaring from somewhere down the hall.

Holly froze when I came into our room.

"I have to go," I managed. My legs, my entire body were numb. Since hearing the news of Madison's death, it felt like the life had slid out of me too.

"How long will you be gone?"

"I don't know. However long it takes."

Holly just hugged me, for once not saying a word.

I pressed my face against the window of the car, remembering the evening more than two years ago when I'd sat in the same spot on my way to headquarters for the very first time. So much had changed since then.

My skin prickled and I sensed that Major was watching me.

The car glided to a stop. I reached for the door but Major's words stopped me. "I know something is going on between you and Alec. I already spoke with him about it. Don't let it endanger the mission."

"There's nothing . . ." I stopped myself. It would have been a lie and some people said Major could smell lies. It was just one of the ridiculous tales people spun about Major because they didn't really know what he was capable of.

We stepped out of the car. My legs felt like jelly as I trudged into the hospital. The tightness in my chest grew with every step I took closer to Madison's room. Voices echoed from the end of the corridor and my muscles began quivering.

I stumbled and Major grasped my arm. "Act natural," he said under his breath. "They should have been gone by now."

We walked through the corridor, closer to Madison's parents, acting as if we had some good reason to be here apart from covering up the death of their daughter.

I busied myself with gazing at the checkered pattern on the linoleum floor, but as we passed Madison's room, my eyes found them: Ronald and Linda Chambers. Linda looked older than in the photos I'd seen—wearier, paler, her blond hair gathered in a messy ponytail. Ronald looked thinner and the gray streaks in the hair at his temples had spread. They clung to each other as they listened to the doctors spewing lies. I couldn't hear the doctors' words but I knew that whatever they were telling them was far from the truth.

The worst thing was the way their faces lit up with hope as the doctors spoke to them. They thought their daughter would recover, that they'd get her back; they didn't know that only a few hours ago they'd lost her forever.

Suddenly, a sense of determination filled me. I'd find the monster who'd taken their daughter away from them. Even if I couldn't give Linda and Ronald Chambers their daughter back, I could at least try to give them justice. We turned another corner and they disappeared from view.

Hawk-Face leaned against the wall a few steps from us. He straightened when he saw us. Major let go of my arm. I hadn't even realized he'd been dragging me along.

"Why are they still there?" Major's scowl made the man recoil.

"I'm sorry, sir. They should be gone any moment."

"They'd better be."

Major started pacing and I busied myself with counting his

steps. His legs weren't long but his stride made him look tall. Hawk-Face peered around the corner, then turned to us and gave a quick nod.

We walked back to Madison's room, my mouth as dry as sawdust. Hawk-Face marched ahead and opened the door. Major beckoned for me to enter. There was no turning back now.

CHAPTER 7

The silence of the machines hit me.

No beeping.

No intake of breath.

I wished I had my iPod with me; anything to drown out the silence in the room. Madison lay on the bed. Nothing had changed—except for her missing heartbeat and the stillness of her rib cage.

"Can I have a moment?" I asked. The words sounded muffled, like they were spoken through a layer of cotton. Major hesitated. Did he have to question everything I did?

I set my jaw, keeping my focus on Madison as I waited for him to leave. When he finally did, I moved to her side. Her eyes were closed, as if she were asleep. I'd always thought that death would be ugly and ghastly and forbidding. Instead it masked itself with peacefulness and quiet.

I reached out, my fingertips stopping an inch from her hand, then closed the gap and touched her cold skin. I sank down beside the bed, my forehead coming to rest on the cool blanket beside her body. There was no sound.

The small ball of unease that formed in my stomach when I

first heard about the mission had now turned into a pulsating fear beneath my skin. Looking at Madison's still form, I was forced to confront the truth. A killer would be after me; someone who cut *As* into the skin of his victims, like an artist signing his work.

Just then, the door opened without warning. I stumbled to my feet, wiping away the tears that threatened to spill over my eyes. I wanted to snap at Major for giving me so little time.

But it wasn't Major.

Alec gently closed the door behind him. I turned away and perched on the bed, my fingertips resting on Madison's hand. Why was he here? Shouldn't he be off saying goodbye to Kate?

He moved closer. "How are you feeling?"

"How do you think I'm feeling?" His eyes rested on me, kind and understanding, and I had to press my lips together to keep myself in check. I couldn't risk breaking down now, in front of him.

"I know it's hard for you."

I stumbled to my feet. "How would you know? Are you about to lie to a family? Are you about to smile at them, laugh with them, all the while pretending to be their dead daughter? Do you have to look into their faces and see the joy of having their daughter back, all the while knowing that it's all a lie?" More words threatened to spurt out; the truth of how scared I was, the worry over making a rookie mistake and ending up dead. But I swallowed them back. If Alec knew just how scared I was, his annoying protectiveness would only skyrocket.

Alec reached out to pull me into his arms but I pressed my palms against his chest. I didn't want his pity, his consolation. He didn't let go. The feel of his hands on my arms, warm and comforting, broke my resistance. I let him embrace me, let his woodsy smell envelop my senses, let it carry away some of the pain. I felt my pulse slowing with his touch, felt my muscles relax for the first time in days.

"Tess, nobody expects you to be perfect, to go through this mission like a machine. You're allowed to be angry and frustrated. And you're allowed to make a few mistakes."

That was the one thing I couldn't allow myself. A slip of the tongue, a single blackout of my Variation and the mission was over—or I'd end up with a wire around my throat.

His fingertips brushed my neck and I melted against him.

"You're doing this for them too, you know? For Madison's parents. You're trying to catch the person who murdered their daughter. Don't you think that counts for anything? This monster is roaming the streets, searching for his next victim, and you're the key to finding and catching him. You have the ability to save lives. Just think about it that way." He brushed back a wisp of my hair. "Everything will be all right. I'll be there for you."

How did he always find the right words to sway me? Or maybe it was the feel of his soft touch on my skin. Maybe both.

"Major is waiting," he said eventually.

I nodded against his chest. Alec gave me a moment to gather myself before he opened the door and called everyone else into the room.

I avoided Major's eyes but I didn't miss the look he exchanged with Alec. Two men who looked like they belonged with the FEA approached the bed, though they could have been undertakers in their black suits and ties. They carried Madison's body off, leaving the bed empty.

I looked at the imprint left by Madison's body on the mattress. "Do I have to—?"

"We'll change it," Major said. A nurse hustled in and busied herself with the bed, stripping it clean and making it up with fresh sheets. She didn't once make eye contact with any of us. After she'd finished with the bedding, she left without a word. Now it was only me, Major, and Alec in the room.

"Here, you should put this on."

I took the hospital gown from Major, the fabric crisp and cold under my touch.

"Would you mind?" I glanced at the gown, then at the door. Major went first and Alec gave me an encouraging smile as he followed close behind.

With shaking hands, I put the gown on the bed and started undressing. This was a job, I reminded myself. It wasn't about my comfort. I peeled off the last of my clothing and slipped the gown over my head. A shiver shot down my back as my body made contact with the cold fabric.

There was a knock on the door. "Are you done?" Major called. He wasn't one for patience.

I climbed onto the bed and covered myself with the blanket. The door slid open and Major walked in. Alec hesitated but when he saw me propped up on the bed, my body safely hidden from his view, he entered.

There was another knock. Madison's parents? I wasn't ready yet.

Major went to the door as Alec sat down on the chair beside the bed. "It's only a doctor."

"But he'll see that I'm not Madison."

Alec nodded. "It's okay. Major decided to tell him. He won't tell anyone."

"How can you be so sure?"

"Major is sure."

A tall man with a bald head entered the room.

"This is Dr. Fonseca. He'll prepare you for Madison's parents," Major said in a matter-of-fact tone. I didn't get the chance to ask what "preparing" meant, as the doctor and Major stepped closer to my bed.

Dr. Fonseca's eyes rose to meet mine before darting back to Madison's patient file. He put more distance between us. A fine sheen of sweat covered his forehead, and his collar was soaked. I didn't have to be a mind reader to know that he too was scared.

"Tessa. It's time for you to take Madison's appearance," Major said.

In front of Dr. Fonseca? The man was gripping his ballpoint pen so tightly his knuckles had turned stark white.

"What are you waiting for, Tessa?" Major snapped.

Dr. Fonseca kept his eyes glued to his papers.

I allowed myself to relax and gave myself over to the shift. Skin loosened and was reshaped, bones lengthened. A gasp burst through my concentration. I closed my eyes, forcing my body to finish what it had started. And when the rippling sensation ebbed away, Tessa had dissolved and been replaced by Madison Chambers.

I opened my eyes and something sour filled my mouth at the sight before me. Dr. Fonseca stood pressed against the farthest wall, the medical files like a shield brandished in front of his chest. Alec's eyes hardened as they settled on Major. I'd never had anyone be afraid of me before. But there was no doubt about what I saw in Dr. Fonseca's eyes. Living with the FEA had let me forget about the true nature of my existence: a freak. A variation from the norm. Not the gifted wonder Major always wanted me to believe I was.

"Doctor?" Major's voice sliced through the silence like a razor.

Fonseca tore his gaze away from me with obvious difficulty and looked at Major, or rather at a point over Major's head.

Major's snarling face reminded me of a rottweiler. "Doctor. Do your job." Apparently, Dr. Fonseca hadn't gotten the memo that you obeyed Major's orders without hesitation. In one split second, Alec darted from the corner of the room to appear by the doctor's side. "What's your problem?" he spat. Fonseca's eyes darted between me and Alec, apparently still not scared enough of him to consider coming anywhere near me. Alec reached for the metal chair and snapped one of its legs in two. "She's not the dangerous one."

I wondered why Major let Alec do it, other than for the sheer pleasure of showing off what FEA agents were capable of.

Dr. Fonseca stumbled in his haste to get to my side. His hands shook as he placed a few electrodes on my arms and chest. I withdrew my arm when he tried to put me on an IV. The way the needle shook in his grip made me nervous. He'd more likely poke an eye out with it than put it safely into my arm.

"Why do I need that?" I jumped at the sound of the unknown voice coming from my lips. It was higher than my own. And my arm—Madison's arm—was so pale and thin. Her muscles must have suffered during the weeks she'd been in a coma. But luckily I didn't feel any weaker than before, only different.

"Because Madison would need medication. Be glad we convinced the doctors that you can breathe on your own," Major said.

I extended my arm. Dr. Fonseca took a deep breath and his hand steadied. I winced when the needle jabbed into the skin on the back of my hand.

"What's in there?" I nodded toward the clear liquid in the plastic bag of the IV.

"Nothing to worry about." Major sounded like he didn't have a worry in the world, but the deep lines around his eyes suggested he wasn't as relaxed as he pretended to be. This was a big day and an important mission, and it was out of even Major's hands. I was the one who had to perform.

My heartbeat picked up, and with it the annoying beep-beep of the machines. Alec approached me. "Everything will be fine." His eyes scanned my face, lingering on Madison's features a moment too long, like he had to get used to looking at them.

I forced the muscles in my—or rather Madison's—face to relax. My fingers traced over the scar on my throat where the killer had strangled her with a wire. It went almost all the way around my neck. Slowly, I let my hand wander lower until I could feel the spot on my rib cage where the killer had left his signature. Shivering, I drew back.

Dr. Fonseca let out a small cough. "I'm done here."

"Good." Major raised a cell phone to his ear. Apparently, the no-cell-in-hospital rule was suspended for him. "We'll be gone in a few minutes." I didn't know who was on the other end or what they were saying, but Major looked satisfied when he hung up.

"Where are Madison's parents?" I asked.

"They're still talking with the other doctors about how Madison's condition has improved and that it might be possible that you're going to wake soon."

The "you" threw me at first. Pretending to be Madison was going to take some getting used to. She wasn't much taller than me but she was thinner, and her chest was even smaller than my own. I picked up a strand of her dark blond hair. It felt smoother than my own and fell in straight lines to my chest.

"Your hair doesn't look right," Alec said.

He pushed his hands into my hair. A tingling shot down my spine and I relaxed against his warm palms. He froze as our eyes met. I couldn't tell what was going on behind them. He broke eye contact and started mussing up my hair. He was so gentle.

"That's better." He pulled away but I immediately wanted his touch back.

Major's cell phone started vibrating. "It's time to go." He opened the door but didn't leave. "Ronald and Linda Chambers will be here at any moment. Remember everything you read about Madison. From now until we find the murderer, you're Madison. Tessa's dead."

Tessa's dead.

Something gripped my insides and twisted. If I could vote to determine who should live and who should die—Madison or me—there was no doubt about the outcome. Madison had parents, a brother, relatives, even an ex-boyfriend who loved her; I had nothing.

What am I thinking?

"Did you hear me?"

I gave a nod, not trusting myself to speak. A sudden wave of calm overcame me, foreign and invasive, and I could feel my body bristle at the unwanted emotion. It wasn't mine. My eyes darted to Major, his form still lingering in the doorway. Had he just managed to manipulate the way I felt?

Alec hesitated as if he wanted to say something. I couldn't stop myself from meeting his eyes. There was worry in them, and something else—something softer I couldn't put my finger on. After a quick glance at Major, he smiled encouragingly, and they left.

Dr. Fonseca stayed. He checked the machines and the IV once more. I winced as the needle moved in my arm, and he apologized quietly. He didn't talk much, nor did he ever look me in the eyes.

One thing was for sure: Major was right, people were scared of our powers, afraid of what we were capable of. That was the first thing he'd taught Holly and me when we'd arrived at FEA headquarters. I'd never felt the truth of his words as plainly as I did now.

Voices outside the door caught my attention. I sank into the pillows and closed my eyes, trying to calm my breathing while watching the entrance through half-closed eyes. The door started to open. This was it. And it was in my hands not to mess it up.

I couldn't mess up. I *wouldn't* mess up.

Tessa was dead, for now.

CHAPTER 8

I cycled through my breathing exercise, trying to calm the pounding of my heart.

In and out.

In and out.

Through the narrowed slits of my eyelids, I watched as Linda Chambers slipped into the room, her steps faltering as she saw Dr. Fonseca. Ronald Chambers stopped behind her, his hands on her shoulders. His eyes were focused on me and I decided it was safer to keep mine closed.

"How . . ." She cleared her throat. "How is she? Dr. Myers and Dr. Ortiz told us there was a chance she would wake today."

"Her condition has improved. She's breathing on her own and she stirred just moments ago," Dr. Fonseca said.

"She moved?" The hope in Mrs. Chambers's voice made me feel like the worst liar in the world. She should be mourning the loss of her daughter, and instead she was being promised a miracle.

"Even if she wakes, don't expect too much from her. After what she's been through, she might have to learn many things from scratch. It might take a while before she'll be able to walk and talk the same way she used to. It's very possible that she won't remember much, maybe not even you." He paused before adding, "It's important that you don't pressure her into remembering." Listening to Dr. Fonseca talk with ease, I wondered how he could lie to them without so much as a quiver in his voice.

"We won't. We'll do everything in our power to help her get well," Madison's father said.

I allowed my hands to twitch and my eyes to flutter.

"I think she's waking up," Mrs. Chambers said.

Steps came closer.

I knew they were watching my every move. I turned my head an inch but kept my eyes closed and let out a hoarse cough.

The mattress dipped. "Maddy? Honey, wake up."

"Cupcake, Mom and Dad are here." Ronald's tone was so soft, so loving, so gentle. I couldn't help but wonder if my own dad had ever talked to me like that, if he'd been happy after I was born, if he ever missed me at all.

I allowed my eyes to flutter open for a moment, enough to see their worried faces hovering above me, before I closed them again. A hand touched my cheek, too soft and small to belong to a man. "Honey?" I'd never thought one word could carry so much love. Linda's palm felt warm and comforting, even though it was a foreign touch. I felt myself relax.

Finally, I opened my eyes. I'd never seen someone look at me the way Ronald and Linda did—like I was the most precious thing in their lives.

"Oh, Maddy."

Linda started crying. I wanted to join her. Overcome with relief and joy, she was emotional for all the wrong reasons. She didn't know her dead daughter had been carried out on a gurney only a few minutes ago while the doctors wove a story about their daughter's miraculous recovery. They didn't know their little girl lay in the cold storage of a morgue, waiting there until the day when my job was done, when they'd finally learn the truth.

Heat pressed against my eyes as Ronald's lips brushed my forehead and he murmured words of comfort. Suddenly, I could no longer hold back. The tears trailed over my cheeks and pooled near my lips.

Linda hugged me, her touch cotton soft as though she was afraid of hurting me. Ronald brushed my hair from my face and wrapped his arms around Linda and me. For a moment I allowed myself to imagine their love was actually for me.

Eventually they pulled back.

I noticed that Dr. Fonseca had left the room. Maybe he couldn't stand watching the happy reunion, knowing the ugly truth behind it.

Ronald pulled a chair up to the bed and sat down. Linda perched on the bedside, holding my hand in a crushing grip. "Do you know who we are, Cupcake?" Ronald's blue eyes were alight with hope but there was still a certain tightness around his lips.

I coughed again because the medical papers had said I'd have trouble speaking after being hooked up to a breathing machine. Technically, I shouldn't have been able to talk properly for days, but there was a killer to catch. Linda's expression grew troubled. "Do you need water?"

I nodded.

Ronald brought me a plastic cup and I started raising my arm.

You just woke from a coma. Move slowly, I told myself, and let my hand drop.

Linda took the cup from her husband. He helped me sit up and supported me while she brought it to my lips and tipped it forward so I could drink. The water cooled my dry throat.

"Better?" she asked.

I gave a nod. Ronald propped the pillows up behind me, so I was sitting upright.

"Do you know who we are?" Linda asked.

Ronald gave his wife a warning look.

"Yes," I barely croaked out. My throat closed up at the sight of their happiness. They hadn't expected me to speak, nor to remember them, and technically I shouldn't have been able to. But Major thought it would speed up our mission if I didn't have to pretend to learn every little thing all over again. He wanted me back at their home and investigating the high school as soon as possible.

"What else do you remember?" Linda asked.

"I'm . . ." I coughed again. "I'm not sure." I forced my face to look puzzled. "I remember Ana, and Devon. I remember Fluffy." I trailed off.

"That's good," Ronald paused. "Do you remember what happened?"

Something dark clouded his eyes and his hands balled to fists at his side. Linda tried to keep her face relaxed but the hand holding mine began trembling.

"No, I . . . I don't know how I got here." I hesitated, the words crowding in the back of my throat.

"What happened?" I asked quietly.

Linda slid off the bed and walked quietly to the window. I wished I could have seen her face, but the way her shoulders shook maybe it was better I didn't. Ronald clutched at his knees. "It's a long story. Maybe we should wait to talk about it until you feel better." I nodded. Neither of them spoke after that. I watched them through half-lidded eyes but Linda kept her face turned to the window. Eventually Ronald went to her and wrapped his arms around her shoulders.

With a short rapping, the door opened and a teenage guy slinked into the room. I recognized him from the photos as Madison's twin brother. I kept my eyes half closed and pretended to drift back to sleep, so I could watch them interact before I was forced to join the conversation. I wasn't yet ready to meet my pretend brother.

Devon was stocky like a wrestler but not as tall as Alec. His blond hair was cropped short and mussed up with styling mousse to give him a just-out-of-bed look. I had to strain my ears to hear him. "How is she?"

Linda's face was red and splotchy. "She just woke up." Devon's eyes widened as he let his mother wrap her arms around him. "She talked to us, she *remembered* us."

"Oh Mom, that's great." He pulled back, his eyes darting back over to me. "Did she remember anything about the attack?"

Ronald shook his head. "No, she doesn't seem to remember anything about that day."

"So she's got no clue who did that to her," Devon said.

"I don't think we should talk about it in front of her," Linda said. She walked over to the bed and began stroking my hair.

"Sorry, Mom." His sneakers squealed on the linoleum floor.

It was probably too soon for me to wake again, but pretending to sleep was harder than it sounded. I wanted to twitch.

I stirred, coughed, and was greeted with startling blue eyes. The photos hadn't done Devon justice. His smile was all sunshine and his eyes almost matched Alec's in their intensity.

"Hey, sleepyhead." His tone was playful and dripping with warmth.

"Devon," I whispered.

His grin turned lopsided but then his eyes darted to my throat and for an instant his face darkened. I fought the urge to touch the scar.

Major had placed both Devon and Ronald on his list of suspects, along with pretty much every other male in Livingston. But if he'd seen their reaction to Madison's recovery, he probably would've changed his mind. It was obvious that they both loved Madison. How could one of them have done her harm?

"Fluffy has been sleeping on your bed ever since you arrived at the hospital," Devon said, a slight edge in his voice. "He even buried a dead mouse in your covers once." I made a disgusted face, which made them laugh. Hearing their laughter filled me with unexpected joy.

There was happiness, there was love, and there was the impostor who didn't belong. How could they not see through the mask?

CHAPTER 9

Over the next few days, Linda and Ronald didn't leave my side. They followed me wherever I went—to every checkup and every X-ray. One of them always spent the night at my bedside. I wasn't used to having someone care for me like that.

Even Devon visited me every day after school. He always told me funny stories from our—it was strange thinking of it like that—childhood. Sometimes it made me wonder if my own brother would have been anything like Devon if we'd grown up together. I couldn't even remember the way he looked. My mother had burned every photo of him and my father. It was just one more thing on the long list of things I resented her for.

I bounced my legs, my feet hitting the bed frame.

"Dr. Fonseca will be here any moment. You can't wait to get home, can you?" Linda's face was alight with joy.

That was an understatement. After three days of being confined in a hospital room and made to sit through a barrage of useless medical tests—the work of Dr. Fonseca—I felt about ready to burst. I didn't care where I went. My nose couldn't take another day of disinfectants and sterility. The smell was burned into my brain forever.

"We're so glad that you've recovered so quickly. Even the doctors said it could take weeks but you proved them wrong," Ronald said. He and Linda shared one of their private smiles. When they looked at each other that way, I couldn't help but feel like an intruder. What they had was something I'd never witnessed before, something I desperately wanted.

Witnessing their happiness and hope was like a constant punch in the gut. I couldn't help but be reminded of how it was all built on lies that were destined to crumble. I knew our actions were necessary in order to find the killer, but I wished there was some other way.

With a knock, the door opened and Dr. Fonseca stepped inside the room. His fingers fumbled with the patient file as he stopped beside my bed. He greeted the family before he turned to me. The edges of his eyes were tight, as if it cost him a great deal to look at me. "How are you feeling today?" he asked. Of course, he already knew the answer.

"I'm feeling great," I said. "I feel like I'm ready to go home."

Dr. Fonseca browsed the patient file, though he wouldn't find anything there that he didn't already know. Major had ordered him to release me today, so that was what would happen.

"Is everything all right?" Linda rose from the chair and stood beside Ronald, who wrapped an arm around her.

Dr. Fonseca looked up from the papers and smiled tightly. "Yes, the blood test results are good. She's in good health. But she shouldn't overstrain herself." He turned his attention to me. "Lots of rest. No extracurricular sports, and no gym at school. Otherwise, I don't see any reason why we should keep you here." The truth was he couldn't wait to get me out of the hospital. I knew it must be hard for a scientist to encounter a freak like me, who made him doubt everything he thought he knew.

"It's incredible," Linda said, unaware of the tension gripping Dr. Fonseca's body. "She's recovering so quickly. It's a miracle."

"A miracle," Fonseca repeated. Coming from his mouth it sounded like a curse. "You're probably right. I've never encountered anything quite like this." I was the only one who noticed the anxiety in his voice and the way he said "anything" with an emphasis on *thing*, like I wasn't human. If he'd been allowed to, he'd have loved to do tests on me. He'd tried to keep one of my blood samples, despite the orders from the FEA to forward everything to them. Major was furious when he found out. I wished I could have witnessed that episode, but I'd had to settle for a secondhand account from an agent disguised as a nurse.

Fonseca's eyes hovered somewhere over my head, never meeting my own. "You can go home now," he finally concluded.

Linda zipped the tote bag shut. She'd already packed it an hour ago.

We left the hospital as a family. Ronald led me with a gentle hand on my back as though he was afraid I'd collapse or disappear.

I was silent during the drive to my new home, trying to memorize every detail along the way. The map hadn't lied; Livingston was an exceedingly small town. We passed row after row of houses with the same anthracite shingles, beige double garages, and patios decorated with flower beds. Vans with visible child seats were parked in front of every other home and I caught the occasional glimpse of a swingset in a backyard, and yet there weren't any children playing in the streets. Had their parents forbidden them to go out-side while a killer was on the loose?

After just a few minutes we pulled onto a street with the same sort of two-story houses that filled the rest of town, only these were much newer versions. Ronald stopped the car in the driveway. As we piled out, I could feel their eyes on me, waiting for a reaction, a sign of recognition.

I'd seen the house in photos but, of course, they hadn't given me a sense of home the way it would have meant to Madison. The red flowers in the flower beds lining the front walkway were with-ered, and from the looks of it, the grass in the front yard hadn't been mowed in a couple of weeks.

"Do you remember?" Linda asked, her voice hesitant. Ronald played with the keys in his hands as he stared anywhere but at me.

I nodded slowly. "It's all a bit hazy but it's coming back."

This wasn't what they'd wanted to hear. I knew this wouldn't be the last time I said something they hadn't expected. The front door of the neighboring house opened and a middle-aged man with a paunch stepped out, holding a garbage bag. The old I-have-to-bring-out-the-garbage-but-really-I'm-snooping trick.

He strolled toward his trash can, only to stop with badly played surprise when he spotted us. I had to stop myself from rolling my eyes. He dropped the bag into the trash can before ambling over to us. He looked at me with barely disguised curiosity.

"How are you? I didn't know you'd come home today," he said. I could see the curtains shifting in a few of the other houses.

"She's fine but she's tired," Ronald said curtly. He squeezed my shoulder and gave Linda a meaningful look. She took my hand and, after shooting a tight smile at the neighbor, dragged me toward the front door.

"Looks like your lawn could use a trimming, my friend," was the last I heard from the neighbor before Ronald stepped into the hall and closed the door.

Inside, the house oozed comfort and love. Everything was colored in warm beige and yellow tones, and family photos covered almost every surface. Light streamed through the huge, arched windows. The overstuffed sofas were beige, too, and looked comfortable enough to sleep on.

"Do you want to go up to your room?" Ronald asked.

They probably hoped I'd know where to find Madison's room. Major had said I shouldn't push the amnesia too far or it would hinder me from investigating, but how far was too far? I tried to recall the floor plan of the house that Kate had drawn after she'd raided Linda's mind, but it was one thing to see it on a piece of paper and another thing to actually be inside the house.

Tentatively, I ascended the staircase. The fluffy carpet softened my steps and I noted it would make sneaking out of the house to meet Summers or Alec easier. With Linda and Ronald keeping such a close watch while I was in hospital, I hadn't gotten the chance to communicate with either of them.

At the top of the stairs I was greeted by a long corridor with three doors on either side. Madison's door was on the right, but which door? Devon's room was beside mine, that much I could remember. I glanced over my shoulder at Ronald and Linda, who followed on my heels. They watched me like I was a toddler about to take her first steps. I was touched by their constant monitoring, but it opened endless possibilities for me to slip up.

Thankfully, Ronald chose that moment to take pity on me—or maybe he just couldn't stand the waiting anymore—and opened the door in the middle. The room was much bigger than any of the ones I'd had back with my mother, and it was spotlessly clean and smelled fresh and faintly flowery.

A vase with white roses waited on the desk beside the bed, the same white roses that decorated the pattern of the blankets and the two large photos hanging on either side of the bed. They must have been Madison's favorite flower. A huge black and white cat lay curled on the pillow—Fluffy. His eyes opened to watch me warily. I walked over to him but as I got close enough to touch him, he jumped off the bed with a hiss, bristling. He scuttled out of the room as if the devil was after him.

A tingling started in my toes and traveled up my ankles. I pressed my legs together, turning away, hoping they hadn't seen the panic on my face. The tingling disappeared as fast as it had come.

Ronald and Linda hovered in the doorway, watching me anxiously. Would Fluffy's reaction make them suspicious? Linda let out a nervous laugh. "He hasn't been himself since you left. I bet if you open his can tonight, you'll be his favorite person again."

"He smells the hospital on you. He'll come around soon," Ronald added.

I touched the soft rose petals. They felt like velvet. "They're beautiful. Thank you," I whispered. That raised a smile from both of them as though I'd given them a beautiful present just by acknowledging their gift.

"We're having chicken casserole for dinner," Linda said. I could feel her and Ronald's eyes on me, waiting for a reaction. What did they expect? Was chicken casserole a cue for something important? Their faces fell.

"Your favorite food, remember?" Linda asked.

"Sorry. Yes I remember. I'm just tired." It wasn't even a lie. Pretending to be someone else 24/7 was already more tiring than I'd expected. Linda came toward me and kissed my cheek. "Get some rest. We'll be downstairs if you need anything." With one last look, they closed the door.

My legs quivered, forcing me to plop down on the bed. The mattress was much softer than the one I was used to at the FEA, and it smelled like roses. Linda probably bought rose-scented softener just for Madison—for *me*. I longed to change back to my own body, to feel the pressure lifted off my shoulders, but I knew that wasn't an option.

My eyes fell on a smattering of photos in a framed collage on the wall over the bed. I got on my knees to get a closer look. The photos showed Madison with her family, on the beach, with Devon on swings. Several of them showed Madison with another girl. Ana—her best friend.

I dragged myself toward the desk and sank into the chair. Madison's laptop looked brand new and took almost no time to load. After logging on to the FEA homepage, I clicked on the file to access my e-mails. Three were new. One from Holly with a smiley face and lots of exclamation points in the subject line, one from Major titled IMPORTANT, and the last from Alec, without any subject heading at all.

I opened Alec's first.

Tess—Keep your guard up. Anyone could be the killer. See you tomorrow. Remember—we don't know each other. Alec

Jeez, couldn't he have said a few nice words? So typical.

I clicked on Major's e-mail, which managed to be even shorter.

Meeting @ Summers's house. Tomorrow 11 P.M. sharp. Expect status update.

Major never bothered with pleasantries. And what did he mean by "status update"? Did he think I'd found any clues already? I hadn't even started searching—not really. Though I was already sure neither Devon nor Ronald had anything to do with the murders.

I opened Holly's e-mail last, but it was several pages long and I only skimmed through it.

I miss you so much . . . How's it going?? . . . Headquarters is boring without you . . . Everyone seems to be busy with something, except for me! . . . Louis is filling in for Summers but Variation training with him is even less fun . . . Kate is as mean as ever . . . Stay safe!

I shut the window with the e-mail, logged out, and closed the laptop. I'd read her update in detail later. For now, I needed to gather information.

Maybe Madison had kept a diary. That could give me hints about her reasons for breaking up with Ryan and tell me if she'd noticed anything strange. Pushing the chair away from the desk, I opened the only drawer. Rummaging through it uncovered nothing but two old pocket calendars, some blank writing pads, and a few faded movie tickets. Madison had been very tidy—unless Ronald and Linda had cleaned before I came home. Besides the vase of roses, the laptop and a stack of school books were the only items on the desk.

Where would I keep a diary if I had one? I got down on my hands and knees and peeked under the bed, but apart from a forgotten sock and something that looked like a toy mouse for Fluffy, there was nothing. I doubted Fluffy would come back to retrieve his toy. From the looks of him, he might never set foot in this room again.

Sitting on my haunches, I looked around the rest of the room, trying to suppress my growing feelings of guilt. Madison was dead and here I was, completely invading her privacy.

A few shoe boxes were piled up inside the open closet. I crawled over to them and opened the one on top. I was greeted with more photos of Madison with friends, particularly Ana. One of them showed Madison with the other cheerleaders, and I recognized one of them as Kristen Cynch, the killer's second victim. Had she and Madison been friends?

I set the box on the ground and opened the next one, which was filled with old picture books. I brushed my fingers over the cover of *The Very Hungry Caterpillar*. The pages were crinkled with use. Linda and Ronald must have read it often to Madison when she was a child. I hesitated for a moment before I finally put it away.

I went through every single box, nook, and crevice but nothing gave me a hint about why Madison had broken up with Ryan, or about her relationship to any of the other victims. I felt slightly defeated, but what did I expect?

That evening I had my very first family meal. Dinner with Linda, Ronald, and Devon was like nothing I'd ever experienced before.

Everyone waited for the others to finish eating, shared the details of their days, laughed at one another's jokes. I couldn't believe I got to be a part of it.

Ronald was a vet and I didn't even have to pretend to be interested in his stories from work, which were truly hilarious. He took a gulp of his root beer. "Today a cat peed all over me." Linda paused with her fork against her lips, eyebrows raised. A piece of chicken got stuck in my throat and I had to wash it down with water. "What happened?"

"A monster of a Persian cat, that's what happened. Hercules." He snorted into his glass. "He isn't one of my usual patients. His owner rented a vacation bungalow in Manlow." He took another swallow of his root beer and relaxed into his chair. "Anyway, the cat's fur was matted because he doesn't like to be brushed, and unfortunately he had a serious case of diarrhea. And with all that fur?" Ronald chuckled. I put down my fork, trying not to giggle. I'd probably end up choking on the chicken.

"Shitty work, I guess," Devon said, with mock seriousness. He pushed another spoonful of casserole into his mouth. I wondered how he managed to chew with that big grin on his face.

"You got it. So Sarah was holding the cat like she always does and everything was going fine until I started the clipper to get rid of the fur. Hercules didn't like the sound, not one bit, and went berserk. Got his shit all over myself just trying to restrain him." Another bite of chicken casserole disappeared into Devon's mouth. Linda pushed her plate away; her eyes were narrowed but the corners of her lips trembled in an effort to hide a smile.

"And then he started peeing everywhere! You'd think the cat

consisted of nothing but urine judging by how much he got all over me."

I coughed between giggles.

"You couldn't wait with that story until we were done eating?" Linda asked with a shake of her head, but she was clearly amused.

Ronald took her hand on the table top. "Sorry. Next time."

Linda sighed as if she'd heard those words before. She stood and began gathering up the plates from the dinner table. I rose to help her, but she shook her head. "Today's my turn."

Devon slumped in his chair, his arms crossed over his stomach. Even with half the chicken casserole inside him, his abs still formed tight ripples beneath his shirt. I looked away.

"Devon, how was school today?" Ronald asked, with a worried glance in my direction. I'd wondered when that question would come up. I knew Major expected me to gather as much local information as possible, but dinner had been too wonderful to ruin with practical questions.

Devon straightened, the lightness slipping off his features. "It was okay. But everyone's talking."

Ronald nodded as if he'd expected nothing else.

"It's the gossip of town."

"My recovery?" I asked, my hands curling around my knees beneath the table.

"Yeah, they're all talking about your miraculous recovery. You know how they are. They need their gossip. The entire school knows you'll be back tomorrow." Great, so I'd be the focus of everyone's attention. Just what I needed.

"Honey, you know you don't have to go if you don't want to. I think it's still too early anyway," Linda said, returning to the table. Part of me wanted to give in and spend more time at home, in the presence of Linda's kind smiles. But Major would rip my head off if I didn't get my ass into gear soon. He wanted results, and judging by the nothing I'd found so far, I obviously wouldn't get them by sitting in Madison's room.

"No, I'm ready to go back," I said. "I really want to see Ana again."

"She called every day to ask about you. She even wanted to visit you today but I told her you needed time to settle in," Ronald said.

I smiled. "Thanks, Dad." The word still sounded strange coming from my mouth. I'd never called anyone "Dad" before.

Devon leaned forward. "Ryan asked about you today." Ronald's forehead furrowed and Linda froze in place.

"What—what did he want?" I asked.

Devon's face was like stone. "Just wanted to know if it was true, if you were coming back, if you could remember everything and all that shit. I told him to stay the fu—"

Linda interrupted Devon with a cough.

"—to stay away from you," Devon finished.

"Why did you say that?" I asked.

They exchanged glances.

"You didn't want anything to do with him after the breakup," Devon said.

Alarm bells went off in my head.

"Are you sure it won't all be too much? All the attention?" Linda asked.

"Don't worry, Mom. I'll keep an eye on her." Devon flashed me that grin I'd been on the receiving end of so many times in the last few days. His eyes reminded me of a cloudless summer sky and I loved the deep dimples that appeared each and every time he smiled. Was it pretense or could he really switch his moods so quickly?

"You're not going to follow me around like a lost puppy, now are you?" I watched their faces for reactions, unsure if Madison had teased her brother like that. Acting out of character would be a dangerous thing, even with pretend amnesia. But they smiled.

"If it annoys you, definitely," Devon shot back.

Maybe this was how it always used to be when Madison was still with them. She must've been so happy.

Linda became serious. She pushed a cell phone over to me. "We bought you a new phone. Your old one was damaged . . ." She trailed off.

"When you had your accident," Ronald said. "But we were able to save your SIM-card so your messages and your contacts are still there."

"Thanks." That would be useful. I'd have to take a closer look at it when I was back in my room, but the police had probably already checked the data, as was usual procedure.

After dinner, I trudged up the stairs, exhausted. I felt as if I'd endured several workout sessions with Alec. Could being in a foreign body cause this kind of muscle ache? I'd never experienced anything like this before but I'd also never been someone else for so long. We hadn't tested how many weeks or months I could hold the shape of another person's body. My Variation had never wavered, had always been in my control from day one. To everyone at the FEA, my Variation was perfect. But I knew it wasn't.

I turned on the phone the moment I was alone. There were dozens of text messages and just as many missed calls from the last few days. I recognized most of the names from the FEA's files as school mates or family members. But two names stood out: Ana and Ryan. While Ana's texts could be summarized as well wishes and words of comfort, Ryan's messages were of a different nature. He, too, said he hoped Madison would get well but he was also desperately trying to get her back. *I miss you . . . I can't stop thinking of you . . . You're the most important person in my life . . . Give us another chance . . . I love you.* Eventually, the tiny letters on the screen started blurring in front of my eyes. Getting this glimpse into Madison's personal life was interesting, but it still left me without any real leads.

As I undressed for bed, I couldn't stop myself from checking my reflection in the mirror on the door. Back in the hospital I hadn't gotten the chance to take a good look at this strange body. With shaky fingers I traced the red *A* under my bra. The skin was rough and tender. It didn't exactly hurt but it was uncomfortable. The scar would never fully fade; the knife had cut too deep.

Hesitantly, I raised my eyes to examine myself. Though I'd gained some weight over the last few days, Madison's body was still frighteningly thin. But even pale and emaciated, Madison looked pretty with her blue eyes, high cheekbones, and long blond hair. I slipped a nightgown over my head and went to close the blinds, when sudden movement outside the window made me pause.

A figure stood on the other side of the street, clearly watching my window. His hoodie hung low over his eyes and the evening fog obscured the rest of him. It was impossible to make out who he was. Spotting me, he turned and took off running down the street.

It wasn't Alec. Who was it? The killer? I doubted he had the audacity to show up in front of my house so soon after my return. It was probably just some curious snoop who wanted to have the rumors confirmed.

I rubbed my arms and let down the blinds, double-checking that the window was locked before I finally crawled into bed.

CHAPTER 10

I woke so early that the sun hadn't even risen. I lay in bed for a while, my eyes taking in my surroundings, my body throbbing dully. I'd managed to keep Madison's form overnight. That was probably why I felt so sore. I smiled. If I could keep it up during a full night of sleep, maybe the next few weeks wouldn't be that difficult after all.

My mind returned to the window stalker from the previous night and goose bumps flashed across my skin. Might it really be the killer or just a local reporter pursuing a good story?

The sound of raised voices downstairs made me bolt upright, but it was impossible to hear what was being said. I slipped out of bed and tiptoed into the hall. The rich fragrance of coffee greeted me. My feet were noiseless on the staircase as I lightly padded downstairs. Linda, Devon, and Ronald were all in the kitchen. I pressed myself against the wall and listened.

"He's only doing his job. They've already interviewed her teachers and friends. At least they waited until she was released from the hospital to contact us. That was very considerate of them," Linda said. Her voice was calm but it was impossible to miss the tension behind it.

"Considerate? They know she doesn't remember anything. They'll only make it worse if they interrogate her," Devon said, and he was anything but calm. It was hard to believe that the same guy with the permanent grin was capable of sounding so upset.

A moment of silence followed before Ronald's deep voice sounded. "I don't like it either. That's why I told the police they'll have to wait a few days. But we're supposed to keep them updated. If Maddy tells us anything, even if it doesn't seem significant, we have to report it."

"If they'd done their job, they would have caught him by now. They don't have a clue. When Sheriff Ruthledge interviewed me, he seemed totally lost. Maddy doesn't even know what happened to her. If she hears all the details, she'll be terrified," Devon said.

"It's in the newspapers and all over town. There's no way we could keep it from her. We have to talk to her before school today. There's no other choice."

Linda's sniffing grew louder. "I don't want her to find out. I don't want her to go to school or out of this house. I just want to lock her in her room until they catch that monster." A chair scraped over the floor. I peeked around the corner. Ronald had moved his chair next to Linda's and was embracing her.

Devon's face was buried in his hands. "Who's going to tell her?" he asked, his voice muffled.

Ronald brushed a wisp of hair from Linda's face before giving a resolute nod. "I will."

I turned and hurried up the stairs, my insides churning.

When I entered the kitchen an hour later, Linda didn't stop fussing, constantly asking if I was sure about going to school, if I felt well, if I'd taken my pills—really placebos that Dr. Fonseca had given me. Ronald looked as anxious as his wife while his gaze followed me from over his coffee cup.

Linda set down a mug in front of me and filled it with coffee. She didn't say a word, her smile fleeting. In my normal life, I didn't drink coffee. Had Madison liked her coffee black or with milk and sugar? That hadn't been in the file. I turned my attention to the plate, giving Ronald time to gather his courage. Linda's homemade blueberry pancakes melted on my tongue, my fingers becoming sticky with maple syrup. Ronald folded the newspaper, smoothing over the edges. His hands shook. I wiped my fingers on a napkin, knowing what would come.

"There's something we need to tell you," he said quietly. Linda and Devon fell silent and may have stopped breathing.

I lowered my eyes, not able to stand the looks on their faces.

"Before you were in the hospital, you didn't have an accident. Your injuries . . . someone attacked you." He cleared his throat.

I hesitated. "I know. I overheard the nurses talking about my scars," I whispered. I lightly touched the bandage on my chest, where the *A* lay concealed beneath it. "Do they know who did it?" I should be nominated for an Oscar.

Linda clutched her coffee pot and Devon glared at the tabletop but it was Ronald who finally shook his head, eyes haunted. "They arrested a homeless man after the first murder but he was in custody when the second murder happened."

"So they don't have any suspects?" I asked softly, my voice scared. It didn't take much of my acting skills to sound that way.

Ronald shook his head.

"And . . . do you suspect anyone?"

"No. You got along so well with everyone," he said in that adoring fatherly way.

Linda put her hand on mine. "They'll find him soon. You don't have to be afraid. Dad and I won't let anything happen to you."

"There's always a police car in front of the school," Devon added.

They watched my face for a reaction. If I acted terrified, I knew they'd never let me out of their sight. "I'm okay," I said. "I don't want to hide. I don't want to spend my time being scared of something I don't even remember."

I could see on their faces that they wanted nothing more than to put the attack behind them, too. If only it were that easy. Finally, Devon spoke.

"We really have to get going or we'll be late. You'll be the center of attention today, so walking the halls will take twice as long." He got up and gathered his car keys and his backpack, waiting for me in the doorway.

My palms felt sweaty at the thought of being under so many people's scrutiny. It increased the chance of someone noticing I wasn't who I claimed to be. But it was also my chance to find out more about the murders, about Madison's friends, and about Ryan. And to try to find, in Major's words, the chink in the perfect armor that was Madison's life.

I rose from the table and Linda held my backpack out to me. "Promise me that you'll always stay with Devon or Ana. Don't go *anywhere* alone."

"Okay, Mom."

Ronald opened a drawer, took something from it, and held it

out to me. "Pepper spray, just in case." I slipped it into my backpack, though I was sure Alec would give me something more effective once we had our first meeting.

I hesitated, not sure what the usual morning routine was. Did Madison hug her parents before she left? Since Devon was watching me expectantly I decided not to rack my brain over it. I followed Devon out of the house toward his car. Ronald and Linda stood in the doorway. I could see on their faces just how much they didn't want to let me out of their sight, and if it hadn't been for Major's impatience, I might have given in and waited a few more days before starting school again.

"Be careful," Linda called as we got into the car.

I waved to them as we pulled out of the driveway. Devon's posture grew tense as he drove. Suddenly, it seemed like his calm demeanor was all an act for his parents' sake. Finally he spoke.

"If anyone's bothering you, tell me and I'll talk to them." His knuckles cracked from his tight grip on the steering wheel.

"When Dad said I got along well with people, I saw you look away," I said. "What was that about?"

"Nobody gets along with everyone."

"Do you think the person who . . . hurt me . . . goes to school with us?"

Devon's expression grew tight. "I don't know. I've thought about it a lot. There are a lot of creeps in school and you always seemed to be drawn to them. First Ryan and then—"

He stopped.

"And then who?"

We parked in the already crowded parking lot beside a gray

building that reminded me more of a prison than a school—a three-story building with a flat roof and rows of perfectly uniform square windows. Devon turned the engine off before his eyes searched my face. With a sigh he shook his head and reached for the door handle. I gripped his arm.

"Who? Who were you talking about?"

A knock on the window made my heart jump into my throat. The door opened and a girl with long, curly brown hair and huge brown eyes beamed at me: it was Ana. Her face was familiar. I'd seen her in so many pictures, but sometimes it was difficult to translate those images to real life.

"Ana!" I said.

She wrapped her arms around me and a small tearful hiccup escaped her throat. I had to force my body to go soft at her touch. "I thought you didn't recognize me." She stepped back so I could get out of the car and close the door. Her eyes darted to my throat. I should have covered it up with a scarf.

"Of course not. How could I forget you?" I asked.

Devon hovered beside the bumper. His hands rested casually in his pockets but his eyes darted over the parking lot—keeping watch. That's when I noticed how many eyes were turned toward me, how everyone had stopped doing whatever they'd been doing to stare at me like I'd just risen from the dead.

Devon positioned himself on my left side and Ana sidled up on my right, sandwiching me between them like my personal bodyguards as we made our way toward the front doors. Some people stumbled over their feet because they were gaping and pointing at me. Had their parents never taught them manners? A small part of me wanted to shape-shift to give them the scare of their lives.

"What jerks," Ana said as we went inside.

The halls weren't crowded, probably because so many people were standing outside, still whispering among themselves. Were they too shy to approach me? I was welcomed by only a few mildly familiar people whose faces I couldn't link to a name. They kept glancing at my throat and I could tell they were curious, but thankfully, they didn't dare to ask. Maybe Devon's glare was what stopped them.

If I'd really been Madison, would it have bothered me? Would this have hurt my feelings? It was likely, but I wasn't sure.

"We have biology first," Ana reminded me.

I'd studied the schedule and even browsed a few of the schoolbooks since I would have to participate in all of Madison's classes. It was the first time I'd ever been in high school. If the situation was different, I might have enjoyed it. But I was out of my league. I didn't know the first thing about how to act like a regular student, let alone a senior.

Ana stopped in front of a locker and entered the combination. The lockers were yellow and matched half of the overly cheerful yellow-and-blue checkered tiles on the floor.

"Umm, that's yours." Ana pointed at the locker next to hers. A piece of paper stuck out of the gap between the door and the frame. Devon grabbed it before I could react, but I snatched it out of his hand. "That's for me."

For a moment, he looked like he wanted to argue. "Who's it from?" he asked. Ana had stopped rummaging and stared at Devon and me. "Do you know my combination?" I asked, but Devon didn't let the topic change slip. He reached past me and turned the lock first right, then left, and then again right. He pulled it open and handed me a scrap of paper with the numbers. "Now spill, Maddy."

People were whispering and watching but no one stood close enough to eavesdrop. Nervously, I unfolded the letter. It was a message from Ryan.

> *Hey Maddy,*
>
> *I know you'll be back today, and I can't wait to see you. I was so worried about you. Your brother didn't want to tell me anything. (You know how he is.) But I can't stay away from you. I miss you.*
>
> *I need to talk to you. Meet me in the parking lot after school. Please?*
>
> *Ryan*

"No. You're not meeting him," Devon said. He'd been reading over my shoulder. "You don't remember how miserable you were because of him. I won't let him use your amnesia to get you back."

I crumpled the letter and chucked it into my locker. "I can take care of myself."

"Please, just once, listen to me. Stay away from Ryan, at least for a few days until everything is settled." I gave a reluctant nod and picked up my biology book and a folder. Devon walked Ana and me toward the classroom. "Is Ryan in biology with you guys?"

Ana nodded. "We share most of our classes."

"I'll be fine, really. I mean, when did I break up with him?"

"Like two months ago," Ana said. The first murder happened around that time.

"So it's been a while. It'll be fine," I said. They didn't look convinced, and who could blame them after reading that letter? "Go," I urged. With a last glance over his shoulder, Devon jogged to his class.

Ana and I took our seats and a hush fell over the room. This was starting to grate on my nerves. I gave them all a smile to show them I was really alive. If they realized I knew they were staring, they might stop. As if someone had just yelled "action!" the girls gathered around my table and the boys slowly followed.

A tall girl, thin as a stick bug, spoke first. "We're so happy that you're back, Madison. People said you were badly injured." She paused as if she thought I might contradict her.

"We were all really worried. The police questioned us after what happened," a black-haired girl added. She looked vaguely familiar; I thought her name might have been Stacey.

"It's incredible how fast you've recovered," Stick Bug said. Her eyes were eager and curious. They hadn't come to welcome me back. They had come to gather fodder for gossip. I forced myself to focus on their hands (were they fidgeting?), their body language (were they tense or sweating more than usual?), and their expressions (were they too sympathetic, too kind, like they were trying to compensate for their lack of real emotion?). I filed the info away. My eyes darted to the people who had stayed in their seats. Were they feigning uninterestedness in order to seem innocent?

Some people were whispering. One boy with blond hair, pale skin, a narrow face, and a haggard body kept his head down. I couldn't see his hands but his shoulders were tilted toward his ears as if he hoped to disappear into his seat.

Another girl touched my shoulder. "Does it still hurt?" She pointed at my throat and the boy beside her nudged her. What a stupid question. I shook my head.

"Do you remember anything?" a girl who'd sneaked up behind Stick Bug asked. Her hair was dark as coal and so were her eyes. Suddenly everyone seemed to hold their breath. Ana made a sound that reminded me of a growl. "Shut up, Franny."

The girl flinched before narrowing her eyes.

Mrs. Coleman, the biology teacher, chose that moment to enter the room, as a few late students scurried in behind her and everyone scattered to their seats. She leveled her eyes on me and gave a curt nod before she turned her attention to the books she'd set down on her desk.

"Wow, what a welcome," I said under my breath. Ana shrugged.

"People want to know the truth. The newspaper has been reporting about the murders for weeks and everyone's scared. You're the only victim that survived and people are making up their own theories about that, how you've come back from the *dead*."

"I wasn't dead," I said.

Ana's eyes turned soft. "No, but you were so still. I was there once, in the hospital. You looked so . . . lifeless." I remembered the way Madison had looked. So small in the hospital bed, so lost.

I smiled at her. "I'm back."

Mrs. Coleman harrumphed, seemingly drawing up to twice her height—which wasn't much—until every gaze settled on her. "Darwin's theory of evolution."

I bit back a groan. Evolution was the last thing I wanted to hear about, especially since the way most humans learned it was wrong. They never learned of nature's slip or whatever you want to call the existence of people like me or Alec or Kate. Variants.

Speaking of Alec. Where the hell was he? I thought he was supposed to arrive at school today and I knew he had biology with me—I'd compared our schedules beforehand. Had he somehow managed to weasel his way out of it? If so, I'd have to have a serious talk with Major. It was unfair that I had to suffer through high school while he was doing God knows what. Probably having phone sex with Kate. The thought of it made me want to puke up my pancakes.

A knock interrupted Mrs. Coleman's bland introduction of Charles Darwin. With a cutting glare that would have made me squirm if I wasn't already used to Major, she turned her attention to the door. Alec—every tall, muscled, self-assured inch of him—entered. The fury instantly vanished from Mrs. Coleman's face. She blinked at Alec, and his gray eyes held her gaze. She was a goner.

"I'm sorry for being late. I'm new and I had to meet with the principal first." He didn't hand her a slip of paper that would have confirmed his statement but she didn't ask him to. In moments like that, I couldn't help but wonder if Major wasn't the only FEA agent with a hidden mental Variation. Or was it really just Alec's good looks that made people react to him the way they did?

Mrs. Coleman nodded and pointed Alec to the sole free seat—next to Franny, one row behind us. Our eyes met briefly as he walked past my table but his face didn't show any recognition. I hoped I'd managed the same. My face always seemed to go still when I saw him. Every girl—even Mrs. Coleman—watched Alec as he lowered himself into his chair. That was why being in love with someone like him was such a bad idea. Even if he wasn't with Kate, there'd still be all the other girls who'd give their right arm to be his.

My eyes met with a pair of olive green ones at the end of the room and the face they belonged to immediately rang a bell. It was Ryan. I hadn't even seen him come in. He must have been among the late arrivers who filed into the room behind Mrs. Coleman. He had dark brown shaggy hair that brushed his ears. His face was unreadable. A girl with a cute bob that framed her oval face tried to get his attention but he ignored her. I turned around, stunned by the intensity of his gaze.

I jumped when Ana's voice pressed against my ear. "Dude, he's so not over you. Before you were attacked he tried to get you back by making you jealous with other girls. Such a jerk."

I was sure the note wasn't the last I'd hear from Ryan.

I tried to focus on Mrs. Coleman, in case she asked me a question. Most teachers would probably cut me some slack because I'd gone through so much but Mrs. Coleman seemed to be the unrelenting type.

Boredom turned out to be my biggest problem during class. Linda and Ronald really had been worried about nothing. I definitely wouldn't overexert myself.

The sensation started with a light prickling in my neck and slowly raised the hairs on my arms. Someone was watching me. That's one of the things you learned to notice during your training at the FEA. A gaze could be something physical, something solid if you focused hard enough to detect it.

I turned around. The blond boy with the hunched shoulders sat two rows behind, his focus squarely on me. When our eyes met he looked down and pretended to scribble on his notepad. His irises were watery blue. They had the same unsettling vibe as Kate's eyes. I remembered his face from the yearbook: Phil Faulkner. He stared intently at his writing as if his life depended on it. I faced the front of the classroom, not sure what to make of him.

Mrs. Coleman had her back turned to the class and was writing something on the chalkboard.

I leaned over to Ana, deciding to play the amnesia card. "What's his deal? Why is he staring at me like that?"

She threw a glance over her shoulder, then turned to me. "Who, you mean Phil?" I gave a nod. Ana rolled her eyes. "Don't get me started. He's such a dork. The guy's hopelessly in love with you, probably since kindergarten. After you broke up with Ryan, he came to your house and told you he was sorry and that he was there for you if you needed someone to talk to. Who does that? I can't believe he'd ever think he'd actually have a chance with you." She snorted.

The sound earned her a glare from Mrs. Coleman.

I glanced over my shoulder once more to get another glimpse at Phil's eyes, but his head was bowed.

I wanted to ask why Madison had broken up with Ryan. If one person must have known, it was her best friend. But biology really wasn't the place to do it.

The lesson dragged on 'til infinity. I fidgeted with my pens, looked around the room, shifted on the uncomfortable plastic chair. It had been too long since I last attended school. Sitting in a classroom and listening to a teacher lecture wasn't what I was used to. I even missed the morning runs and push-ups. Hell, even taking a swim with a straitjacket would have been an improvement over *this*.

The moment the bell rang, I stuffed my books into my backpack and jumped out of my chair.

"Whoa, you can't wait to get out of here, can you?" Ana asked, scurrying behind me.

I slowed. I should have waited for her and not stormed out of the classroom but the walls had started to close in on me.

"Sorry, I just needed to move. I hate sitting still for too long." Ana eyed me carefully as if what I'd said was out of character. We walked through the crowded halls toward our next class. I felt a twinge of nervousness but quickly convinced myself that it wasn't enough to make her suspicious.

"Is it because you were confined to bed for so long?" Ana asked. I stopped in the doorway to our next class.

"Yes, I guess that's why. I just feel like there's too little time to spend it sitting around doing nothing." A heavy silence spread between us, but then Ana's face lit up.

"Don't let Mrs. Coleman hear that."

"Have you noticed anything strange about Phil?" I asked, not able to get over the way he'd looked at me.

"Why?" she asked. "Do you remember something?"

I shook my head. "It's just . . . his eyes, they creep me out."

"They creep out everyone. Rumor has it that he's got a cataract."

Creepy eyes didn't make someone a suspect. But I decided I'd keep an eye on him anyway.

•   •   •

Eyes and whispers followed me all the way to the cafeteria. Ana glowered at anyone who dared to look at me for longer than a second. I really liked her. She reminded me a lot of Holly.

"Can we sit somewhere quiet? I need to talk to you," I whispered after we'd purchased our slices of pizza. Ana led us to a table at the end of the room, delightfully close to the bathroom. No wonder no one had chosen it yet. But it was perfect for my purposes, as it also gave me a fantastic view of the room.

We sank into the hard plastic chairs and I started chewing my pizza. Too much cheese with the texture of chewing gum, dotted with unidentifiable pieces of some kind of sausage. Bleh. I dropped the slice on my plate. Ana hadn't even started hers yet. She was too busy watching me.

I wiped my greasy hands on a napkin, buying myself some more time to word my question. "Um, why did I break up with Ryan?" So much for eloquence.

Sadness flashed on Ana's face. She smiled tightly. "You never told me." She shrugged as if it wasn't a big deal but her voice and eyes told another story. She was hurt and disappointed to be left out. "I've always thought it was because he cared more about his buddies than you, but you were kind of secretive about the whole thing." Her eyes searched my face.

I'd hoped for another answer. If Devon wouldn't talk, that left only one other person who might know why I broke up with him—Ryan. And I wasn't sure if talking to him about it was the best choice.

"So you really don't remember?"

I shook my head. "I have a lot of blanks in my memory. I wish I could remember more."

"Maybe it's good that you don't remember everything." She picked the pieces of sausage from her slice and arranged them in a tiny circle on her plate.

"No, it would help if I remembered. Then maybe the killer wouldn't still be out there." The words came out harsher than I'd intended.

Ana's eyes grew wide and her hands froze. "Sorry, of course. I just meant—" She trailed off, her eyes darting away.

I reached out for her hand. "I know. It makes me nervous to think of what really happened. You really don't know anything else, like if Ryan and I had a fight or something?"

Ana's hands balled to fists. "No. I mean, you told me you and Ryan had grown apart, but never anything about a specific incident. Though there were the other rumors."

"Rumors?"

"About you and another guy."

"Who?"

"I don't know." She kept glancing at a table across the room. The popular kids—it was easy to tell who they were because the entire lunch room seemed to center around them. Ryan and the girl with the bob haircut sat there. Another familiar face was beside them—Franny. She was throwing glances our way.

I'd never attended high school before but I knew enough about hierarchy, which was Major's favorite topic. Madison must have been one of the popular kids to date Ryan.

"Why aren't we friendlier with them? Weren't we part of their group before I was attacked?"

Ana's face darkened. "No, we left their group a while ago." She began fumbling with the remaining sliver of her pizza slice.

"Why? What happened?"

Devon entered the lunch room with a group of boys and smiled when his eyes found me. He sat with his friends, but I could tell he was keeping an eye on me. I allowed myself a look around the rest of the cafeteria. A group of goths sat behind Devon and his friends. The table to their right was occupied by two chubby girls wearing nearly identical outfits, and at the edge of the room, all by himself, was Phil. His eyes darted up to meet mine for a millisecond before he returned his focus to his plate.

"Like I said, when you broke up with Ryan some people thought it was because you'd cheated on him. Franny apparently saw you one night—with another guy."

"With who?"

Ana grimaced. "I don't know. No one does, Franny couldn't tell. She just said the guy was shorter than Ryan and definitely wasn't him. Franny likes to hear herself talk. She's a liar. But the group was on Ryan's side and so we left and just did our own thing. They called you a skank and a whore. I hate them."

"You left your friends for Ma—me?" I'd almost said Madison but managed to catch myself before the name escaped my lips.

"They weren't real friends or they wouldn't have talked shit about you."

"Was Kristen one of them?" I asked, following a sudden intuition.

"Yeah, she was the worst, always talking shit about you. She and Franny were best friends." Guilt flashed across her face. "I got in a big fight with Kristen a day before she died. I called her horrible things. I still feel really bad about it."

"You couldn't have known what would happen." I took her

hand. "So did Franny take the tragedy very hard? She doesn't look like someone who lost a friend a few months ago."

"She broke down crying when she found out and wasn't in school the following week, but when she returned she acted like nothing had happened. She's trying to keep up appearances. I don't know how she manages. I was a wreck while you were in the hospital. I'm so glad I didn't lose you."

But you did. I looked down at the table top. "Did you tell the police what you just told me?"

"Yeah, but not in that much detail. They asked about you and Ryan but it wasn't something that seemed very important to them."

"Why not? Shouldn't an ex-boyfriend make the top of their suspect list?"

"You would think, but I guess it's because of the other murders." She gnawed on her lip, her eyes becoming distant. "It really doesn't make sense. Why would someone do this?"

My cell phone buzzed. I pulled it out of my backpack. It was a text from Ryan, asking if I'd gotten his letter and if I was going to meet him. When I looked up, both Ryan and Devon were staring at me, but after a moment Devon followed my gaze to glare at Madison's ex. Ryan didn't notice. He only had eyes for me, his expression hopeful. I almost felt sorry for the poor guy.

"A text from Ryan?" Ana asked. I looked up, startled. "Yeah, he really wants to talk."

She bit her lip. "It's up to you, but I think you should listen to your brother." I typed a short reply, telling Ryan that I got the note, but I couldn't make it.

The moment everyone's attention shifted, I knew Alec had

entered the lunch room. He scanned the rows of tables and our eyes met. He was wearing the Chucky shirt. It was physically painful to pretend not to know him. I wanted to wave him over but someone else was faster.

Franny rushed over to him, a saccharine smile plastered on her face, and suggestively touched his arm. *Paws off, Franny*, I thought. But to my surprise Alec actually followed her to the table with Madison's former friends.

Jealousy burned in my stomach. I knew he was only trying to gather information from them, but I didn't like it, especially the way Franny half shoved her impressive chest into his face.

Ana leaned in and whispered conspiratorially. "That's the new guy. He just moved here with his mom. His name is Alec."

I was glad that Major had decided to let Alec keep his name. That way at least I wouldn't call him the wrong thing by accident. People seemed to believe his and Summers's story. Maybe Summers had also seen to it that the police didn't insist on interviewing me right away.

I crammed the crust of the pizza into my mouth, though I wasn't even hungry.

"He's watching you *again*," Ana said.

I hoped she was talking about Alec. Swallowing the gooey clump, I asked, "Who?"

"Phil. Why can't he get a grip on himself?"

But when I turned his way, he buried his face in a book.

CHAPTER 11

I decided to talk to Franny after our last class of the day, but on my way out of the school, I came across none other than Phil, who was waiting in front of the doors.

He straightened the moment he saw me and his face reddened. I stopped, unsure of what to say.

"I'm glad you're back," he said, shuffling his feet. He held out a large round tin with a picture of a goose painted on its lid, still staring at the ground.

I took it. "For me?"

"My grandma baked brownies for you."

"Why?" I burst out, resisting the urge to back away. Was he the secret guy Madison had been seeing? His skin flushed an even deeper red as he glanced up, his watery gaze meeting mine. "Your mother told my grandma you'd be back in school today. You know, neighborly chitchat."

"You live with your grandma?" I asked. Only after I'd said it did I realize that it might have been an awkward question.

He looked away. "Yeah. I have to go. It's good to see you, Madison." Before I could say another word, he hurried over toward the idling school bus. I bet the other kids gave him crap for taking the bus.

I spotted Franny in the parking lot and made a beeline toward her. For once she wasn't surrounded by her enormous group of friends. I didn't want them around, least of all Ryan or his replacement girlfriend, bob-haired Chloe. She'd given me the evil eye for most of the day. Maybe she knew that Ryan still carried a torch for Madison.

As I approached the car, Franny pushed the key into her red VW Beetle convertible.

"Hey Franny," I called out. "Can I talk to you?"

She jerked the key out and opened the door. "Don't call me that."

Any sympathy that I might have seen on her face back in biology class had completely disappeared.

"I'm sorry. That's what Ana called you earlier. I . . . I don't remember your real name." I tried to look as apologetic as possible. I needed her on my good side if I wanted to coax information out of her. She eyed me suspiciously over the car door. "So you really don't remember?" I forced my lips to quiver as if I might burst into tears at any moment, then shook my head. It seemed to work.

Her expression softened a tad but it was still cool. "My name is *Francesca*. And I really need to get home now."

I took a step forward. "Just a minute, please? I want to ask you about something."

She tightened her grip on the keys. "What about?"

"I heard a rumor . . . that you saw me with someone a while back, a guy who wasn't Ryan. Who was it?"

The parking lot hummed with the sound of engines and conversation, and the stench of exhaust lingered in my nose as more people set out to drive away. Ryan leaned against a car on the other side of the parking lot, watching us. Apparently, he still hoped we could talk despite my text message. And maybe he'd get his wish— if Devon didn't turn up first.

Francesca drummed her fingers lightly on the steering wheel, her face closed off. "Listen, Madison. It was dark, and I didn't see much."

The tips of her ears turned pink. Liar. She put the key in the ignition and started the engine. I gripped the edge of her door. "Please, Francesca. I need to know."

She looked at me, contemplating, and for a moment I was sure she'd tell me but then she shook her head. "Look. If I knew, I would tell you, but I didn't recognize him. I wasn't close enough, and it was late. All I know is that the guy was definitely *not* Ryan. That's all I saw. I can't help you." She closed the door and I had no choice but to step back or the tires would have rolled over my toes as she drove off. Ryan started in my direction, a smile building on his face, but then he stopped. Steps crunched on the concrete behind me.

"What was that about?" Devon appeared at my side. Francesca's car vanished around the corner.

"We were just talking."

He narrowed his eyes at Ryan. Before he could ask any more questions, I trudged over to his car. We both got inside but Devon hesitated, his hand on the key in the ignition. "Don't believe everything Francesca tells you; she likes to gossip."

If she had told me *anything*, I could have followed his advice, but as it was I was just as clueless as before. Why was it so difficult to find out who the other guy was? When I'd started my preparations for the mission, I'd thought Madison's life looked easy, but now it seemed as if there were countless trap doors just waiting for me to fall into them.

The car slipped out of the parking lot with a stutter and we pulled onto the main street.

"Do you know anything about some other guy I'd been dating?"

Devon almost steered the car into oncoming traffic. His fingers curled around the steering wheel. "Why?"

He clenched his jaw. He wasn't giving anything away. "Because I need to know what really happened and I can't remember. Was I dating someone else after Ryan?"

"No, you didn't have another boyfriend." The way he worded it made me think that maybe there was more to the situation. Why would nobody tell me anything? Devon probably wanted to protect his sister, but didn't he realize that keeping secrets would only make it easier for the murderer to prevail? As I glanced over at Devon, my stomach dropped. My heart drummed in my chest as count-less questions swirled in my brain. There were so many secrets to expose, and who knew how much time I had before the killer tried to finish what he started?

"You know, what if something happens to me because you won't tell me?"

He winced. "I'm trying to protect you, Maddy. I'm really trying but you have to let me."

We pulled into the driveway and I knew the conversation was over. Linda was already waiting in the doorway. Had she even left that spot?

That night, we all ate dinner as a family again. It seemed to be a daily ritual. After dinner, Ronald came into my room. He lingered in the doorway, his hands fumbling with a little red package.

"When you were little, only five, we gave you a necklace for Christmas and you've worn it ever since. Until . . ." His Adam's apple bobbed up and down. He never finished his sentence, but of course I knew what he was talking about. He held out the little packet and I took it with shaking hands. I opened the lid to find a golden necklace with a rose pendant. I brushed my fingertip across the delicate chain.

"Let me." Ronald took the necklace out with trembling fingers and fastened it around my throat. The gold felt cool against my breastbone.

"Thanks." My voice came out raspy and shaky. I'd never received such a lovely gift before.

Don't get emotionally involved. Major's stern face accompanied the words in my head. But as a lump formed in my throat, I realized it was too late to heed his warning.

I wrapped my arms around Ronald and he kissed the top of my head. Why couldn't my dad have been more like him?

"Umm, Dad? Can I ask you a question?"

He smiled. "You just did."

"Phil Faulkner. Do you know him?"

"Of course, he lives down the street with his grandmother. You and Devon used to play with him when you were younger but over time you drifted apart. Come to think of it, I haven't seen him around in a long time."

"Thanks," I said. He ruffled my hair. I had a feeling Madison might have hated it if someone ruined her hair like that, but I couldn't bring myself to say anything.

Long after he left, I still stood there, clutching the little gold pendant.

Sometimes glimpses of the past flashed in my mind. A time when my brother and father had lived with my mother and me. A time of laughter and happiness. I couldn't even say if they were memories or figments of my imagination.

I closed the door and turned the lock. Madison's face stared back at me from the mirror on the door. I shut my eyes, though it wasn't necessary for the shift. The familiar rippling washed over me. Bones lengthened. Sinews stretched. Face reshaped. But there was a tentativeness to the shift that shouldn't have been there, like the stutter of an old engine before it starts to purr.

The sensation died down, and I risked a look at my reflection. And it was all wrong. I'd tried so many times to shift into my dad in order to see his face, to hear his voice and help me remember, but it was a useless struggle. The data had been washed away, as faded and distorted as my memories in years gone by.

Whatever I'd turned into resembled a badly done figure from Madame Tussauds. Skin waxen, eyes blank, my face generic and indistinct. I let the rippling sensation wash over me. Within seconds I was back in my own body.

I peeked through the gaps in the shades, but no one was there. At least, no one I could see. Maybe the stranger I'd seen outside my window before was the same person Francesca had seen Madison with?

As I stretched out on the mattress the ache in my muscles was close to unbearable. My body was tired from days of pretending. Glancing at the door, I made sure the lights were already out in the hall. Madison's nightgown fit snuggly around my chest. Falling asleep in anything but Madison's body was a risk, I knew. But I was so, so tired and my body needed the rest. Clutching the pendant, I closed my eyes.

Just a few minutes.

I woke to the sound of hammering. Blearily I looked around, searching for the source of the noise until I saw the shadow behind the window shades. I swung my legs out of bed, untangled them from the blanket, and gripped the edge of the nightstand. Someone was in front of my window.

Panic wormed its way through my body.

"Open the damn window. I'm freezing my ass off."

Alec.

I padded over to the window and pulled up the shade, trying to calm my pounding heart. The frame was warped, but with Alec's strength it was easy for him to pry it open and slip inside.

It was dark in the room but the gray of his eyes and the white of his teeth still shone in the dim light. "What are you doing here?" I whispered.

His eyes wandered over me. I wrapped my arms around my chest as I remembered the skimpy nightgown I was wearing. The last time alone in a room with him had ended in a debacle. I wasn't keen on a repeat performance.

"Shouldn't you be Madison?"

I hurried past him to check my reflection in the mirror. Even in the dark I could see that my hair was definitely not blond. I'd forgotten to change back to Madison before checking the window. That could have ended badly. "Shit."

He came up behind me and touched my shoulder, his fingertips soft against my skin. Even with the space between us, I could feel his warmth against my back. I wanted to lean against his chest, wanted him to wrap his arms around me. He didn't say anything, his face shrouded by shadows, but he didn't remove his hand. His warm breath ghosted over my neck, raising the tiny hairs on it. *Kiss me,* I thought.

But then he stepped back and pulled something from his jeans pocket. "I came to give you this." He handed me a small cell phone and a Taser. "E-mail isn't a good way to communicate. It's not fast enough, and it isn't safe on someone else's computer. We must be able to reach you at any time. And I want you to keep the Taser with you no matter what."

I slipped the phone under my pillow and the Taser into my backpack. I'd have to find a better place for it.

"Do you know what time it is?" Alec asked. I could hear a smirk in his voice.

I scanned the room for the clock. Eleven fifty. No wonder I was tired.

"Major's furious."

"What? Why?"

Alec raised his eyebrows.

I slapped my palm against my forehead. "Oh, shit. I forgot about the meeting." Ronald's gift had clearly distracted me even more than I'd realized.

"Yeah, I thought as much. Major wasn't happy but I told him there wasn't anything substantial to tell, so it didn't matter."

"Thanks." The mission had just started and already I was screwing up.

"Don't worry."

"So did you find anything?" We asked at the same time. I smiled and so did he, but he quickly stepped over to the window, bringing some distance between us.

"You start," I said, my smile gone.

"Nothing interesting. Just talk. That guy, Ryan, has been watching you a lot. It seems Madison had some kind of an affair with someone else, but no one seems to know who. Francesca and the second victim, Kristen, spread rumors about it in school."

"That's what I heard too. I tried to find out who it is but nobody wants to tell. I think Devon knows but he's keeping it a secret."

"Maybe you can pry it out of him."

"I'll do my best. What about Ryan?"

"What about him? He doesn't like me. Probably thinks I'm competition." That made him grin.

"I found a letter from him stuck in Madison's locker this morning. He wants to talk. I think he's really trying to win Madison back." I propped my butt up on the desk, tired of standing. "Do you think he could be the murderer?"

Alec leaned against the window frame. "I'm not sure. What reason would he have had for the other murders? I mean, I guess he had a reason to kill Madison, but then why would he try to get back together with her? And what about the janitor or the doctor or that Kristen girl?"

I sighed. "I don't know. Maybe there was some other reason we don't see. Had he ever dated Kristen?"

"No, he'd been with Madison for over a year and before that he wasn't serious with anyone."

"And the pediatrician, Dr. Hansen? Was she Ryan's doctor?"

Alec laughed darkly. "I don't know, but probably. Livingston's a very tiny town. Hansen's practically treated everyone here at least once in their life."

We were going nowhere with this.

"I noticed a guy in school today. His name's Phil Faulkner; have you seen him? He's got really abnormal eyes."

"And?"

"I mean, some Variants have strange eyes. Look at my freaky eyes." I thought it best not to mention Kate's unsettling amber-copper color.

Alec took a step closer. "Your eyes are just fine." My body flooded with warmth.

"So," I said. "You don't think Phil could be a Variant."

"We're not here to look for Variants, Tess. We're here to look for motives."

He looked as tired as I felt. I glanced at my bed, wondering how it would be to fall asleep beside him, cuddled against his chest, encircled by his arms. My fingers found the pendant again.

"So, how are you getting along with Summers? Is she a good mom?"

Alec shrugged and continued to stare out the window, his face solemn. "I guess. I wouldn't know."

Beneath the bitterness, there was a vulnerability that he seldom showed. I jumped off the desk and walked up to him, my bare feet soundless on the carpet. He didn't turn to face me. Without shoes on, I barely reached his shoulders. I linked our fingers and squeezed. "I know it's hard. But the FEA is our family and that's enough." I was trying to convince myself as much as him.

A tremor went through his body and I wrapped my arms around him, though I half expected him to push me away. He didn't. I relaxed against him. After a moment, he pressed his palm against my lower back. Perhaps one day he'd realize that I was a better choice than Kate. He tensed. "There's someone on the sidewalk, watching your window. A man."

I quickly shifted back to Madison's body before approaching the window. There was a lone figure, obscured by the darkness. "He was here before," I whispered.

Alec pushed open the window. The frame groaned as the man whirled around and fled. I could only hope the rest of the household hadn't heard the noise. Alec swung out of the window, not bothering to climb. Falling one floor wouldn't hurt him. He took off running in the direction the stranger had gone. Alec was stronger and faster than a normal human. If the guy didn't have a bike or a getaway car somewhere nearby, he didn't stand a chance.

"Text me," I hissed but he had already crossed the street and disappeared into the foggy night. Cold wind blasted into the room, making me shiver. I wanted to run after them but in the time it would take me to get dressed and climb down, they'd be too far away. I closed the window, sank down on the bed, and clutched the cell phone in my hands.

My eyes began to blur from staring at the dark screen. Finally, a half hour later, the little phone glowed and Alec's name appeared.

He got away. Lost him in fog. Talk tomorrow.

That was all? Nine words? I'd hoped for a call or at least a warmer text. He must have known that I wanted to learn every detail. After all, it wasn't an easy feat to outrun Alec. How had the stranger managed it? I had no choice but to wait until tomorrow to find out.

My first class of the morning was English literature, one of the few classes Alec and I didn't share. That meant I had to wait even longer to get an explanation from him.

Ana and I took our seats in the front row, the only class where we occupied such a prominent position. "Why the first row?" I asked as we unpacked *Wuthering Heights*, a book we were apparently reading. I'd never read it and hadn't found the time to make up for it yet.

Ana tipped a pen against her lips, smearing her lip gloss all over it. She was always getting lip gloss everywhere, leaving her shimmery fingerprints on everything. If only the killer had been into wearing shiny makeup.

"You chose the seats," she said. "Because of how much you love literature." She eyed the yellowed pages of the book in front of her as if they might bite her. "Personally, I think it's boring. The only reason I agreed to the front row is for the view."

"The view?"

Ana winked. "You forgot the best thing about lit class? Just wait, you'll see."

As soon as the lit teacher, Mr. Yates, entered the classroom, I knew exactly what she'd meant. He was cute and very young for a teacher, maybe in his early- to midtwenties. His brown hair was short and curly. He wore a light-blue shirt and black trousers and was lean, but built like an athlete. Perhaps he was a runner.

"He's new. It's his first year as a teacher," Ana whispered. "Everyone totally has a crush on him."

Mr. Yates stopped behind his desk before he turned and allowed his focus to settle on me. His eyes flitted to the scar around my throat. "We're all happy to welcome you back, Madison. I'm sure you'll be caught up in no time."

"Thank you," I said, feeling the heat rise to my cheeks as every pair of eyes in the room focused on me. He gave me a tight smile and picked up his copy of *Wuthering Heights*. He began reading an excerpt from somewhere in the middle of the book but I wasn't listening anymore.

A minute before the bell rang, I started packing my backpack, eager to get out as fast as possible. There wasn't much time to squeeze in a talk with Alec before the next class started. The bell rang and everyone began streaming out of the room.

"Madison, can you please stay behind for a moment? I want to discuss the assignments you missed while you were gone."

So much for talking with Alec . . .

Ana mouthed "good luck" before she disappeared.

Mr. Yates and I were alone in the classroom. I hoped I wouldn't have to make up work for all the classes I'd missed. I really had better things to do. Maybe someone from the FEA could do the homework for me.

"Could you please close the door? It's getting loud outside."

I did as he asked. My steps were the only sound as I made my way back to the front of the room where Mr. Yates was waiting.

He stood behind his desk, fidgeting with a few papers. Something about the way he looked at me made me uncomfortable. It was off. There was something too familiar about it. It wasn't a look I'd ever been on the receiving end of. And it was certainly not a look I'd expected from a teacher. His eyes searched mine and I had to fight the urge to look away.

He walked around the desk. "I was so worried. It was torture not to be able to visit you in the hospital." A horrible suspicion wormed its way into my mind. "I missed you so much," he whispered. "I thought I'd never see you again."

Goose bumps flashed across my skin. I looked up at him, though I dreaded what I'd see in his eyes. There it was: affection.

And I thought the FEA was twisted.

His eyes moved to the scar on my throat. "I wish I could have protected you."

"Mr. Yates," I said, my voice like a squeak.

Hurt flickered in his eyes. He grabbed the edge of the desk as if he needed something to hold on to. "You don't remember."

"I'm sorry. I—" I whispered, then stopped myself. Why the hell was I apologizing to a teacher who obviously had some kind of inappropriate relationship with his student?

He began rearranging the pencils on his desk. The silence expanded until it felt like it might crush me. His fingers hovered over a stack of papers, shaking slightly as he picked one up. "That's for you in case you're thinking about catching up."

It was a summary of the last book they'd covered. I couldn't care less.

"Mr. Yates . . ."

"Owen." His voice was strangely raspy.

"Owen." The word tasted strange in my mouth. "Can you please tell me what happened between us?" He handed me the stack of papers. I took it but didn't pull my eyes from his face. He turned abruptly, leaving me to stare at his back. "You'd better go. Your next class is about to start."

I waited, hoping he'd say more.

"Maybe it's for the best that you don't remember." His voice betrayed the lie buried beneath it, and it gave me an opening. Gingerly, I leaned toward him and put my hand on his shoulder. He didn't shy away from the touch. "Please. I want to remember."

He turned his head, his expression a mixture of dread and hope. The bell rang, marking the beginning of my next class. No one had entered. Maybe this was his free period.

"Please," I whispered, my eyes pleading with him. I was sure he'd refuse me.

"I'll tell you everything if you come to my house today." *To his house?* "I need to talk to you without the risk of being seen or interrupted," he said, his eyes hopeful.

I swallowed my concerns and ignored the alarm bells going off in my head. I needed to know more about Madison's relationship with him. Maybe it was the missing puzzle piece that would lead us to the killer. Maybe Yates *was* the killer and was luring me to his home to finish what he'd started?

"Okay," I agreed.

He looked relieved and far too happy. "Meet me at five. Do you remember where I live?"

I shook my head.

Yates scribbled down his address and handed it to me along with a slip of paper excusing me for being late to my next class. "I'm looking forward to talking with you," he said as I swung my backpack over my shoulder and trudged into the hall.

I couldn't say the same.

———————————————

CHAPTER 12

"You're not going to that meeting," Alec said the moment I'd stopped talking.

I glanced around. We were alone in the parking lot but I could hear laughter in the distance. It was lunchtime. People were milling around, and though it was still cold outside, some of them were enjoying the first sunshine of spring. "I have to. It could be crucial to our investigation."

Alec shook his head. "Don't you get it? He could be the murderer. Do you want to get yourself killed? For God's sake, Tessa. That guy had an affair with his student. Don't you think he could've killed in order to keep it a secret?"

Of course I knew that was a possibility, and I hated how he made it sound like I was too naive to realize it. "That doesn't explain the other victims, or do you think he had an affair with them too?"

His eyes narrowed at the challenge in my tone. "Maybe. But what about this theory: The janitor caught Yates and Madison red-handed after classes and Yates decided to get rid of him so he couldn't tell anyone. And that girl? Maybe he had an affair with her too, and that's why she had to die. Or maybe he wanted to silence her because she was talking shit about Madison and possibly about him too. How does that sound?"

He really made it sound like a logical explanation. At the very least, Mr. Yates seemed to have a more plausible reason to dispose of the victims than Ryan or Phil.

"It doesn't matter. If we want to get proof, I'll have to talk to him. Maybe he's got nothing to do with it," I said.

"I won't let you go there alone."

"Alec, don't be stupid. Do you think he'll talk to me if you're around?" I joked, knowing full well what he meant.

He wasn't amused. "I'll wait outside. If something goes wrong you'll scream or make yourself noticeable. If you don't return within thirty minutes, I'm coming in."

"Suppose my talk with Yates takes longer than thirty minutes."

"You'd better make sure it doesn't."

That was the last word on the matter. Alec had that stubborn glint in his eyes that I knew all too well. He was in protective mode and it was useless to argue with him.

Ana drove me home that day. She kept throwing worried glances my way and I could practically feel the tension rolling off her.

I needed an alibi for my meeting with Yates—Linda wouldn't let me leave without an explanation. But asking Ana would make her even more suspicious. Not that I had many options. "Could you do me a favor?"

She hesitated. "Sure, what is it?" Her voice was light but her lips thinned out.

"I need you to cover for me. I'm meeting someone this afternoon and I can't tell my mom about it. Can I tell her we're meeting at your house?"

Ana narrowed her eyes. "Who are you meeting?"

"Please, Ana, I can't tell you yet but it's important. Please."

She swallowed twice, thickly, like she was trying to push back the words that threatened to rise into her mouth. "You know, these last few days I've been holding myself back, swallowing my feelings, telling myself it would get better, that you needed time to recover. Actually, I've been holding back for months, ever since you started keeping secrets from me. But I'm just sick of it. I'm sick of being lied to and left out. I thought we were best friends. I abandoned everyone for *you*. And now you won't even let me in." She took a deep, shaky breath and wiped at her eyes.

I opened my mouth but closed it again, unsure of how to respond. I agreed with what she'd said. If Holly had kept so many secrets from me, I'd have been just as hurt and angry. But I couldn't tell Ana the truth now, not even half of it, no matter how much she deserved it.

"I don't know why you don't trust me," she said. I could feel that I was losing her, that she was pulling back, and I couldn't let that happen. I couldn't talk to her about Yates, much less about the rest. But maybe I didn't need to.

"I trust you," I stammered. "It's just . . . complicated. The new guy, Alec." I hesitated and looked down at my lap, trying to feign discomfort.

"What about him?" There was a flicker of excitement in her voice and it was all the encouragement I needed.

"I'm meeting him this afternoon."

"Like, a date?" Ana slowed the car until we were crawling along at a snail's pace.

I glanced up, hoping I looked appropriately embarrassed and excited. "Kind of. We're hanging out. I'm not really sure what it is yet."

"But when did that happen? I've never even seen you guys talk!" Every bit of resentment and disappointment I'd seen on her face earlier seemed to evaporate.

I thought about the times I could have spoken to Alec in school without Ana's noticing and there weren't many; she and Devon seemed to be glued to my sides. "Actually, I met him right after I was released from the hospital. I went for a walk around the neighborhood to get some fresh air."

"Your parents let you out alone?"

Shit. "No, I snuck out once, so please don't mention it around anyone." I waited for her to nod before I continued my tale. "Alec was jogging near our house and we kind of just started talking. And during lunch break today, I met him in the parking lot and he asked me out."

"What are you going to do?"

My mind drew a blank and a panicky feeling wormed its way into my head as I struggled for a semi-intelligent reply. "Umm, he's picking me up in his car and we're going to drive around a bit and familiarize ourselves with the area. I mean, since he just moved here and I don't really remember much about it." Gosh, I was a rambling idiot.

"Okay, but please be careful. You don't know him very well.

Keep your cell phone in your pocket and call me if he's acting like a douche. Promise me," she said. Her brown eyes fixed me with a stare that reminded me of Kate's when she rummaged in other people's brains.

I snorted, unable to help myself. "You sound like my mom."

"Maddy, I'm serious."

"I know."

She relaxed against her seat.

"Don't tell your mom we're meeting at my house. If she calls and my mom picks up the phone, she'll know it was a lie. Tell her we're spending the day in Manlow. I wanted to head there anyway to go to the mall," she said.

That was one of the moments I wished I were just a normal girl. A girl who could go shopping and hang out with her friends instead of doing the kind of work that would terrify any normal person.

"Thank you," I said.

"And don't think I'll let you off the hook so easily this time. I want a detailed account of your kind-of-date."

"And you'll get one, I promise. I know I've been a bad friend . . . and I'm trying to get better, but I'm still trying to figure things out myself. I don't even know what my life was like before. I don't even remember why I broke up with Ryan or why I dated him in the first place. Do you know how hard that is? It's like living someone else's life."

Guilt filled Ana's face. "I'm so sorry, Maddy. Sometimes I almost forget what happened. It's easier that way, you know?"

"I know but it's my life. I can't pretend it hasn't happened." I knew I had her. This was my chance to pry more information out of her. "Can't you just tell me more about Ryan and me? I need to know what's been going on before I can allow myself to consider dating someone new." I made a mental note to tell Alec about all this later so our stories would line up.

Ana bit her lip and nodded. "You'd been dating Ryan for a year and a half and you were the dream couple. And you really were happy, at least from the outside. But then, maybe three months before you and Ryan broke up, something changed. I don't really know what happened. You never said anything about it, but I could see something wasn't right." She glanced at me and I tried to keep a straight face. "I thought you and Ryan were drifting apart. It happens. I mean, we're only in high school, you know? But then Franny and Kristen told everyone they saw you with another guy at the lake, and it was all downhill from there."

"How did Ryan react to the rumors?"

"It's actually funny. He should have been furious but he never showed it. I think he didn't believe it. He's one of those guys who is so full of himself, it's like he couldn't imagine his girlfriend would ever want someone else."

I nodded as if I understood. But the truth was, I didn't know Ryan well enough. I hadn't even talked to him yet. "Thanks, Ana," I said. I wondered why Madison had kept her in the dark when she seemed like such a good friend.

We pulled up to the Chambers' house, where, just like every other day, Linda was already waiting for me in the front yard. New flowers had been planted in the flower beds—purple geraniums—and the lawn was freshly mowed.

"Oh, and Ana? Could you please keep my date with Alec to

yourself? Devon is uberprotective at the moment. I don't want him to threaten Alec or something. That would be too embarrassing."

"My lips are sealed, don't worry," she promised.

We hugged goodbye and I slipped out of the car. I suspected she wouldn't forgive me if I didn't tell her every little detail about my date. I would soon have more lies to keep track of.

Inside, Linda had prepared a tray with three different kinds of sandwiches. I told her about school, editing out my search for info and my talk with Mr. Yates. She listened to me, her eyes practically glued to my lips, that loving look on her face like I could do no wrong. What would she say if she found out about Madison's affair with her teacher?

"I told Ana I'd meet up with her again at five," I said between bites.

Linda wiped her mouth with a napkin. "Where did you girls want to go?"

"Just to the mall in Manlow."

Linda dropped her sandwich. It fell apart, sending lettuce, bacon, and tomatoes sliding onto the table. Her hands shook as she picked them up. "Don't you think it's too dangerous to drive to Manlow all alone? Wouldn't it be better to stay in Livingston? You could invite Ana here and order a pizza."

"Ana will be with me the whole time, and the mall is full of people. I really want to go out. I can't hide inside forever."

She picked up the phone. "I'll call Devon. He can join you."

That was the last thing I needed.

"Mom, don't. He has practice. Don't make him come home because of me."

"He doesn't mind. He's as worried about you as I am." She started dialing but I pried the phone from her hands.

"Please. I don't need a babysitter. It's bad enough that Devon keeps an eye on me at school. Ana and I will be at a crowded public place. There'll be security cameras and people. Nothing is going to happen." I touched her hand. "Please."

She looked away, her lips trembling. I felt horrible for doing this to her.

"Take your cell phone and the pepper spray with you. Stay in the mall and don't let Ana out of your sight. I want you two to stick together. And promise to call me as soon as you get there and again when you leave."

I kissed her cheek. "I will."

At four forty-five I made my way downstairs, trying not to feel guilty at the sight of Linda's worried face. "Don't forget to call." She hugged me goodbye and waited outside until I'd turned the corner. Ana lived well within walking distance, so I didn't have to come up with an excuse for why I didn't want Linda to drive me.

Alec waited for me behind the steering wheel of a black Jeep. I gave a quick glance around before I got in to make sure nobody was watching.

"I told Ana that I was going on a date with you," I blurted the moment I got inside.

"Why?" He didn't act as surprised as I thought he would.

"She wanted to know what was going on with me. Apparently, she was sick of Madison lying to her, so I had to come up with something. She's also my alibi for leaving the house, so this seemed like the easiest explanation. I don't think she'll ask, but if she does, just tell her we cruised around in your car."

"Wow, what an exciting date. Can I at least add some backseat action?"

I knew he was trying to be funny, but with everything that had been going on between us lately, the laughter died in my throat. He looked away, jaw locked, and started the car. I was glad when the sound of the engine cut through the thick silence.

Alec parked a couple blocks away from Mr. Yates's house, so there was no chance that he'd spot us together.

"Be careful. And don't let him feel you up," he said with his usual professionalism.

"Jeez, thanks for the advice." My sarcasm made him scowl, but before he could reply, I got out of the car and jogged toward the house. Though I didn't look over my shoulder, I knew Alec was following close behind.

The lawn in Yates's front yard was neat and freshly cut; there wasn't a single blade of grass that stood taller than an inch. The mailbox and the shingles framing all the windows glowed white like they'd been painted hours ago, and not a speck of dirt could be seen on the light beige clapboard. From the looks of it, I wouldn't have guessed that it was the home of a single man.

As I walked up to the front door, I wiped my sweaty palms on the legs of my jeans. I didn't really know anything about the guy. Was he married? I hadn't noticed a ring. Would he be a difficult opponent in a fight? He'd looked like an athlete. Maybe this was it. Maybe I was willingly putting myself alone in a house with a guy who strangled people. I didn't know if he had a Variation, or if

I'd have any chance at defending myself against it. My leg muscles twitched with the impulse to bolt. But I didn't have a choice. Lives depended on me.

Squaring my shoulders, I pressed the button beside the door.

A second later, the door creaked open and Yates stood in front of me. He must have been watching my arrival from a window or waiting in the entrance hall. He ushered me inside, with a quick glance outside, probably making sure that none of his neighbors had seen me. I brushed my palm across the Taser in my bag.

The hall smelled of chocolate.

"I made chocolate chip cookies," he explained as he led me into a big, stainless steel kitchen. A baking sheet with fresh, golden brown discs sat atop the spotlessly clean counter. Why the hell had he baked cookies?

"They're your favorite." He smiled tentatively. Had Madison liked that he took care of her? Sweat glistened on his skin. Was it from nerves or because of the heat streaming out of the oven? He picked up the tray with a dish towel and held it out to me. His hands shook. "They're still warm. Do you want one?"

They smelled delicious and looked even better. Would a taste really hurt?

"No, thank you, I'm not hungry. I just ate a sandwich," I said. It was the truth.

His smile disappeared and he returned the baking sheet to the counter.

Perspiration made my back slick. It was too hot in the kitchen. He rested his eyes on me, not once breaking his stare. "Could we go somewhere else?" I asked, taking a step toward the hall.

He seemed conflicted. Was it such a difficult request? His eyes flitted around the kitchen, over the still-steaming cookies, the empty coffee cup on the round glass table, and the enormous knife-block resting on the counter. I had to stop myself from touching the A over my rib cage. Had Yates used one of those knives to cut his victims?

A droplet of sweat trickled down my spine. Alec was outside. He'd come if I screamed. I felt the Taser again through the fabric of my purse.

I took another step back. Yates shook off whatever stupor he'd been in and walked past me, his shoulder brushing my arm and sending a shiver through me.

I followed him into the living room, where it was thankfully ten degrees cooler. He looked around before gesturing for me to sit on the sofa. It was soft and I sank down into it. It would be difficult to make a quick escape.

Yates filled two glasses with water and set them down on round coasters before he sat down beside me, his leg pressing against mine. I inched to the side but the armrest stopped my escape. I could still feel Yates's warmth seeping through the fabric of my jeans. I rubbed my hands over my legs to chase it away. Yates stared at me, his eyes once again lingering on my scar. It was strange to think that Madison had seen something in him, that she might have welcomed his attention.

"Did we meet here often?" My voice came out hoarse. I took a sip of water, remembering too late that it might be tainted. Hastily I put the glass down. Yates stared at it for a moment before shifting it slightly so it sat in the middle of the coaster. He wiped a few droplets of water from the wooden table. He was obviously thorough, the kind of person who wouldn't have any trouble covering his tracks.

Then he shook his head, looking almost embarrassed. "Only twice. We usually met in Manlow or at the lake." He flinched, his eyes taking up their dance around the room again like a nervous twitch. Madison had been found on the shore of the lake. He must have seen something flicker on my face because he looked like he was going to be sick.

"Did we meet at the lake on the day of my attack?"

He ran his finger over the crease in his pants. "So you really don't remember anything?" I detected a hint of relief in his voice.

"No. Now stop avoiding my question."

"We were supposed to meet that day," he said slowly.

"Before or after the time of the attack?"

"I–I'm not sure. I was late because my wife and I had a fight and when I arrived at the lake, I didn't see you anywhere. I thought you'd left. If I'd known you were there waiting for me . . ." He trailed off and inched toward me.

Wife? I leaned on the armrest to put more space between our bodies. "Did you see anyone?"

"It was a misty day. Not many people were around."

"Was there a reason for our meeting? I mean, it was pretty cold for a date at the lake."

Red crawled up his neck. "Why are you asking all these questions? I feel like you're interrogating me. Do you think I'm the one who attacked you?" He let out a laugh but it sounded forced.

I shrugged. "It would be bad if people found out about us."

Something flickered in his eyes—anger or fear. He put his hand on my knee. "Maddy, maybe we should just forget what happened."

Next to the couch there was an end table, with various photos on it. Framed in sterling silver, Yates posed with a tall, curly-haired woman. They looked happy.

I jerked away from him and stood up, causing his hand to slide off my leg. "Is that your wife?"

He buried his face in his hands and let out a sigh before he spoke. "Yes."

"Did I know about her?"

"Yes."

I didn't get it. How could Madison have had an affair with him? It was one thing to date your own teacher but a whole different thing to date a teacher who had a wife.

"My wife and I married too young. We care about each other, but we were never a good match. We have an estranged relationship. We barely talk anymore."

I didn't sit down again and Yates didn't try to make me. From the corner of my eye, I kept track of his movements while I tried to catch a glimpse of Alec outside. "What happened between us?"

Yates pressed his head against the backrest, his eyes darting around the room. "I don't think—"

"Just tell me."

"It . . . it started four months ago." Four months? Madison had broken up with Ryan only two months ago. Six weeks before the murderer had attacked her.

"You were one of the few students who showed genuine interest in my class and we often talked afterward about the books we'd covered."

I couldn't look away from the smiling photo showing him with his arm around his wife's shoulder. When was that picture taken? Had his smile been fake?

A question rose up in my throat but wouldn't make it past my lips. It seemed glued to my tongue. I knew I had to ask. I swallowed my reluctance. "Did we . . . did we sleep together?"

He hesitated. Was he thinking about lying? It was too late for that. His hesitance was all the answer I needed.

"We did," I said, leaving no room for protest. Madison was eighteen—only two years older than me—and yet she was so much more experienced. I hadn't even kissed anyone yet and she'd already slept with this man and probably with Ryan, too.

He jumped up, alarm on his face. "No—I mean, we did, but it's not like that. You were okay with it. You wanted to, I didn't pressure you."

This was so wretched. More questions crowded my mind, trying to burst my skull. "And is that why we were meeting on the day of my attack?"

He pressed his hands flat against his body but they were still shaking. "No, we were meeting because you wanted to talk."

"About what?"

"I don't know," he said, avoiding my eyes.

He reached for my hands but I stepped back. I didn't want him to touch me, didn't even want him to stand that close.

"What do you want to do now?" Strain lined the edges of his eyes. They weren't as soft as moments before. He gripped my hands.

This time I wasn't fast enough to pull away. "You can't tell anyone, Madison. I could lose my job. It's against the school code."

His grip tightened, becoming uncomfortable. His face was on the verge of despair. "This isn't a game. We were both invested; you know that."

I shook him off, keeping my eyes glued to him as I edged backward out of the living room. "Don't worry. I won't tell a soul."

Though he deserved to be punished, I didn't want Linda and Ronald to find out about their daughter. I'd tell Major, and maybe he could find a way to remove Yates from his position without people finding out the whole story.

He followed me into the hall but kept his distance, as though he could feel the waves of disdain rolling off me.

"I really need to go," I said as I fled through the front door, not looking back, though I knew that he was watching me.

My steps echoed on the street. One block away, Alec was already waiting for me in the car and drove off as soon as I was inside.

"What did he say?" he asked.

"Give me a sec," I hissed, needing some time to get my thoughts in order and the sick feeling out of my stomach.

"Did he do something?" He slowed the car as if he was going to turn back to the house and beat Yates up.

Though I liked how protective he was, it was unnecessary. "No, I'm fine. It's just . . . he has a wife. How could he sleep with his student?"

Alec relaxed in the seat. "So he actually slept with her? It wasn't just flirting?"

"Not just flirting." It gave me a queasy feeling. Maybe it was because I realized that despite all our preparations, I didn't know Madison at all, and apparently neither did her friends and family.

"Madison was at the lake that day to meet him. He said they were meeting because she wanted to talk. I think he's keeping something from us." Alec reached over and touched my hands, which I had balled into tight fists on my lap. "I'll tell Major about it. Maybe he can find out more about Yates."

I nodded, but my mind was far away. I couldn't stop thinking about Madison and who she'd really been. How many secrets had she taken into the grave with her?

Alec parked a few houses from the Chambers' home and turned to me. His mouth was tight with worry. "Will you be all right?" My skin warmed under his palm and, as usual, I immediately felt calmer. Nobody else had that effect on me.

"Yeah. I just need to think everything through. I'll have to find out more about Madison's past, what really happened. Maybe I should try to talk to Ryan."

Alec's expression turned grim. "Alone? I'm not sure that's the best idea. I bet the guy holds a huge grudge against Madison. No surprise, considering the girl had been cheating on him."

CHAPTER 13

When I pushed the key into the lock, I expected to find Linda waiting in the hall, but no one was there. Relief washed over me, even though the feeling made me guilty. Linda was lovely, caring, and everything I'd always wanted in a mother, but right now I didn't need her fussing and questioning. My head felt about ready to burst.

The entire thing with Yates—seeing his photos, having him reach for me in the house he shared with his wife—made me feel sick. I trudged up the stairs and caught a glimpse of my face in the mirror hanging on the wall. Blue eyes, long blond hair, and the thin red line around my throat. Who was Madison Chambers? I couldn't help but wonder if anyone knew. Major had wanted me to find a chink in her armor but what I'd found felt more like a crater the size of the Grand Canyon.

Holly had sent me two more e-mails and I hadn't even read her first one completely yet. I was a best friend failure. Despite the tiredness lingering in my bones I clicked on her latest e-mail—I wouldn't treat Holly the way Madison had treated Ana.

Rubbing my eyes, I started reading.

Hey girl,

I hope you're okay? I'm worried about you. Major's been gone most of the time, so I haven't had the chance to ask him how things are going with you. And you know him (*rolls eyes*), he wouldn't tell me a thing anyway. I'm even more distracted than usual. Louis is throwing a fit because my Variation is a total mess. I almost miss Summers. But don't tell her I said that. ;)

Anyway. That's not why I'm writing. It's been kind of strange at headquarters in the last few days (and not just because you and the others are gone). The older agents are whispering to each other all the time BUT I caught snippets of their conversation. They seem really worried. And not about the Livingston killer. They mentioned a group of Variants that's been causing trouble. I think these people, whoever they are, have been threatening the FEA. Something about old enmity. It almost sounded like these Variants want to destroy us. Apparently, two external FEA agents have disappeared, without a trace. Even Major looked really upset the last time I saw him. It was kind of scary.

I'll keep my ears and eyes open, and will let you know if I find out anything else.

Miss you so much. Write back if you can!

xoxo

Holly

It took me a few minutes to digest what she'd said. A group of Variants was giving the FEA trouble? I knew that some Variants preferred to live in hiding because they were unwilling to submit to the FEA's rules; Major'd said they were mostly Volatiles—Variants who weren't capable of controlling their powers or else just didn't want to. But those were loners, not a threat to the FEA. An organized group of Variants was another matter altogether. Why had Major never mentioned them? It made me wonder what else he was keeping from me.

I wrote a quick reply, telling Holly I was fine—just tired and super busy—before I let myself fall on the bed, my mind whirling with thoughts. If the group of Variants had started kidnapping agents, shouldn't Major have warned us? Especially me. I was now an external agent.

I took a deep breath and released it slowly. I couldn't let this distract me from what was really important. I checked the messages on Madison's cell phone; I'd received a text from Ana, asking about my date, and two from Ryan, saying that he really needed to talk to me. I couldn't avoid him much longer, even if Alec and Devon didn't want me alone with him.

I took Madison's iPod, pushed the buds into my ears, and turned the music as loud as it could go. I wasn't familiar with the song, but the beats blasted the worries from my head and that was exactly what I needed.

Cuddling into the softness of the mattress beneath me, I closed my eyes, allowing myself to feel and think nothing, and with every beat of the music I felt myself being pulled deeper and deeper into sleep.

Just as I had drifted off, something dropped on my legs, pressing them down. I jolted upright, earbuds ripping from my ears, and screamed. The scream died abruptly when I saw my attacker. Fluffy was sitting on my legs, blinking at me with the accented indifference only a cat could muster. He didn't budge when I shifted to get into a more comfortable position. If my scream hadn't scared him away, nothing could. Had he forgotten that I wasn't really who I pretended to be? I reached out to pet him and earned myself a hiss.

Steps pounded up the stairs and a moment later Devon appeared in the doorway. He looked around wildly as if he expected to confront an attacker. He was wearing workout clothes—a tight T-shirt and gray shorts—that clung to his sweaty body.

"I heard you scream," he said, noticeably relaxing when he saw me sitting on the bed.

"Fluffy startled me."

He nodded but his blue eyes stayed tense as they scanned my face. "Hard day?"

You have no clue . . .

"Fight with Ana?"

I shook my head no. "You're home early. Did mom call you?"

"Yeah, she was worried about you." He sounded like he agreed with her.

"That's why you didn't shower after practice? Because she wanted you here when I got back?"

He glanced down at his soaked T-shirt, which was doing wonders to accentuate his toned chest. I forced my eyes to stay on his face. "Nah, she and Dad haven't been on a date for weeks. I told them they should head out early, that I would stay home and look out for you."

"That's good. But I hate how much you're all worrying."

His eyes softened. "Maddy, you almost died. I've never seen Mom and Dad so devastated." He paused for a moment, searching for some way to lighten the mood. "You look like you need cheering up. Let's order some pizza and watch a movie." I felt a twinge of homesickness. Movie night with Alec or Holly had been an inherent part of my life since I'd joined the FEA.

I managed to wriggle Fluffy from my legs and followed Devon downstairs.

"When did you come home? I didn't hear you," I said after he'd ordered a family-size pizza called "hot mess." I didn't even want to know how it got that name.

"Around twenty minutes ago, but you were fast asleep. I'm gonna grab a shower. Mom left some cash on the counter; you can use it for the pizza if it comes before I'm done." With that, he dashed up the stairs, taking them two at a time.

The doorbell rang ten minutes later and I still heard the sound of water running above. I grabbed the money and opened the front door to find myself face-to-face with Ryan. He wasn't holding a pizza box.

"What do you want?"

He took all the space in the doorway, his shoulders squared, his feet set apart. "I want to talk." He glanced over my shoulder into the house. "You alone?"

"No, Devon's here."

He propped himself up on the doorframe, blocking the light with his body. "Listen, I know you've been avoiding me, but we really need to talk." I didn't like the commanding tone he used, or the way his eyes bored into my skull. If he'd always treated Madison like that it wasn't surprising that she wanted to get away from him. He was trying to intimidate me.

"I really don't have time now. How about we talk tomorrow during lunch?"

Upstairs, I heard the water stop. I had a feeling Devon and Ryan would get in a fight if they confronted one another. I'd noticed the scowls they exchanged in school. I started to close the door but Ryan thrust his foot forward, blocking it. Maybe Madison had let him act like that but the new version of Madison was not going to let that fly. "Move your foot or I'll break it."

He took a step back in surprise, something changing in his olive eyes. I'd never threatened anyone before, had never thought I could, but it felt good. "Why are you acting like this? You know I love you," he said. The pizza guy chose that moment to drive up on his moped. I relaxed. The pizza carton was wider than his shoulders. Good God, what kind of monster had Devon ordered?

"Please leave," I told Ryan again and this time he listened. He hunched his back on the way to his car, and he was so distracted that he barreled into the pizza guy. He looked up, startled, and hurried on without an apology.

I paid and carried the hot cardboard into the living room, my thoughts still lingering on my encounter with Ryan. Did he really love Madison? And what had he wanted to talk about? I set the pizza box down on the living room table and opened the lid. "Hot mess" deserved its name. The toppings consisted of jalapeños, bacon, peppers, pepperoni, sausage, and lots of cheese. At first it burned my taste buds but after the second bite I'd gotten used to it, and I was too hungry to care.

"Leave some for me," Devon teased as he walked into the room. His hair was wet and disheveled and his shirt clung to his body. Wrestling had really shaped him up nicely. I tore my eyes away and took another bite. The real Madison would've never ogled her own twin brother.

Devon went to the shelf that held the DVDs and pushed one into the player before plopping down on the sofa beside me and grabbing a pizza slice. He threw his feet up on the table and started the movie. "*Terminator*. Sorry, Maddy, but I'm not in the mood for a chick flick."

"I love *Terminator*," I said before I could stop myself. Tessa had spoken, not Madison.

He looked at me, his eyebrows half disappearing into his hairline. He still hadn't taken a bite of the pizza. "Uh, since when?"

I shrugged and stuffed the crust of the pizza into my mouth. "Delicious," I said between bites. "You should have some before I eat it all."

He leaned back and shoved almost half the slice into his mouth, staring at the screen. After he'd swallowed he spoke again. "You're kinda different, you know?"

This was exactly what I'd dreaded. I picked a piece of sausage off the pizza and popped it in my mouth while I tried to keep my eyes directed at the movie. "What happened kinda got me thinking," I began, trying to come up with a logical explanation. "Life is so short. I decided to change a few things."

Devon seemed to buy my story. We watched the movie in silence. But even one of my all-time favorites couldn't keep me from thinking of Yates.

"After I broke up with Ryan . . ." I tried to sound casual, keeping my eyes glued to the screen where the Terminator had just killed a guy. I could feel Devon's eyes on me. His shoulder leaned against mine and his warmth crept into my body, stirring something in my stomach. "Was there someone else?"

I'd asked him this question before, but he was relaxed and un-suspecting now—the best time to take him by surprise and startle a reply out of him. Not that I still needed one, now that I knew about Yates, but if Devon had known about the affair, that changed the situation.

He wrinkled his forehead like he was thinking really hard about it. I placed my hand on his forearm; the touch—skin on skin—sent a shiver up my back. My head jerked up and our eyes met. He looked puzzled, as if he couldn't quite believe what he was seeing.

A horrible thought crashed into my mind. Had I changed back to my own body by accident? But no, it couldn't be. Devon didn't look freaked out enough for that. If he'd seen his sister shape-shift into a stranger, his face would have shown something much greater than puzzlement. Still, something had happened. A nearly imper-ceptible spark had soared through my body at his touch.

"So . . . was there?" I asked to cut through the tense silence. I felt his muscles shift beneath my fingers, making me acutely aware of the fact that I was still touching him. I pulled back.

"I'm not sure if I should tell you," he said carefully, setting down an untouched slice.

He *knew*.

"My teacher."

He grimaced. "Yeah. I tried to talk you out of it but you wouldn't listen."

Devon leaned forward, resting his elbows on his thighs. "Is it over now or do you still feel something for that . . . guy?" I could tell that he'd almost called Mr. Yates another name and frankly I couldn't blame him. The whole thing creeped me out. How much worse must it have been for him to witness it unfolding?

"It's over. I don't remember him as anything but a teacher," I said, for once telling the truth.

Devon scanned my face. "You mean it?"

"I mean it. It's like I never had feelings for him in the first place."

Dimples flashed in his cheeks. My body flushed with heat. He grabbed a cold slice of pizza and ate it in just a few bites.

Tucking my legs under me, I rested my head on the back of the couch, close to his shoulder. He smelled of soap, clean skin, and something warmer—cinnamon maybe. I had to stop myself from burying my nose in his shirt. *That* would've looked really bad. I could just imagine what Major would do if he found out I'd failed the mission because I wanted to *smell* Devon. What the hell was wrong with me?

The Terminator found his temporary end in a junk press and my eyelids began to droop. Sleep sounded like a good plan. After all the heavy food and excitement of the day, it couldn't come fast enough.

"So you really can't remember anything about the day, you know, you were attacked?" Devon's voice crashed through my slumber-like trance. I jerked my head up. There was something odd about the way he asked.

He was facing the TV but his expression was so tense it resembled a stone mask.

"No," I said. "It's a huge black void in my memory."

He nodded but his lips and the muscles in his neck visibly tightened.

"Why do you hate Ryan so much?" I blurted.

He stiffened. "I don't hate him. I just never liked how possessive he was. He was jealous and a control freak, and he still hasn't gotten over the breakup."

The end credits scrolled up the screen but they blurred before my eyes. What had been a comfortable silence now felt like the moment when the birds go quiet in the forest and you know something terrible is stalking you.

I stood up. "I'm tired."

Devon didn't follow me; instead he kept staring at the black screen.

My steps echoed in the hallway. Linda and Ronald would return any moment from their dinner. It was dark in my room—no, Madison's room. Rain pelted against the window, creating a nice change from the silence in the corridor. I wished Holly was there to give me one of her pep talks. That was something I could have used.

I went over to the window and pried it open. The frame groaned but with a jerk the window slid up and cool air streamed in. The fresh smell of rain in the night was one of my absolute favorites.

A shadow shifted on the street. I poked my head out. Even in the rain, the hooded stranger waited on the other side, staring at my window. I grabbed my cell phone from the nightstand and the pepper spray from my purse, slipped into my ballet flats, and rushed out the room and down the stairs. Devon appeared in the hall, his eyes bleary. I didn't stop to explain.

My feet carried me outside where the rain plastered my hair down and soaked through my clothes. The stranger turned the corner as I crossed our front yard.

I pumped my legs. I heard Devon's steps behind me and his

shouts of confusion, but I turned a corner and then another until it appeared that I'd lost him. I stormed into the forest at the edge of our neighborhood, where the stranger had disappeared just moments before.

From up ahead, the sound of twigs breaking kept me on the trail. Devon must have given up or lost sight of me because I didn't hear him behind me.

Without streetlights, the forest's darkness was absolute. Rain rattled the leaves, and twigs snapped under my shoes. Shape-shifting while running was difficult and straining, but with Madison's short legs I'd never catch the guy. Who was he? The killer? And I was alone in a dark forest with him. Maybe not my best plan.

I let the rippling wash over me. Tearing, stretching, twisting, remodeling. My clothes strained and ripped. I stumbled a few times over my lengthening legs but then, with Alec's body, I gained on the stranger. Wind howled in my ears and for a moment I lost my bearings as he disappeared from view.

Up ahead, something flashed in the blackness like a beacon. He'd turned around to check if I was still following. My breath rasped in my throat as I jumped over a fallen trunk. The forest was cloaked in mist, concealing the outline of the mysterious figure.

I was startled by a sudden buzzing from my pocket. My foot caught on a rock, sending me flying. I landed face-first in a bed of leaves, the wind rushing out of my lungs. I stumbled to my feet but the stranger was gone and so was the mist. Over the steady drum of the rain, I could no longer make out his footsteps.

I took the phone from my pocket, and saw I had an incoming text from Alec.

Meet me at the bus stop at 11

A glance at my watch revealed that it was ten fifty-five. Alec seemed to forget that my legs weren't quite as long as his.

Now that the adrenaline had left my body I realized just how tightly my clothes—luckily sweatpants and an elastic shirt—fit, how even my shoes had stretched, and how the wristband of my watch had cut into my skin. I shape-shifted back into Madison's body. The seams of my shirt were partially ripped and a cool draft wafted against my butt. Apparently I'd also made a hole in my pants.

I wished I'd grabbed a sweater from my dresser before I'd started my chase. I looked around for the pepper spray I'd dropped but it was too dark. Shivering, I trudged through the forest in the direction of the bus stop, roots and stones digging into the thin soles of my flats. My cell phone buzzed again.

Where are you?

I ignored him. After a few minutes the trees thinned out and eventually I was back in our neighborhood. The asphalt felt good under my feet.

When I rounded the corner near the bus stop, Alec was already waiting for me, tapping his foot impatiently. His eyes scanned me from head to toe. He rushed toward me and grabbed my shoulder, making me wince. He pushed my ripped shirt aside to check the spot I had bruised with my fall. His fingertips were gentle as they traced the injury. A bluish spot was already blooming on my skin. The leaves hadn't cushioned my fall as well as I'd thought.

"Are you okay?" he asked, hands brushing back the hair from my face and lingering against my cheeks. His palms felt warm and rough.

"I'm fine."

He removed his hands slowly. "What the hell happened? You look like you had a fight with a bear."

I slumped against the street sign, trying to take my weight off my feet. "I was trying to catch my stalker. He was watching my window again."

His eyes flashed. "You shouldn't have followed him. You can't just do things alone! It's too dangerous."

"If it weren't for your stupid text, I would've caught him. I was so close until you startled me."

A muscle in his jaw twitched. "There's been a new development."

CHAPTER 14

"What do you mean?" I whispered.

"FEA pathologists examined Madison's body and detected a growth—"

"She was sick?"

"No. Pregnant."

"Is Yates the father?" I asked.

"We don't know. But she wasn't far along. The pathologists estimate only four or five weeks. It's quite possible that Madison wasn't even aware of it yet."

Strange certainty cut through me. "No. She knew." Alec raised his eyebrows, so I continued. "I think that was the reason for her meeting with Yates at the lake. He said they wanted to talk."

"So you think she wanted to tell him about it?"

I paused. Yates had acted oddly when I'd talked to him about the reason for their meeting. "I'm not sure. I think he might've known about the pregnancy. Maybe they wanted to discuss their options."

"I bet Yates would've wanted her to have an abortion," Alec said.

"I'll ask him about it. Maybe I can get it out of him."

"I don't want you alone with him again."

"I'll approach him in school tomorrow. I'll just pretend that I suddenly remembered the pregnancy."

Alec frowned. "All right. But there's more."

More?

"I had a discussion with Major and we agree that aside from Yates, Devon is our prime suspect."

"Devon? Are you kidding me?"

"Today when he was supposed to be at wrestling practice, I saw him sneaking around the places where the last two bodies were found. I don't know what he wanted there but he was definitely looking for something."

"But why would he return to the crime scene? Maybe he's trying to solve the case. After all, it's his sister who was attacked. Or maybe he was just jogging."

"He wasn't there to jog and I don't think he's investigating. He went to the exact spots where the bodies were found. What could he possibly find there after the police already searched the place several times?" He paused. "Sometimes murderers return to the place where a murder happened because it gives them a kick. It's a compulsion. And what's more important, he knew *exactly* where Madison's body was found. The police never disclosed the exact location."

Dimples-in-his-cheeks Devon was a killer?

"That's ridiculous. Devon loves his sister." I couldn't stop myself from getting defensive.

Alec narrowed his eyes. "You're not supposed to let them get under your skin. Not Devon or the rest of the Chambers family or any of Madison's friends. This is a job. Don't get emotionally invested."

I was so tired of hearing that. I looked away, my muscles heavy and aching.

"Don't ever be alone with Devon or Yates. I mean it, Tess."

"You haven't even told me why Devon would kill those people. He doesn't have a motive."

"We'll find out, but until then, keep your guard up."

Didn't I always? With a tired nod, I turned and dragged myself back home. Two minutes later I arrived, just as a car turned onto the street. Linda and Ronald.

Luckily, I was able to slip inside before they noticed me. But Devon cornered me in the hallway.

"What the hell was that?" he hissed. His eyes blazed with anger and I felt a twinge of nervousness. But just as suddenly, his fury disappeared, replaced by softness and worry. "Get into your room before Mom and Dad get inside. You look like you've been in a fight. If they see you like that, they'll freak out." He shook his head. "You really owe me an explanation for this, Madison."

That was the one thing I couldn't give him. Not after what Alec had told me.

I raced into my room just as the front door opened. I peeled my wet clothes off and hid them in the wardrobe. I'd find a way to dispose of them tomorrow, but for now I needed sleep.

I locked the door, my fingers frozen stiff from the cold rain. Better safe than sorry.

What if Devon hadn't been at the crime scene to look for evidence? What if Alec was right? An image of Devon's smile, eyes alight with laughter and dimples showing, popped into my head and suddenly I felt guilty for ever buying into Alec's suspicions. Ryan or Yates or even Phil with his freaky eyes seemed so much more likely to have killed Madison. If I could only find out why.

The next day during lunch, I strode into Yates's classroom without knocking. He turned around, about to chide whoever barged in, but his reprimanding-teacher expression slipped when he saw it was me.

"You shouldn't be here. If someone sees us—" he didn't finish the sentence. He came around his desk but made no move to remove me from the room.

"You never minded in the past."

His face twisted like he wished I would forget about it, or maybe that he hadn't reminded me in the first place. I closed the door behind my back and leaned against it. My nerves churned like winding snakes in my stomach but I forced myself not to let it show.

"What do you want?"

"Did you know about my pregnancy?"

The color drained from his face. The backs of his legs bumped against the edge of his desk and slowly he sank down onto it. I couldn't tell if he was shocked because of the pregnancy itself or shocked because I knew. "You . . . you're . . . pregnant?"

Maybe I was wrong, but it sounded like he'd almost said "still."

"I was." I softened my voice, made it hitch. "I had a miscarriage following the attack."

Relief flashed in his eyes and he made no attempt to hide it. He didn't say he was sorry.

"Did you know? Was that the reason for our meeting at the lake? Did you want to talk about it with me?"

He stood. "I didn't know."

I stared at him, wishing I could wrangle the thoughts from his mind. "I don't believe you."

His shoulders went slack. "I'm not lying. I—the day before our planned meeting, you mentioned you were late with your period." He went on faster than before. "But I wasn't worried. I thought it was normal for a girl your age. You weren't that late, and I didn't even know you had taken a pregnancy test." His eyes darted around the room, he twisted his hands, and the first signs of sweat patches showed in his armpits. But it wasn't proof of him lying. Any guy who just learned he'd impregnated his secret girlfriend would likely break out in a sweat.

"But you knew it was a possibility. It would've made things really complicated for you. People would've started wondering who the father was."

"I don't even know if it was mine."

Anger surged through me. "What are you trying to say? You think I was cheating on you?"

"You cheated on Ryan. What am I supposed to think? There's no proof." He was right. Madison had cheated on Ryan but the way he tried to put the blame on his student really rubbed me the wrong way.

"You're right. The proof was destroyed when I almost died," I said quietly.

He swallowed and looked down. "Did you tell anyone about it?"

"No."

But what if Devon knew? Or maybe Dr. Hansen? What if Madison had gone to her to ask about the pregnancy? Yates could've killed Dr. Hansen in order to silence her.

The school bell rang once—only five minutes until the next class started—and Yates released a breath. I turned to leave, but he grabbed my arm. "This is a new chance for both of us. My wife and I have started marriage counseling. We should leave the past behind. Just think what people would say about you if they found out about us."

I couldn't believe he was trying to make Madison feel guilty and threatening her reputation. Disgusted, I shook him off and stormed out of the room. Nobody paid me any attention as I hurried away. My brain was struggling to wrap itself around what had just happened when Ryan stepped in my way.

"We need to talk," he said. I wasn't sure if I was in the mindset for another difficult conversation but I nodded anyway.

"Let's go somewhere private," Ryan said, turning on his heel. At the other end of the corridor, Francesca made a face that would have impressed even Kate. She gave me the evil eye as I followed him; gossip would be floating around school soon.

Ryan led me into an empty unlocked classroom, closed the door, and leaned up against it. I braced myself for an argument as I waited for him to speak. He pushed himself off the wall and began moving toward me but then stopped and ran a hand through his hair. He looked nervous. "Listen, Maddy."

The way he said it, his voice softer than I'd ever heard it, his face warped with regret, I knew this conversation wouldn't take the turn I'd thought. I let him take my hand in his own, which were big and calloused. It wasn't quite as bad as Yates touching me, but I didn't want Ryan to be this close, either.

"I'm sorry for what happened. It was stupid of me and it won't happen again. I really want you back."

What wouldn't happen again?

"Please, Maddy."

His other hand came up to my neck and that was too much. I tried to pull away, but his hands tightened around me like vises.

"Let me go," I hissed.

"Don't be like that, Maddy. You know I love you. We were the dream couple—why ruin it all?"

His hand on my neck drew me toward him, trapping my hand between us. He was so close I smelled the staleness of cigarettes on his breath. "Let me go," I said, shifting my weight to get a better stance. "You've got a new girlfriend, go be with her."

"Chloe? Please. I was just trying to make you jealous. It's nothing. I want only you."

Our lips were inches apart. I struggled against his grip, but with a thrust he pulled me into his arms and pressed his lips against mine. His fingers dug into my skin. Images from my training with Alec flashed in my mind. I clenched my mouth shut and jerked my knee upward. Bull's-eye.

With a feral noise—half yowl, half groan—he let go of me and staggered backward before sinking to his knees as if he was about to pray.

A shudder went through my body. *That* had almost been my first kiss.

"What the hell's gotten into you?" he panted. "Why'd you do that?"

"Because you don't understand the meaning of no," I said, careful to stay out of his arm range. He was strong and tall. The element of surprise was what had given me an advantage, but that was gone now.

He closed his eyes. I couldn't read his expression. Was he angry or apologetic?

"What happened before I broke up with you?" I demanded. The bell rang a second time. I'd be late for class.

He cradled his crotch in his hands, looking up at me with damp eyes. He pressed his lips together. For a moment it looked as though his eyes had clouded over. Had I hit him that hard?

"You okay?" I asked stupidly.

"No, I haven't been okay since you broke up with me."

The door opened, hitting Ryan in the back and making him stumble forward.

Alec poked his head into the room; his eyes darted between Ryan and me before he stepped inside and closed the door.

"Get out. This is private," Ryan growled, a fine sheen of perspiration on his face.

Alec ignored him. "Are you okay?"

I nodded. "We were just talking."

"Is this your new boyfriend? That took all of five minutes." Ryan staggered to his feet, his shoulders hunched from pain. He looked like the answer would really crush him. But there was something else at play.

"That's none of your business," Alec said before I could say no.

Ryan took a step toward me, his face conflicted.

Alec pushed him back. "Get out before you lose more than your pride."

They were almost the same height, but Ryan didn't know that Alec was stronger than any normal human. He straightened as if he wanted to fight but pain still contorted his face. I had landed a good hit. With one last look at me, he left.

"Looks like you just made a new enemy," I told Alec.

His face turned dark. "I can deal with him."

Following the line of Alec's eyes, I saw the finger marks Ryan had left on my wrist. Good thing that Alec couldn't see my neck from that angle. It felt sore, too. Ryan took getting Madison back a bit too seriously.

I rubbed my wrist and leaned against a table.

"Why did you follow him into an empty classroom?"

"Because he came to my house yesterday to talk. He wasn't going to give up unless I finally spoke to him."

"He was at the house? Why didn't you tell me? He could've come to attack you."

"I'm not stupid, Alec, and Devon was home anyway."

Alec shook his head. "Oh great, is that supposed to calm me? That guy is as much of a suspect as Ryan."

I shushed him. We couldn't risk being overheard.

"Devon is innocent."

"Do you really believe that?"

"I think Yates knew about Madison's pregnancy."

"Are you sure?"

"No. I'm not sure. He didn't admit anything, but he was jumpy and tried to guilt me into not talking about the affair or the pregnancy with anyone. I don't know what to make of him."

Alec closed his eyes and exhaled through his nose. "I'll talk to Major."

"We need to get to class," I said, knowing the look on his face too well. I turned to exit the classroom.

"You're risking too much," Alec whispered.

"I'm just trying to do my job, Alec. We always knew it would be risky."

The following weekend I met the rest of Madison's family, at the barbecue Ronald organized to celebrate her recovery.

Madison's paternal grandparents arrived first, with presents—chocolate truffles, money, and books. It felt wrong to accept anything from them, but I did anyway. Madison's grandpa had a laugh like dry leaves, and he put his cigar down only to light a new one.

The spicy smell of tobacco mingled with the smoky smell of the steaks sizzling on the grill. It was a cold and cloudy day, but even that couldn't dampen the mood. There were about twenty people there, but we could have easily fed twenty more with the amount of food piling up on the dining room table, not to mention the stack of steaks waiting by the grill. Madison's cousins, aunts and uncles, godparents, and great aunts were all in attendance. There were so many guests that I couldn't even remember half their names. Luckily most of them just asked me if I was well and hugged me before they moved on to grab something to eat. They were a hungry bunch. Only Uncle Scott, Ronald's older brother, and his wife, Aunt Cecilia, stuck to my side like super-glue.

Uncle Scott, who had a mustache that curled around his lips like a constant frown, told dirty jokes about nuns and penguins that made my ears turn pink, while Aunt Cecilia giggled at each one as though she was hearing it for the first time. Watching them interact made me laugh even more than the jokes.

The whole house buzzed with laughter, conversation, chewing, and the occasional burp—from Uncle Scott. I couldn't remember a time when I'd been happier. The smile seemed to be permanently carved into my face, my muscles aching from unfamiliar use. Was this how my life could have been if I had been normal? In that moment, I wished more than anything that I could keep them, that I was more than an impostor with a borrowed family.

I turned around, feeling like I'd suffocate if I stayed with them for a moment longer. I headed for the kitchen, hoping to find a moment alone but instead found Linda frosting a huge buttercream cake. She didn't hear me enter over the chatter coming from the rest of the house and I stopped for a moment to watch her as she spread the icing with a spatula. She had a small, happy smile on her face. Instinctively, my fingers closed around the rose pendant over my breastbone, drawing comfort from it.

Linda turned and dropped the spatula, clapping a hand over her heart. "Good God, Maddy, you scared me."

"Sorry, I didn't mean to. I just needed . . ." I trailed off, not sure how to tell her I needed a reprieve from her family. She gave me a knowing look.

"I know. They can be quite overwhelming," she said as she

picked up the cake stand and headed toward the dining room. "I'll be back in a minute."

I stared out the kitchen window, still clutching the pendant. A flash of white-blond hair had rounded the property and stopped behind the fence. As he took a step closer, his face came into view: Phil Faulkner. He seemed to be glancing up at something. My window? I knew he lived close by, but I'd never seen him loitering around the neighborhood before. Could he be the guy watching my window? What was his deal?

His eyes moved down toward the kitchen window, where he caught my gaze. He was holding something in his hand, but from my vantage point I couldn't see what it was. He hastily turned and hurried away. And then I saw what he was carrying: a fishing rod. The pathology report had said the victims were strangled with a wire. What if it was a fishing line?

I debated whether or not to follow him when Devon walked into the kitchen, carrying an empty platter. It was the same one I'd seen piled high with steaks and spareribs in the living room just a few minutes ago. "Do lots of people go fishing in this area?"

He opened the fridge and piled up even more meat on the tray. "Many people do. The lake is a good fishing ground."

I frowned at the pile of meat. Dimples dented Devon's cheeks when he noticed me staring, and his eyes had a mischievous glimmer in them.

"Don't tell me you want to barbecue them," I said, following him through the living room and out into the backyard, where a pillar of smoke rose into the sky.

"Dad asked me to take his place for this round," Devon said as he loaded the grate with steaks the size of dinner plates. The meat sizzled when it touched the hot surface, and a new wave of smoke bubbled up into the air.

"But Mom's already taken the cake into the dining room. I thought it was time for dessert." I mean, the hungry bunch had already eaten half a cow at least.

Devon turned the steaks with barbecue tongs. "Maddy. A Chambers barbecue isn't over until every piece of meat has been cooked and gobbled down."

Oops. That seemed like something I should have known.

"What's up with Uncle Scott's facial hair?"

Devon grinned and suddenly I could breathe again. "You mean his porn-stache?"

I laughed and so did he. So much in fact that he didn't notice how his hand was inching dangerously close to the hot grate. I opened my mouth to warn him, but it was too late. His hand bumped against the barbecue. He jerked it back, dropping the tongs and letting out a hiss of pain.

My stomach plummeted. Burn wounds could be ugly, and this would be bad. Devon cradled his hand against his chest and bent down to pick up the tongs as if he was going to keep right on grilling. I wrestled them out of his grip. "Let me see your hand."

He turned away, his shoulder forming a shield between us. "It's nothing, Maddy. I didn't even touch the grate."

"Don't be stupid." I gripped his arm and pulled his hand back toward me. I turned it around but the skin was only a bit red, as though nothing had happened at all.

He pulled away and took the barbecue tongs, resuming his

work. "I told you it was nothing. I was just startled. I barely touched it."

Had my eyes played a trick on me? Maybe he hadn't really touched the grill. But I could have sworn I'd seen it happen. Seen him grimace in pain.

Ronald poked his head out the back door. "Are the steaks done? Uncle Scott's moved on to his sheep jokes. It'd be great if we could get him busy chewing again."

I raised my eyebrows at Devon for an explanation. He smirked. "Don't ask. Believe me, you don't want to know."

It was almost midnight when the last visitors left. I felt drained from all the happiness and the knowledge that it was fleeting. Soon I'd have to exit this world and leave only darkness in my wake, when Linda and Ronald would learn the truth about their daughter's death.

Once the lights were turned out, I crept down the stairs and tiptoed into the garage. I used a small flashlight to illuminate my surroundings. Slowly, I guided the beam over the workbench and the camping equipment. There was nothing suspicious—no knives, no fishing lines, no wire. Relief flooded me. A creak sounded behind me. "What are you doing?"

I whirled around, my heart thrashing against my rib cage. The beam of the flashlight caught on Devon's frown and he squinted. I lowered my arm. "I thought you were asleep," I said.

He peeked over my head into the garage. "You didn't answer my question."

"I couldn't sleep and then I thought I heard a noise and got scared," I said quickly.

Concern flashed across his face. "You should have woken me or Dad. You shouldn't sneak around in the dark," he whispered. He glanced at the stairs; the voices of Linda and Ronald carried down from their bedroom. Had we woken them? I'd thought they were sleeping.

"I know," I said. "But I didn't want to worry you. I already feel like enough of a burden."

I hugged Devon and leaned my cheek against his chest, not sure if that was a sisterly move. His arms wrapped around me. He felt warm and strong and he smelled like skin and cotton and comfort. I pressed my nose into his shirt, hoping he wouldn't notice. I knew without a doubt that he wasn't the killer, no matter what anyone else said.

CHAPTER 15

I slipped out of my clothes, turned on the shower, and stepped under the steam of water. Goose bumps erupted all over my body, and for one glorious moment my mind felt empty. But then it started. At first in my toes, then my calves, and up to my thighs. My skin rippled, undulated, stretched; my bones shifted, cracked, repositioned. Shock kept me rooted to the spot. The rippling moved higher until it had taken over all of me. Shifting without volition—that wasn't supposed to happen. Not now, not ever.

I willed it to stop, for my body to obey my orders. My skin rippled and shifted in small waves, like there were bugs crawling under its surface. That wasn't normal. It had never happened before.

Grabbing a towel, I got out of the shower stall and stumbled as my legs shortened a few inches. My knees collided with the tiled floor, sending sparks of pain through them. I held my arms out in front of me. I shuddered, which ushered in a new wave of rippling through my body as my skin grew paler.

I gripped the washbasin and pulled myself to my feet. I staggered to the mirror to see my reflection. My face was shifting, remolding slowly. It was still Madison's face but my eyes were turning turquoise.

First one, like one of those Siberian huskies with different-colored eyes, and then the other. My lips twisted, my bangs lengthened and turned auburn. It was happening to me. I could see it happening, could feel it happening, but I was powerless to stop it.

I pressed my eyes shut, refusing to believe what I saw. Why wouldn't it stop? Rippling, tearing, stretching, and then it was over. I looked at my reflection. It was no longer the one it was supposed to show, the one I'd gotten used to.

Freckled nose, auburn locks, turquoise eyes. Madison was gone.

I shivered. A puddle had accumulated around my feet where water dripped from my body and hair. I felt more drained than if I had just run a marathon. Even if my body obeyed me now, I doubted I'd find the strength to shift back into Madison's body.

I heard steps coming up the stairs. I stumbled toward the door and turned the lock.

"Maddy? Everything okay?"

Choking down my panic, I turned on the faucet, hoping desperately that the sound of running water would drive Linda away. I pressed against the far wall beside the toilet, as far away from the door as possible.

"Maddy?"

If I answered her, she'd realize it wasn't Madison's voice. What was I supposed to do?

Her steps halted in front of the door. "Maddy?" She knocked. "Maddy, honey, are you okay?" She wouldn't leave until she knew I was all right.

Clearing my throat, I tried my best to sound like Madison. "I'm just taking a shower before bed. I'm fine." It wasn't a very good imitation but hopefully the sound of the running water would help to drown it out.

"Are you sure?" I could hear the concern in her voice. She turned the knob but the door was locked.

"Yep, just taking a shower. Don't worry, Mom."

The *Mom* slipped so easily from my lips, it scared me.

"Haven't you already showered?"

Think, Tessa, think.

"I started but I heard my phone, and I got out to see who texted me."

There was silence on the other side of the door. "Who was it?"

"Ana."

Just go away, I thought. *Please.*

"Okay. Wake me if you need anything."

She waited a moment longer before her steps moved away from the door. I turned the shower back on and waited until I was sure everyone was safely in bed. Once I was sure nobody was around, I hurried into my room and locked it. My own reflection stared back at me from the mirror on the door. Shadows spread under my eyes. My fingers brushed over my unblemished throat. I'd gotten so used to feeling the scar there.

I needed to change back into Madison. Closing my eyes, I tried to trigger the rippling sensation but I didn't feel anything, not even the slightest tingling. Droplets of sweat mingled with the water from my hair and gathered in the towel around my body.

Exhausted, I sank to my knees, still Tessa. It was midnight. I'd been trying to shift for almost an hour.

I fumbled for my phone and punched in the speed dial for Alec. He picked up after the second ring.

"Hmm?" His voice was gravely with sleep and the sound sent a pleasant shiver down my back. "Tess?"

I tried to speak, but the words crowded in my throat.

"Tess, what's up?" His voice was thick with worry.

"I'm losing it, Alec. I can't shift back. I don't know what to do." I took a deep breath, trying to get a grip on myself.

"Calm down. Tell me again, but slowly this time."

"I—I'm not Madison anymore. My body changed back to myself and now I can't shift back. I don't know what to do. What if I'm losing my Variation?"

I heard rustling in the background and imagined Alec getting out of bed.

"Where are you?"

"I locked myself in my room. Linda was suspicious but everyone's asleep now."

"Hang in there. I'll be there in a few minutes." More rustling. He was probably getting dressed.

"I could climb through the window."

"Wait 'til I'm there. I'll make sure you don't break your neck."

Before I could offer him a witty comeback, he hung up. I cradled the phone against my chest. It would take him maybe ten minutes to get here.

Looking down at my shivering body, I realized I was still wrapped in a towel. I grabbed some clothes from the dresser and slipped into them. The clothes clung to my body, better suited to Madison's tiny frame.

My phone rang once—Alec. My cue to open the window. The hairs on my arms rose as the cool air hit my damp skin. Alec waited below, dressed in black and one with the darkness. I scrambled out of the window and held on to the windowpane as I slowly lowered myself down.

"Let go," he said, and I did.

He caught me with ease. I breathed in his scent, allowing my cheek to rest against his chest. He didn't set me down immediately but I wasn't going to complain. I could have stayed in his arms forever.

"Your hair is wet. You'll get pneumonia if we don't get out of the cold," he said, briefly tightening his grip on me before he put me down. I could have sworn he'd smelled my hair. Sometimes I wasn't sure what was real and what was merely the result of wishful thinking. Sometimes I didn't want to know.

We kept to the shadows as we hurried toward his car, which was parked around the corner. The windows in the neighbors' houses were dark. Apparently, people in Livingston didn't keep late hours. We closed the car doors quietly, and I slumped against the seat as Alec keyed the ignition. I could only hope the Chambers household would sleep through the night without noticing I was gone. Though, nothing could be worse than if they caught me as Tessa.

Alec looked over at me. "Tell me again what happened."

As I recounted the story, every word seemed to drain me. He carefully weighed my words before responding.

"Why does it happen? Why do you lose control?"

There could be so many answers to that question. Emotions. Stress. Distraction. Because I couldn't get him out of my mind. Or because I felt happier in my pretend life inside someone else's body than I'd ever felt before. Or maybe because I worried we still had no clue who the killer was. The list could have gone on and on.

"I don't know. Maybe it's the pressure," I said eventually.

"It can happen to anyone," he answered. "Don't worry, you're doing a great job." It was as if he could read my thoughts.

"I'm not. Something is wrong with me."

"You just need to relax. Let's do something to get your mind off things." I hoped the darkness of the car hid my burning cheeks. I didn't want Alec to know what I wanted to do, what his words made me think of. "There's a drive-in movie theater just outside town."

I'd heard the other girls talk about it in the locker room, and from their stories it didn't seem like the movie was the real entertainment. That could be pretty awkward. But I heard myself agreeing nonetheless.

Alec pulled up next to the ticket booth, where an old man sat slumped against the wall. He looked old enough to have fought in the Revolutionary War and had the scars to show for it. His face looked as if someone had run a rake over it—repeatedly. His chin rested on his chest and I could hear the snores coming from his parted lips even through the walls of the booth. Did he spend his nights like that?

Alec had to knock twice on the window before the old man woke. It took him even longer to wake up enough to serve us. Alec paid for the tickets and a huge bowl of popcorn—reheated and slightly stale. As the buttery smell made its way around the car, Alec circled the lot in search of a good spot. As he eased into a vacant space, I felt the tension leaving my body.

The theater was nearly empty, and we had a prime spot with a perfect view of the screen. Alec placed the popcorn on the console between us. I wasn't sure if it was to keep us from getting too close or just so I could reach it. I decided to go with the second option.

The movie was *Alien*.

I had seen it dozens of times and I was glad that we wouldn't have to watch anything remotely romantic. I knew the whole movie by heart, but when the alien found its first victim I still shuddered.

"It seems we never get tired of this one," Alec chuckled.

We'd seen it at least five times together. "Seriously. Every time I see it, I love it more. Sometimes it takes some time to appreciate every detail about something. Like the more you see it, the more you come to like it," I said. I glanced over at him. His eyes looked so intense. They seemed to glow in the dark of the car.

"That sounded stupid," I said with an embarrassed laugh.

He didn't laugh, didn't even crack a smile, just stared at me.

"It's not stupid. You're completely right." He took a handful of popcorn but didn't eat it, just held onto it in his hand. "Do you remember the first time we watched this together?"

I nodded. Of course I remembered. I'd been living with the FEA for only a few weeks and tried to call my mom for the hundredth time. I'd been worried something had happened to her because I could never reach her, but on that day she'd actually picked up. I'd been so happy and relieved, eager to tell her about my new classes, my new room, my new friend Holly, until she'd cut me off mid-sentence and told me to never call her again. Something had shattered in me that day, a feeling I felt unable to share with anyone. I'd hidden in the pool house, behind the bin of wet towels, alone in the dark, and bawled my eyes out. That's where Alec found me.

He sank down on the dank floor beside me and let me cry into

his chest. I barely knew him, but I felt so comfortable in his presence. Later, once I'd calmed a little, he told me the story of how his
parents had abandoned him in a mall during the Christmas holidays
when he was only five years old. He said the pain got better after a
while, that time dulled the memories and repaired the scars. He said
he understood how I felt and that it was okay to feel the way I did.
Afterward we'd watched all the *Alien* movies in a row until sunrise.

"That was the first time I realized how much I wanted to keep
you safe," he said. "It was the first time I met someone who understood me. Nobody understands me like you do."

I stopped breathing and forced myself to swallow my last piece
of popcorn. It was a miracle it didn't get stuck in my dry throat. His
eyes flickered toward me and I saw that for the first time in a long
while, they were vulnerable and unguarded.

He reached over, his thumb brushing across my cheek where
a damp strand of hair had stuck to my skin. Heat bloomed under
his fingertips, spreading all over me and pooling in my belly. His
fingertips halted, unsure. I licked my lips and his eyes followed the
movement, a muscle in his jaw moving in response. I could see the
struggle on his face, feel the hesitation in his touch. Would he pull
back? The air felt stifling, but I was barely breathing anyway. His
hair was as black as the night around us.

His hand still rested on my cheek but slowly it began to move
downward, trailing over my throat until finally it rested on my collarbone. He drew small circles on my skin.

Something changed on his face, like he'd lost the fight, and he
leaned in as the popcorn bucket tumbled over, spilling its contents
all over the floor of the car. Neither of us made any motion to pick

it up. And suddenly there was no space left between us. His eyes darted to my lips and then, just like that, he closed the gap. His lips were on mine, soft and probing at first, and once I got past my shyness, demanding and hard. I ran my hands through his hair and down his back, feeling his muscles ripple under my fingertips. He felt so good; kissing him felt so right.

His fingers drifted over my ear, my neck, my rib cage. His touch left fire in its wake. A strange whine escaped from deep in my throat as his palms moved under my shirt and grazed my stomach. His skin felt lava-hot yet raised goose bumps wherever it touched.

Alec was kissing me. The real me—not an impostor, not Madison, not some fake version of Kate.

"Tess." He whispered the word against my ear and throat. His kisses lost their frenzy. My heartbeat slowed. He buried his face in the crook of my neck. I listened to our ragged breathing and placed my hand over his hand, which rested over my rib cage. His hand was so huge it nearly spanned the entire width of my chest. I bet he could feel my heart pounding against his palm.

"I've wanted to do that for so long," he murmured against my throat.

Happiness erupted like fireworks inside my body. There it was, the one thing I'd wanted to hear from him for so long. A small voice in my head wanted to ask him, "Then why the hell haven't you done it sooner?" But I knew where that would lead us and I didn't want to go there—yet. He pressed another kiss against my collarbone before he straightened in his seat. His hair, I noted with satisfaction, was thoroughly disheveled from my fingers, and his lips were swollen from our kisses.

The shrill sound of ringing almost sent my heart flying through my chest. Alec fumbled in his pockets for his cell and rolled his eyes when he saw the screen. The caller ID read "Mom." I thought Alec hadn't seen his parents since he'd come to the FEA.

"What do you want?" As soon as I heard his tone I realized how stupid I'd been. Of course, it wasn't his real mom. It was Summers, his pretend mom for the mission. "Jesus, Summers, you sound like a nanny." I couldn't hear her response, but it must have been something equally insulting because Alec grinned. I wanted to reach out and grab him, just to make sure I wasn't dreaming, but I wasn't sure if our kiss gave me the right to keep touching him.

His face tightened at something she said. "Okay. Tell him I'll be home soon." He ended the call.

"I never thought Summers was the motherly type," I said.

"She isn't, believe me. She's not happy without someone to boss around and she's worried I'll bust our cover if I'm not home like a good schoolboy. And Major showed up a few minutes ago. Apparently, he wants to talk to me." He looked anxious at the prospect.

I touched his cheek, the stubble prickling my fingertips. "It'll be okay." Without thinking I leaned over and kissed him on the lips. For one heart-stopping moment I thought he'd pull away, but then his arms came around me.

"We need to get you back home," Alec said after a moment. "Can you shift?"

I tried to relax against the seat and closed my eyes, acutely aware of Alec's gaze on me. I reached for my Variation, tried to coax it.

Nothing.

"You can do it." Alec's voice was calm and full of confidence, and suddenly I felt it too. Calm and confident. It was like his words had crept into me and washed away all the doubt and worry.

The rippling started in my toes and snaked up my body and after a few seconds it was over.

"And?" I asked.

He smiled. "You did it."

I couldn't resist. I leaned over and kissed him again. I never wanted to stop.

CHAPTER 16

The next morning, Devon remained silent during our ride to school. I was exhausted. I hadn't dared to fall asleep all night, scared I'd change back into my own body again. He looked like he hadn't slept much either, like something was bothering him.

"Is anything wrong?" I asked. My voice was suddenly loud in the silence of the car and Devon cringed in surprise as if he'd forgotten I was beside him.

"Why do you ask?"

"You look tense," I said, watching his face for a reaction.

"I didn't sleep much." Then, as if a switch had been turned, he gave me the grin that seemed to lighten everything around. "Don't worry, Maddy."

We eased into the parking lot, where Ana stood waiting for me. Devon scuttled out of the car before I could ask him anything else. His behavior didn't really help to stifle my curiosity. Something was definitely wrong. Ana approached us as I climbed out of the car, but Devon was immediately on his way toward the school building. It looked like the devil snapped at his heels.

"What happened? You look suspiciously happy," Ana said.

My stomach exploded with butterflies as I thought about seeing Alec again.

I shrugged. "I'm just happy, I guess."

"You guess? Did you have another date with Alec? You didn't even tell me anything about the last one. What's going on with you guys? I'm your best friend. I deserve to know!"

"I'll tell you soon. I promise. I'm kind of distracted at the moment, freaking out over a test later." That was a lie of course. But maybe I could at least tell her about the kiss. If Alec and I got together, everyone at school would find out anyway. I wondered if he'd already broken up with Kate. Would he tell her about us?

My eyes were drawn toward the teacher parking lot, where Yates was rummaging around in the trunk of his car. "Just a sec," I said to Ana as I craned my neck to get a better view. There were a few items strewn around the trunk—sneakers, a tennis racket, some books—but my eyes came to rest on a huge bottle of disinfectant. Did he need it to cover up evidence?

I turned around and hurried away. I'd have to talk to Alec about it. Ana fell into step beside me as we made our way into the building and toward our first class. Alec wasn't in his spot yet but we still had a few minutes until the class started. Mrs. Coleman swept into the room. Her dress, with its giant collar and garish floral pattern, was probably deemed a crime in some countries.

"She's got some sense of style," Ana whispered. I let out a laugh that I turned into a cough when Mrs. Coleman's angry eyes settled on me. My thoughts returned to Yates. The evidence against him felt overwhelming. He'd had an affair with Madison, he'd been at the lake near the time of the attack, and he seemingly had the most to gain from her disappearance. It was almost too easy. I had to figure out why he'd kill the others.

The bell rang just as Alec entered the classroom. I sat up straighter, trying to catch his eyes. He took his seat without a single glance in my direction.

I looked over my shoulder at him, while Mrs. Coleman began scribbling on the blackboard. He busied himself shuffling his schoolbooks and notepad but eventually he had no choice but to meet my eyes.

Whatever had been between us yesterday was over and forgotten. His face was as unmoving as a statue, his eyes hard and emotionless. My lower lip started to quiver. The look on his face softened. It looked filled with regret, mixed with something like guilt and sympathy. I wanted to be on the receiving end of none of them.

I listened to Mrs. Coleman, feigned interest, nodded when it was appropriate, laughed when it was expected, and took notes. But inside, I felt hollow. The moment class ended, I sprang out of my seat, swung my backpack over my shoulder, and hurried out of the room. Maybe I should have waited for Ana, but I couldn't risk meeting Alec when I knew his words would crush me.

A rippling started in my toes and panic washed over me. Not here. Not now.

I dropped my backpack—it hit the ground with a thud, but I couldn't be bothered to care. I began sprinting, my feet barely touching the ground as I pumped my legs. The corridors grew crowded as people streamed out of their classrooms. Some of them stopped to stare. I bumped into them, pushed them out of the way, ignoring their curses.

The undulating reached my calves. I heard someone call my name.

I burst through the front door of the school. Finally outside, I picked up speed until my sides burned and my lungs constricted. Rippling snaked its way into my thighs, through my upper body.

Soon I'd be back in my own body. In the middle of the school courtyard. Within plain view of anyone who cared to look outside.

The rippling turned into a quivering that nearly sent me flying to the ground. In the last moment I caught my fall against a tree. Leaning my forehead against the rough bark, I took deep breaths, trying to regain control of my body. My fingers clutched at the tree. Its rough edges bit into my skin, cutting, burning. The rippling stopped somewhere around my chest and slowly ebbed away. My breathing calmed. I loosened my hold on the tree and stood up straight.

Steps crunched on the rough asphalt. Not Ana's heels. Long, certain strides. He was close. I could feel his presence right behind me like a shadow.

I braced myself for the words that would inevitably come.

"We need to talk," Alec said, in a quiet voice. "I don't know what came over me yesterday. I'm sorry."

He knew better than to touch me but he was so close I could smell his aftershave.

"You're sorry?" I whispered. The words came out shaky. Not because I was going to cry. For once, I was past that point. This time I was shaking from anger. Anger at him for toying with me, for ignoring months of tension, then kissing me and acting like it meant nothing. Anger at Major for forcing us to work together, though he knew something was brewing between us. But most of all, I was angry at myself for being so stupid and so weak.

I whirled around to face him. "So what, you just change your mind from one day to the next and I'm supposed to accept it just like that?" I snapped my fingers. How could he do this to me? He'd said he'd wanted to kiss me for so long. He'd said nobody understood him like I did. Had he been lying?

"I—" He shook his head. "I lost control and that can't happen again. I talked to Major—"

"You told Major?!" I'd thought what happened was something sacred between him and me, something special.

"No, he already knew. It wasn't that hard to guess with me gone in the middle of the night and all. Anyway, it doesn't matter." He took a deep breath. "You have to forget what happened yesterday. It'll only endanger the mission." His tone was so controlled, so completely unemotional that I wondered if this didn't mean anything at all to him. How could he switch his emotions on and off like that when I felt like I'd lost control altogether? "It shouldn't have happened. It was a mistake."

You're a mistake. That's what he meant. After everything we'd been through, I'd thought that he of all people wouldn't hurt me like this.

"Yes," I said harshly. "You're right. It was a mistake." Refusing to look at him, I breezed past him, but he reached out and touched my shoulder. I jerked back. "Don't touch me ever again." I wanted to hate him, but even now the look in his eyes stirred something inside me.

He lowered his arm. "I'm very sorry." Before I was out of earshot I heard words I was sure weren't meant for me to hear. "For more than you'll ever know."

Inside, the corridors had cleared. The next class was about to begin and I was still shaking with emotions. I had no clue where to find my backpack. It wasn't where I'd dropped it.

I walked to my locker, trying to stop my throat from constricting. I was *not* going to cry. Not here, not now, and certainly not because of *him*. He didn't deserve my tears.

I opened my locker and leaned my head against the door.

"I picked up your stuff."

The voice was familiar. I jerked my head up, not caring how upset I looked. Phil Faulkner stood in front of me, holding my backpack. Had he been following me? Had he been watching Alec and me? I took it from him with a curt "thanks." I knew I should have said more but making small talk was the last thing I was in the mood for.

"What happened?" His eyes—that creepy watery blue—were too inquiring, his expression too sympathetic. Something wasn't right with him. He was always watching me, always hovering nearby. His hand twitched toward my own but then he let his arm drop to his side. I tried to take a step back but bumped against the wall. I brushed past him, careful not to touch him. "I really need to get to class, but thanks again."

CHAPTER 17

That night, I busied myself with online research, though I didn't expect to find anything. Other, more experienced agents had perused the case files ad nauseam and surely would have noticed if something was off, but I needed to distract myself from the hollow sensation in my belly.

The FEA database contained some seriously disgusting and creepy photos from the crime scenes, shots so disturbing it was clear why I hadn't been given them before.

One was a headshot of the janitor, Mr. Chen, who'd been killed in the backyard of his house. The photo was blurry, but it looked as though blood trickled from his ears and nose, and his eyes were wide and bulgy. His expression—pained and tired—made me think that he'd struggled a long time before death. The killer hadn't used a wire to strangle him and the FEA hadn't yet figured out how exactly he'd done it.

The ping of an incoming e-mail interrupted my search. I clicked on the little envelope from Holly, which was likely a response to the rambling e-mail I'd sent her about Alec.

Hi sweetie,

I'm so, so sorry. I can't BELIEVE that happened. I want to wring his neck.

Why the hell can't Alec pull his head out of his ass and finally realize that you're perfect for each other? Though now he doesn't deserve you after all the shit he's put you through. I just don't get it. He's never been an insensitive asshole before. Maybe Kate brainwashed him during their mission a few months ago. That would explain why he endures her bitchiness. I wish I was there to distract you.

Hugs,

Holly

P.S. I dyed my hair fury-red in your honor.

I closed the e-mail and blew my nose before I returned to the crime database. Two of the victims—Madison and Kristen—had been found close to the lake. There were pictures of the A's the killer had cut into the skin of his victims. They all looked exactly like the one on Madison's rib cage. I touched the spot under my bra.

There *had* to be something else here, some detail the killer forgot to cover. I searched Google for more mentions of the murders and found a few articles on the website of a local rag.

The first was about Mr. Chen.

"Mr. Mendoza was on his nightly jog when dense fog forced him to take a shortcut past the victim's backyard . . ."

Dense fog? There had been fog the first night I'd seen the stranger watching my window and then again when I'd followed him into the forest. And fog had kept Alec from catching the guy. And hadn't Yates said it had been a hazy day when Madison was attacked?

I clicked on an article about Kristen Cynch and glanced through it until I found what I was looking for.

"The retrieval of the body of high school senior Kristen Cynch (17) was complicated by mist that blanketed parts of the northern shore."

My hand shook when I opened the next report about Dr. Hansen.

"The neighbors didn't find the body until early the next morning, after the fog had lifted."

The articles about Madison also mentioned fog. Livingston was notoriously rainy, but it couldn't be a coincidence that every murder was accompanied by a curiously thick mist.

Fog. That had to be the hint we'd been searching for. What if the killer was a Variant who could control the weather in some way? I jumped up from my desk chair and turned out the lights before I slipped out the window, almost breaking my neck when I lost my grip on the ledge. I was already running late for the meeting. Summers wouldn't excuse tardiness—not even a broken bone would change that.

My ballet flats were noiseless on the wet asphalt as I weaved my way through Livingston. I turned a corner and stopped dead when fog spread before me. Milky, intangible fingers of haze dusted against me, making me shiver. Mist coiled around my legs and arms, snatching at my skin and hair. It felt like a living, breathing thing. Like something more than nature.

I shied away. A chill wound its way around my ankle like tentacles, cold and slithery. *It* didn't want me to go. I whimpered but the fog swallowed the noise. Nobody would hear me if I screamed. I steeled myself and kicked out. My feet went right through the veil of mist but the grip around my ankles disappeared. I sprinted into the haze, not breathing, not pausing, not once glancing over my shoulder to see if someone—or something—was following me. Icy wetness slithered across every inch of exposed skin, seeping into my pores. It took hold of me, made me feel cold inside and out.

Shaking, I stepped onto the porch of Summers and Alec's home, and as I turned to look back in the direction I'd come, the streets were clear. *It* was gone.

I unlocked the front door with trembling hands. I was a few minutes late for our meeting but I couldn't bring myself to care. Not after what had just happened. Voices were coming from the living room. I slipped out of my shoes—something Summers was very adamant about—before I followed the sound. Major, Summers, and Alec were seated around the dining room table. So Major was back in town. They stopped talking when they spotted me.

Alec leaped from his chair and rushed toward me, his face alarmed. "What happened?" His hands rested on my shoulders and I didn't have it in me to shake them off. My body felt numb. I couldn't even feel my legs anymore. The walls tipped around me and suddenly I was in Alec's arms.

"You're freezing," he said. My head fell forward, my cheek pressed against his chest, and I looked up at him. Though I wanted to speak, no sound left my lips. Another head appeared beside Alec's. Summers rested her calloused hand on my forehead and I leaned into the touch. They were all so warm.

"Run a hot bath," Summers ordered and Major obeyed without hesitation. Alec carried me into the bathroom. When he began to lower me onto the edge of the bathtub, I clutched at him, a choked sound of protest shuddering from my mouth.

"Don't leave."

Alec met my gaze. He looked like someone had stabbed him and was twisting the blade. My fingers curled around his collar. "I need you," I whispered, the words as wispy as mist.

Summers pried me away from him. I'd nearly forgotten she was there. She panted with the effort of supporting my body. Alec had carried me as though I weighed nothing.

"Alec." Major's voice thrummed in my head. Turning his eyes away, Alec slowly left the bathroom, shutting the door after him.

Summers set me down on the toilet seat. Like a puppet without its master, I slumped down into a heap. Summers didn't speak as she held me upright and removed my clothes. Slowly, she lowered me into the tub, where the running water scorched my skin. She sat down on the edge. I sank farther down into the water, trying to cross my arms over my chest. It took me three attempts before I succeeded.

Summers crossed her legs, the leather of her pants squeaking as it rubbed together. Her face was tense. "This meeting was intended to get you and Alec back on track, to stop your personal problems with each other from getting in the way of this mission." I ignored her words, instead watching the way my skin turned lobster-red from the scalding hot water. I didn't think she expected me to talk and I wasn't sure if I could.

"We knew this mission would be difficult for you in many ways. We knew making you part of a family was going to be uncomfortable, but it was a risk we had to take." I wasn't exactly sure where this was going. My thoughts were still fuzzy and I needed to tell them about my discovery. "I need you to listen to me. Later, when we join Major and Alec, you can tell us what happened. But I want to say this now. I probably won't get another chance to talk to you alone any time soon."

The feeling slowly returned to my legs and they began to prickle.

"I've seen the way you look at Alec."

I closed my eyes as if that could stop her from saying more.

"It's not good to want something or someone you can't have. It's self-destructive, and believe me, I know what I'm talking about." I saw hurt beneath the hard lines of her square jaw. If she really knew how I felt, then she also knew that I couldn't switch my emotions off. Summers sighed. "You know, you're still in Madison's body, have you even noticed?"

I hadn't. The rippling started in my toes and traveled up my body. It took a full minute to shape-shift back to my own body. I was still weak.

I slumped against the tub. The rippling sensation washed over me again—this time without my volition. Twisting, warping, stretching. Water sloshed over the edge and Summers let out a startled gasp. I didn't have to look into the mirror to know I'd changed back to Madison.

What the hell was happening? First I couldn't change into Madison and now I couldn't return to my own body. But the worst thing was the way I didn't even mind. Madison had allowed me to live a life I had only dreamed about: a life with a family who loved her.

Summers handed me a towel, her expression blank. "You're losing yourself in Madison. You have to accept that her life can never be yours. It's important that you don't forget that. Everyone wants to be someone else sometimes, but it's crucial to be able to move on."

A few minutes later, we returned to the living room. I was still in Madison's body, dressed in clothes Summers had given me. Major and Alec stopped talking when we entered.

"You look better," Major said. "Now tell us what happened."

I told them about the mist, about the newspaper articles, about my suspicion. The words spewed out of my mouth without pause.

"I need a drink," Summers said as she got up and went into the kitchen. She returned with something that looked and smelled like tequila, along with a hot chocolate for me. Maybe Summers had more maternal instinct hidden behind her hard shell than I'd given her credit for.

Major and Alec talked quietly about the possible Variations of the killer, how to find him, and how to better protect me. I sipped at the hot chocolate. Apparently, my input wasn't expected. Summers disappeared into the kitchen again, probably for more tequila.

Eventually, Major turned to me. "Alec will try to keep a closer eye on you. But remember, even if the evidence points toward Yates as the killer, Devon is still very high on our suspect list. You should avoid being alone in the house with him."

That wasn't as easy as it sounded, but I didn't try to argue with them. It would have been futile to try. I just wanted to get into my bed and forget that today had ever happened. I wanted to see Devon's dimples, to hear Linda's laughter, to listen to Ronald's stories. Sometimes it felt like I wanted their company more than anything else.

"Alec reported that there's a party the day after tomorrow," Major said. I nodded. Ana had mentioned Francesca's party in passing but I'd had so much to deal with that I hadn't paid much attention. "I want you and Alec to keep an eye on things. You should attend as a couple. That way you can easily talk and leave together without drawing attention."

Wasn't that a little hypocritical?

"That's it for today. Keep us updated on any further developments. You're doing a fine job," Major said. That was the most praise I'd ever heard from him.

"I'll take you home." Alec rose from his chair.

"No," I immediately protested.

Summers took her car keys from a side table. "I'll take her."

Without another glance at Alec, I followed Summers out the door and to the car. She didn't try to talk to me during the ride and dropped me off a few houses down from home. I snuck back into the house without a hitch.

The next day, Summers's words still ghosted around in my head. Even if they weren't at the forefront of my thoughts, they crouched at the edges of my consciousness, waiting to catch me by surprise.

You're losing yourself in Madison.

But why not? Madison was dead. She would never come back. Maybe I could spare Linda and Ronald the heartbreak of finding out about her death. I could stop being Tessa and just be Madison. Her body already felt like home, her family like the one I'd always wanted.

Could I live the lie for years and decades?

But one troubling thought haunted me. It wasn't me they loved, it was Madison.

It's important that you don't forget.

There were so many things I wanted to forget, to wipe from my memory once and for all. Like the day my mother's third husband came home drunk and locked me in the closet, forcing me to listen to him beating the crap out of my mother. Or the day my mother said she wished I'd never been born.

I picked up the small hand mirror from its place on the nightstand. Madison's face stared back at me. It wasn't the face I was born with, and yet it felt so familiar, almost like my own. My skin rippled, my features warping, twisting, shifting, breaking until it was my own face in the mirror, my own turquoise eyes, always slightly south of normal. I should have felt relief at being myself for a moment, should have felt a sense of coming home, but I didn't. I felt nothing.

The rippling started again. My face transformed into Madison's and back to my own—then back to Madison's and back to my own. A blur of blond and brown, of freckles and scars, of blue and turquoise. I was starting to feel dizzy but I couldn't stop.

If being someone else on the outside came easily to me, why couldn't it work the same way with who I was on the inside? Why couldn't I simply decide to *feel* like someone else?

The two faces swam before my eyes until I saw a strange combination of the two in the mirror. Despair squeezed the air from my lungs, made me lightheaded. My grip on the handle tightened, grew painful. With a cry, I flung the mirror away. It collided with the dresser and clattered to the floor, the shards littering the ground.

I crossed the room, and as I stood over the remains of the mirror, my face—Tessa's face—was splintered into dozens of pieces. For once, a mirror reflected how I felt inside, how I *looked* inside. Fragmented, broken, torn.

Shaking, I sank to the ground and started picking up the pieces of glass. I wasn't careful enough, and one of the shards cut into the skin on my right palm, creating a tiny crimson river of blood. Someone knocked at the door. I stood, my legs still shaky, and let the rippling bring Madison's body back. Just as I'd completed the shift, the door opened and Devon poked his head in. His eyebrows pulled down in a frown but when he saw my hands, now bloody from the glass, concern took over. He crossed the room and stood before me, cradling my hands in his.

"What happened?" he asked. He looked at me as though he thought I'd done it on purpose. I wanted to rest my forehead against his chest but stopped myself.

"The mirror shattered." I nodded toward the shards of glass on the floor and in the trash can. I didn't even feel the pain, still felt strangely removed from my body.

Devon shook his head, his fingers gentle on my hands. "We need to disinfect this and bandage it up. I'll go get the gauze. You stay here. I don't want Mom to see. She's been worrying enough about you lately."

"Who's been worrying enough lately?" Linda stood in the doorway. When her eyes fell to my cuts, the color drained from her face. She took my hands, her touch gentle.

The worry on Linda's face was too much. I stared at my palm. The gash seemed to be much smaller than I remembered and had nearly stopped bleeding. Maybe my transformation back to Madison's body had helped to heal the wound.

Linda tended to my hand without speaking, but I could feel the questions and worry roll off her in waves. Eventually she was finished. She hugged me, barely leaving room for my breathing. After a moment, I hugged her back with just as much force. It felt like some of the broken fragments inside me had mended, too.

Closing my eyes, I allowed myself to pretend that Linda was really my mom, that her love and worry were for me and not for the mask I'd put on. I dreaded the day this would all be over.

"You have to be more careful. Please, Maddy."

I pulled away from her embrace. "Don't worry. I will."

CHAPTER 18

The morning after the mirror incident, Linda accompanied me to Sheriff Ruthledge's office. Before we entered the building, she paused and wrapped her arms around me. "It'll be okay. Just tell him what you remember. Even if you think it's not important, it could be helpful for the police. Everything could help lead them to that . . . that person." She pushed a strand of hair behind her ear with trembling fingers. "Maybe something you say will give them a lead and then all of this can finally be over."

Sheriff Ruthledge was a short, stocky man with thinning red hair and pockmarks on his cheeks. He rose from his chair and shook my hand across his desk before he gestured at the vacant wooden chair. I sank down onto it.

Linda sat off to the side, out of sight where she couldn't influence me, but her presence was calming.

"Thank you for coming today," the sheriff began. "You don't have to worry. I'll ask only a few questions. If you don't remember something, then tell me and don't feel any pressure to add anything just to give a response."

I nodded and relaxed against the chair. Sheriff Ruthledge's deep, calm voice dispersed the rest of my nerves.

He went over my name, birthday, and place of residence before the real questioning started. "That day, March second, what did you want at the lake?"

I'd learned about police procedure in FEA classes, so I doubted he'd ask any questions that would surprise me. "I—I think I was there to meet someone."

"You think? Or you remember?"

"I don't remember, but I know I often met with friends at the lake."

"With your friend Ana for example?"

I hesitated. "Yes."

"But you don't remember who you wanted to meet that day? Are you sure?" His eyes were sharp but not unfriendly.

I shook my head and looked at my lap. Major didn't want the police to interfere with our investigation, so I had no choice but to lie.

"It's okay. Dr. Fonseca told me that you're suffering from amnesia." Summers had spent the last few days diverting the police's attention. She'd once demonstrated the full extent of her Variation, which left Holly and me so befuddled that we hadn't been able to find our room, though we knew our way around every inch of headquarters. I was willing to bet my interrogation would have been very different without Summers's intervention.

"Do you remember what happened when you were at the lake?"

"No. I've been trying so hard to remember, but it's all gone." I let my voice come out shaky and nervously wrung my hands.

The sheriff scribbled something on his notepad. "Did you have a fight with someone before you were attacked? Or was there some-one you didn't get along with?"

"I don't think so. I know that I broke up with Ryan a while be-fore the attack, and Ana told me that we had a rift within our group of friends because of a fight, but I can't remember what caused it."

He nodded, satisfied—Ana had probably said the same thing. He asked a few more questions about my relationships with Ana, some of the other students, Devon, and my parents, but I could feel that there wasn't the usual urgency behind them. Summers had said that Major wanted the police to believe the killer was an out-of-towner. She'd already begun turning their suspicion in that direction. If nothing else, it was now overwhelmingly clear that the local police wouldn't be getting in the way of the FEA.

Alec kept his eyes firmly on the windshield, fingers tapping an erratic rhythm on the steering wheel. "Listen, I don't like this cha-rade any more than you do, but Major's right. It'll be less suspicious this way. Ana thinks we've gone on dates before, so it makes com-plete sense that we'd show up together." He really had no clue how much I'd have liked being his date if it was the truth, and not one more lie in our elaborate game of deceit.

We pulled up in front of Francesca's house. The driveway and most of the curb were already crowded with cars, so we had to park a block away. It wasn't necessarily a bad thing considering the sullen looks on our faces, which didn't scream happy new couple. The house was bigger than the surrounding homes, with a huge porch illuminated by small lanterns. As soon as we were within sight of the other guests, Alec took my hand in his. It felt warm as always, and my belly flapped with butterflies when he smiled at me.

Inside, the party was in full swing. A wave of smells flooded my nose as we entered: beer and smoke and something sweeter—pot? Apparently most guests weren't adhering to the "smoke outside" rule, and Francesca wasn't stopping them. To my surprise, she had invited us all to the party, though she'd still been giving me the evil eye every day in school.

In the corner of the living room, Francesca's arms were wrapped around Devon and her head was flung back, laughing at something he was saying to a small crowd. I'd thought Devon couldn't stand her, but apparently at parties all bets were off. Her skin was flushed and her eyes looked glassy, like she'd already had one drink too many.

The music was almost a physical thing. The bass vibrated in my body and made me want to grind and swing along with the other partygoers. The living room was huge, with several couches and armchairs and even some lawn chairs thrown into the mix. Most of the furniture was pushed up against the walls to make space for a dance floor.

Alec dragged me through the crowd of dancing bodies to where Ana sat on a couch with her date, Jason. I'd barely spoken to him before, but I knew he belonged to the same group of friends Devon always hung out with.

There was room for one more person on the couch. Alec let go of my hand and nodded toward the open spot.

"You can sit on his lap!" Ana suggested, the way she slurred the *S* making it clear that the beer in her hand wasn't her first.

I looked at Alec and time began to stretch. Ana and Jason were staring up at us, not drunk enough to miss the strange tension in the air. Suddenly Alec grinned and in one fluid move scooped me up and settled me on his lap. Heat surged through my body at the feel of him so close. Our kiss from a few days ago flashed in my mind and all I wanted was to repeat it.

"When did this thing start? It looks like the party's been going on for hours," I said.

Ana took another gulp from her cup. "Nah, not so long ago. Most people were already drunk when they got here." She stood, surprisingly not yet swaying. "Bathroom" she mouthed before she disappeared from my view.

Alec and Jason began talking about the upcoming football game while I tried to focus on observing the other guests. But it was incredibly difficult with Alec's legs pressed against my butt, his chest warm against my back.

Ryan sat in one of the lawn chairs with Chloe, shoving his tongue down her throat. He pulled away and looked at me as if he could feel my eyes on him. My skin flushed after being caught staring and I quickly looked away.

A cup materialized in front of my face, startling me half to death. I rammed my elbow into Alec's stomach. Of course, it hadn't hurt him but I apologized anyway. I took the cup from Ana's outstretched hand. A sniff revealed it as beer.

"Since your date is too busy to take care of you, I'll do his job," she said with a grin.

I raised the cup to my lips. Alec put his hand on my thigh, squeezing. It was a warning, but my body interpreted it in a very different way. Alec's eyes locked on mine. I tipped the cup back and took a gulp, still holding his gaze. It wasn't much, but the taste was enough to make me shudder.

Alec's lips tightened. The angry glint in his eyes made me want him even more. Why was it that I was unable to resist him, no matter how often he pushed me away?

I took another swallow. Alec squeezed my thigh again and leaned in close, his lips against my ear. "That's a bad idea." His hot breath against my skin, his hand on my thigh, his chest pressed against my chest. His smell. His warmth. It was all too much.

I put the cup on the table beside the couch. My hands moved to Alec's shoulders, my eyes dropped to his mouth, and I leaned in for a kiss. I could feel his breath on my lips, could feel my heart slamming against my rib cage, my stomach tightening in anticipation, until he turned his head away and my lips grazed his cheek.

It felt as though the air had been sucked from my body. I stumbled to my feet, knocking the cup of beer off the table. Alec's eyes looked alarmed but there was something else in them, something much worse. Pity.

I entered the kitchen, where two boys were mixing vodka and juice in a huge plastic bowl. Their words and laughter warped in my head and eventually became lost in the rest of the buzz. I opened the fridge. It was filled to the brim with beer. I grabbed a bottle, opened it, and began to guzzle it down. After the first few gulps the taste became bearable, but the alcohol did nothing to correct the abyss that had opened up in my stomach.

Ana leaned against the counter beside me. She didn't seem that drunk anymore. "Do you want to talk?"

"No. I want to forget," I said.

"He's stupid if he doesn't want you. There are plenty of other guys who'd jump at the chance to make out with you." She wrapped her arm around me and I leaned against her.

The stench of puke wafted through the open window. Someone must've thrown up in the garden.

Ana handed me a cup with the fruity mixed drink. "Here, take this. It's good."

Surprisingly it tasted better than the beer, if a bit too much like cough medicine. But after the first swallow, I stopped. Being angry with Alec was one thing but I couldn't risk losing control. What if my Variation stopped working once I was drunk?

Ana waved her hand in front of my face. "Hello? Did you hear me?"

"Sorry, I wasn't paying attention."

"I said it looks like your brother's getting lucky tonight." She pointed at the stairs.

Devon and Francesca ascended the staircase, their arms wrapped around each other. One of Francesca's hands rested in Devon's back jeans pocket. It made me want to gag. They disappeared from my view, on their way to do God-only-knows what. At least the party hostess was having fun. The way my life was going, it'd never be my turn to get lucky.

I took another gulp of the fruity vodka mix. It left a trail of heat in my throat that spread all the way down to my stomach.

Ana glanced toward the living room, where Jason stood waiting for her in the doorway.

"It's okay if you go to him, you know," I said.

She looked conflicted but after an encouraging smile from me, she dashed off, leaving me alone with my drink.

Seizing the moment, Ryan strode into the kitchen and propped himself up on the counter. He sipped his beer, never taking his eyes off me. "So, are you and that Alec guy together, or what?"

"No. I mean, not really."

Ryan leaned closer until our shoulders were touching. "I'm sorry about the other day," he said. "But when I see you, I can't think straight."

"We broke up months ago."

His face tightened. "I know. And I hated every minute of it. I can't stand the thought of seeing you with another guy. I want you back, Maddy. I want a fresh start."

"I don't think that's possible. We both need to move on."

"But I can't!" Frustration flashed in his eyes. "Don't you get it? I don't think I can ever feel the same way about anyone." He grabbed my hand but Alec was on his way into the kitchen. Ryan glared at him before storming out of the room.

"What did he want?"

"The usual."

"Is that vodka you're drinking?" Alec crossed his arms with disapproval.

He took the cup out of my hand and sniffed. His lips twisted. "Vodka," he said, as if he was addressing a small child.

"Stop patronizing me. I'm not a baby."

"You shouldn't be drinking."

I stared pointedly at the cup in his other hand. He was giving *me* a lecture? "You're not allowed to drink either, but you are."

"No, I'm not. I dumped my beer and refilled it with apple juice because I want to stay lucid. I *pretend* to drink because I want to do my job of fitting in. You still realize that this is a job, right? Sometimes I think you forget that."

Even though he didn't say it outright, I knew he was also referring to the incident in the living room.

"You sound like Major." I pushed past him. "I'm off to *pretend* to have fun. Sometimes *I* think you've forgotten what 'fun' means."

I pushed past him and into the throng of people grinding against each other in various stages of drunkenness. I spotted Ana, her body entwined with Jason's, their lips locked as they rocked back and forth to the music. Ryan wasn't in the living room. He probably needed time to cool off.

Someone tapped me on the shoulder and a scowl immediately blossomed on my face. It was Phil. Had Francesca actually invited him or was he a party crasher? He pushed his hands into his pockets and looked at his feet. "Hey. Do you want to dance?"

My eyes darted over the crowd, looking for Alec. What would he say if I danced with someone else? The bass was working its way through my body along with the vodka. A haze spread in my head. Phil took a step back, embarrassment crossing his face. "Never mind. Forget it. I shouldn't have asked." He turned to leave, but I gripped his arm, only to shy back as a strange sensation prickled in my fingertips. Our gazes locked and his eyes grew wide. We stood too close but I was unable to move.

"Leave her alone." A tall shape appeared in front of me, causing Phil to stagger a few steps back. Alec. I took a step forward to stop him. Shock rendered on Phil's face, but for a moment it looked like he considered fighting back. "Go," I said. He hesitated, the flush spreading further on his cheeks before he stormed away.

"What the hell was that? Why were you looking at him like that?" Alec hissed.

"He asked me to dance." I didn't mention the strange sensation I'd felt when I'd touched Phil.

"Dance?" His mouth twisted. "He was looking at you like he wanted to devour you."

Was Alec really jealous of *Phil*? "So what, Alec? Why do you even care? You've made it very clear that you don't give a shit about me."

I pushed past him and fought my way through the masses and over to the stairs. Thankfully the bathroom wasn't occupied. I shut the door behind me and slumped against it. Thinking about Alec made my head hurt. Why did everything have to be so complicated?

I splashed some water on my face and looked up at my reflection through the water droplets clinging to my lashes. Dark blond lashes, dark blond hair, and blue eyes. I realized I wasn't even surprised to see that face anymore. It had become a part of me, the same way Madison's parents, her quirky uncle, and her best friend had all become my world.

Outside the narrow bathroom window, something caught my attention and I stopped to get a better look outside. The lights streaming out of the house illuminated only half of the vast backyard. A figure was making his way across the lawn, and in the last few moments before the figure was swallowed by darkness, I could make out who it was: Devon.

What was he doing out there?

I'd thought he was in Francesca's room, having fun. I checked my watch. It had been an hour since I'd seen him come upstairs with her. They were probably long finished with whatever they'd done.

Suddenly, screams ripped through the constant boom of the music, through the drunken laughter and singing. They multiplied, mingled, rose in volume. It was clear that they weren't shouts of glee; they were cries of terror. I flung open the door and dashed down the stairs, then out of the house and into the garden where the noise was coming from. More and more people were gathering in the backyard.

Alec appeared at my side.

"What's wrong?" I asked.

"I don't know," he said slowly. He stretched to get a look over the heads of the other guests who hustled around us. But my eyes dropped to the ground, where a fine trail of mist curled around my ankles.

The feeling left my legs.

A sudden hush fell over the crowd.

"Is she dead?"

"What happened to her?"

"She's not moving." The whispers carried over to us and then the sobbing began.

There was a figure lying on the grass. She was completely still. And I knew without a doubt that this wasn't a person who'd passed out from one too many drinks.

The killer had been here. He'd found his next victim.

CHAPTER 19

Another murder. Right under our very noses.

"Oh God," someone whispered. "She's dead."

Alec pushed past the growing mass of spectators. My body bristled at the thought of getting any closer, but I followed. We fought our way to the middle of the circle that had formed around the body. Alec crouched beside the body and I stopped short behind him. He pressed two fingers against her throat, searching for a pulse. That's when I saw her face. It was Francesca. Killed in her own home.

A wire curled around her neck. Blood trailed down her throat, trickling to her bra. Her shirt had been torn and an *A* had been cut into the skin above her rib cage. Hints of dewdrops and white frost dotted her clothes—the remnants of fog.

Francesca's face was turned toward me, a cold and hollow look in her lifeless eyes. They were accusing. If I'd worked harder, maybe then she'd be alive.

I turned away, lost in the whirlwind of voices around me. I pushed my way through the crowd, elbows rammed into my sides, shoulders against my back. In the distance I could hear the sound of sirens.

I made it a few steps away from the other guests, to the part of the yard that lay shrouded in darkness, and leaned against an old tree, the rough bark pressing into my forehead. Devon had disappeared into the unlit part of the backyard just moments before the screams had started. He'd been outside when Francesca had been killed, and he'd been the last person I'd seen with her.

"It's not your fault. You're doing your best. We all are."

I jumped at the sound of Alec's voice. Couldn't he leave me alone for one effing moment?

"Oh, so that's what you think now? You sounded really different there in the kitchen."

He raised his hands. "Whoa. Calm down." He lowered his voice. "I'm just worried about you."

A police car and an ambulance pulled up at the curb and Alec turned to watch them. I used the moment to slip away; I couldn't stand to be around him right now.

I turned back toward the house. The police officers and the paramedics ran straight to the backyard, where Francesca was pronounced dead.

Ana stood on the front porch, her face blotchy and her eyes red-rimmed. She stumbled toward me. I wasn't sure if her wobbly gait was due to alcohol or shock. She bumped into me, nearly knocking me over. I hugged her and she slumped against me. My own legs felt like they might give way.

"Oh god, Maddy, did you see her? He was here! He killed her. Killed her." Her words came out jumbled and mingled with sobs.

I pulled away, my eyes searching the throngs of people on the porch and in the doorway. There wasn't a sign of Devon anywhere.

I doubted he had returned but maybe someone had seen him moments before the murder.

"Have you seen Devon?"

Ana rubbed her eyes. "No. Haven't seen him in a while. Why? Do you think he's safe?"

No, I thought. He just might be the killer.

I kissed her cheek. "I just want him to take me home. I'll go try to find him. Do you have a ride home?"

"My stepfather's taking me." She nodded toward one of the police cars. Right. I'd forgotten that he was a police officer.

"Be careful," I warned before I made my way through the crowd that had gathered on the porch. The inside of the house was a mess. Empty beer bottles, broken glass, spilled alcohol, and crumbled chips littered the floor. The rug squished under my feet from all the beer that had been spilled on it. I carefully climbed to the stairs, only to discover that nobody was on the second floor. I peeked into a few rooms until I found Francesca's. Not surprisingly, the blankets were ruffled as if someone had been sleeping in them—or doing other things. Why had Devon brought her up here to make out—in front of everyone—if his plan was to kill her afterward? It was reckless. But killers didn't always act reasonably.

Francesca's window overlooked the backyard—now the murder scene. Police officers, paramedics, and Sheriff Ruthledge were gathered around the body. Alec and Major, dressed as a civilian, hovered a few steps away. The party guests had been pushed to the edges of the yard, but many of them still watched the scene like it was a crime show on TV.

The hinges groaned and I whirled around, almost losing my

footing. Ryan stood in the doorway. Anxiety crawled up my spine. I shouldn't have gone upstairs on my own.

"What are you doing here?" My voice came out hard.

"Calm down, okay? I saw you go upstairs and just wanted to check on you. What are *you* doing here?"

"None of your business." I crossed the room, wanting to squeeze past him, but his arm shot out, blocking my escape.

I balled my fists. "Get out of my way." The collar of his shirt shifted, revealing a series of small bruises on his left shoulder. He followed my gaze, and red blotches blossomed on his cheeks. He pulled up his collar. "You know how hot-tempered my father gets. . . ." He trailed off. But my eyes were no longer on his bruises. There was blood on his right hand. "I cut myself," he said quickly, and turned his hand around to show me the gash in his palm.

"How did that happen?" I asked.

"Broken beer bottle. What? Do you think—" he stopped as we heard the sound of steps pounding up the stairs. He dropped his arm, making room for me to leave. I hesitated. The cut didn't look like a bottle had done it.

"Madison?" Alec called, and it took me a moment to realize he was talking to me. I ran out of the room and found Alec halfway up the steps. "Where have you been? I was looking for you," he said. His eyes narrowed when they landed on Ryan, lingering in the hall, his hands in his pockets.

I needed to get outside, to go somewhere I could breathe. Alec followed me but waited until we were out of earshot of the crowd before he began talking. "You have to be more careful, Tess. Being alone with Ryan isn't the best idea."

I paused to glower at him. "He followed me upstairs. I didn't invite him."

Alec ignored my snide tone. "You're already in enough danger with Devon around, but as long as we don't know for sure that he's the murderer, you should avoid being alone with guys. All of them."

"You're a guy."

"Tess, I'm serious," he said with a hint of exasperation.

"Are you done with your lecture now? I'm not stupid. I can handle this myself." And I realized it was true. I could handle this. I didn't need Alec or anyone else. I'd played Madison for weeks now without anyone growing suspicious, I'd faced Ryan and Yates *and* kept them in check, and I'd figured out the fog connection. I could do this.

He opened his mouth to say something, but no words came out.

"Just drop it, okay?" I said. "I think Ryan is the killer."

Alec frowned. "Why? What happened?"

"I just noticed a cut on his palm. It looked like it was caused by a wire. I think he cut himself when he strangled Francesca."

"A cut. That's all?" Alec shook his head. "What about Devon?"

"Well, I saw him walking around outside shortly before they found Francesca—"

"You saw Devon at the crime scene?"

"Not exactly. I saw him leaving the yard. But at the time, he wasn't with Francesca."

"How can you defend him? Don't you realize what you're doing? You're so desperate to prove that Devon is innocent that you're drawing incorrect conclusions."

He nodded toward a black Jeep parked at the end of the street. "Major wants to have a talk with us."

"Why? Did you already tell him how you think I'm messing up?"

He released a breath and turned his head away, leaving me to stare at his profile, at the way his tendons strained in his throat. "You act like I'm some kind of traitor. I'm not telling Major every-thing, you know. I'm just trying to do my job and keep you safe."

Major watched us with a grim face as we slid into the backseat. Alec and I told Major what we'd seen, and despite Alec's earlier rebuff, I voiced my suspicion about Ryan. Finally Major spoke.

"I agree with Alec. And I think it's time for us to focus our efforts on our main suspect."

I knew who that was.

"You saw Devon with the dead girl just moments before her body was found, and now he's gone. We finally have to act on our suspicions. My instinct tells me that he's the Variant we're looking for."

He paused, searching my face. My fingernails dug into my palms.

"I want you to search Devon's room. It's possible he's hiding something that'll prove his guilt, or perhaps you can find out who'll be his next victim. Look through his belongings, corner him, watch for unusual behavior. Change into him and talk to his friends if you must. Do everything that's necessary to stop him."

CHAPTER 20

The following day, I spent most of the morning at the police station and the rest of the day with Linda, who didn't let me out of her sight. I hadn't seen Devon yet. Ronald had taken him to speak with the police on his way in to work, and he'd been closed off in his room since the moment he got home. I had a feeling that he was purposely avoiding me.

A clattering came from the kitchen—the sound of pots being placed into the cupboards. I followed the noise downstairs and stopped in the doorway. Linda's blond hair was in a high ponytail, revealing the chain of her matching rose necklace. She wiped her hands and gave me that smile that made me feel like I was the best thing that had ever happened to her.

I looked away.

She scanned my face. "You look pale, sweetheart." Her blue eyes crinkled with worry.

"I'm fine, Mom. Just a bit tired."

"Are you sure it's nothing serious? Maybe we should go to Dr. Fonseca."

"It's nothing." *Except for the fact that your son is the main suspect in our murder case.* It would kill her if it was true. How could parents possibly survive something like that? Finding out about their daughter's death and then that their other child was the killer.

Linda's eyes searched my face before she nodded reluctantly. "Let me make you some hot chocolate."

Her skin was sickly pale. She'd broken down crying when she'd found out about Francesca, and it hadn't helped matters that I had been at the same party. The whole town was in a state of panic, some families going so far as to evacuate the area. If we didn't catch the killer soon, people would tear down the police station.

The smell of chocolate wafted through the kitchen. Linda sprinkled a few mini marshmallows into the cup before she handed it to me. It was the best hot chocolate in the world.

Steps pounded down the staircase and Devon bounded into the kitchen. Dark shadows were spread under his eyes. My hands started shaking, so I had to put my cup down.

Linda kissed his cheek before she pressed another cup into his hands and made him sit down across from me at the table. I stared at the tabletop, not wanting to look into his eyes. I'd have to face him soon, but not in front of Linda.

You can't protect her forever, a tiny voice whispered in my head. But I wanted to try. I was still haunted by Linda's terrified expression when she heard about the latest murder.

I could feel Devon's eyes on my face, prodding, searching, but I didn't look up to meet his gaze. Bringing the cup to my lips, I took another gulp, braced myself, and forced my face into an expressionless mask. I raised my eyes. He frowned. After a glance over at Linda, who was rinsing the hot chocolate pot, he mouthed, "What's wrong?"

"Nothing," I mouthed right back.

He didn't buy it.

"Tired," I whispered, surprised how calm my voice sounded.

Linda dried the dishes, unaware of the tension right across the room. When she was done, she turned to us. "I'm heading to bed. I don't feel well." She took a bottle of sleeping pills from the drawer below the sink and popped two into her mouth. She smiled apologetically. "I guess I've had trouble sleeping lately."

I sat the cup down on the table and stood. "I should probably try to catch up on rest too." It was still early evening, but I didn't want to stay in a room alone with Devon. Even if I still questioned his guilt. He stared at his cocoa, not even glancing my way.

When I'd left the kitchen, I heard Devon's chair scrape over the floor. I didn't have to look over my shoulder to know he was following me up the stairs.

"What's the matter with you?"

"You've been acting weird," I said, stopping in front of my room.

"You're one to talk. It's like I don't even recognize you sometimes," he shot back.

"What do—" I stopped myself. "Do you have any idea what I've been through?" I shook my head. "Forget it. I'm tired." I stepped into my room and closed the door, and he didn't try to stop me.

Devon was our main suspect. Alec had said it and Major agreed, so why couldn't I shake the feeling that I was missing something?

I listened for Devon's footsteps in the corridor, expecting him to head into his room. Instead he went downstairs, and the front door fell shut. This was my chance.

I tiptoed into the corridor. The house was silent. Ronald would be gone all night, keeping watch over a dog with a gastric torsion. His and Linda's bedroom door was ajar. I peeked in to see Linda sprawled out on the bed, her lips drifting apart as soft snores echoed from them. I closed the door carefully and moved on to Devon's room.

Devon was surprisingly tidy for a guy, with all of his belongings seemingly in place. I'd seen rooms inhabited by boys at the FEA that had given me a rash just from looking at them.

I wasn't sure where Devon had gone or how long he would be, so I had to hurry. I didn't know what Major and Alec expected me to find. Many serial killers kept souvenirs of the victims as trophies to remind them of their success. Months later, I still remembered the photos and descriptions of different serial killer cases I'd studied in class. Some had been so horrible that I still had nightmares about them. One guy kept body parts of the women he'd killed. The police had found tongues, fingers, and even eyes in his freezer.

But I still couldn't imagine Devon killing someone—much less his own twin sister.

Kneeling in front of the bed, I lifted the mattress and found . . . a *Playboy*. I looked behind the posters on his walls and in his wardrobe. But there was nothing interesting.

My eyes fell on the desk. It was an obvious spot and the last place I'd hide something I wouldn't want anyone to find, but maybe he thought nobody would look.

I hesitated, my fingers resting on the knob of the desk drawer. *Get a grip*, I thought. *It's not like you're going to find body parts. There's probably nothing in here.*

And so I opened it.

A stack of photos was on top. Regular photos, from some party: Devon with his friends, Devon with Ryan—had they been friends before the breakup? Devon with Francesca, smiling and locking lips.

They hadn't officially been a couple, but apparently that hadn't stopped them from hooking up on more than one occasion. I put the photos down and froze. In the drawer, beneath where the photos had been, was a pile of snippets from newspaper articles. All of them appeared to be about the murders—articles about the victims, printed-out *Wikipedia* pages about serial killers, and information about the case. Had he been trying to keep this stuff hidden? Information about Mr. Chen the janitor, Dr. Hansen, and Kristen Cynch were scribbled down in Devon's handwriting. It was hard to decipher in places, but he'd gathered a wealth of information about each of them: their habits, family members, friends, and daily routines.

I carefully placed the evidence back into the drawer and scanned the room for other hiding places, but there didn't seem to be anything else suspicious. As I crossed to exit the room, the tip of my shoe caught on something uneven. One of the wooden floorboards seemed to be raised. I nudged it and the wood jiggled—it was loose. I pried my fingernails into the gap, and with a tug the board popped out. I dropped it, hands shaking, and reached for what was hidden beneath, but my fingers stopped before I could touch it.

It was a necklace with a rose pendant, identical to the one Ronald had given me. Madison's necklace. It was encrusted with something black—dried blood. I didn't dare move it. Gasping, I sank down onto my butt. Devon must have taken the necklace when he killed Madison. As a trophy. That was the only explanation. I'd read the reports. Madison had been found at the lake without it.

I couldn't believe it. Devon was the killer. He'd always been so nice, so caring and attentive, and I'd even started feeling attracted to him in a very unsisterly way. That alone should have been proof something was wrong with him.

I'd been so sure Devon wasn't the killer, had been so sure Alec's suspicions were founded on dislike or jealousy. Why hadn't my instincts lead me to realize the truth? Alec wasn't jealous of Devon after all. Alec didn't let his emotions get in the way of our mission. He was the better agent, the better person, the better everything.

I'd almost forgotten to watch the time when I heard footsteps on the staircase.

I looked around for a place to hide. If Devon found me here, he'd know I'd been spying on him and would have every reason to come after me. There was a creak in the hallway.

I dropped to my knees and squeezed under the bed. A moment later, Devon's sneakers came into view. He hesitated in the doorway. I held my breath but my pulse pounded in my ears.

He stepped inside and closed the door, his calm breathing the only audible sound. I held my breath and watched his shoes—black with the white Nike logo. Dew drops glistened on them as if he'd waded through fog. They moved past me and toward his dresser.

He crouched down and loosened another floorboard. If he turned around, he'd see me just as clearly as I could see him. I steeled myself as he reached into the hole in the floor and pulled out a hunting knife. Had he used it to cut the *A*'s into his victims?

He straightened and came toward the bed. I tensed my legs, preparing to kick him if he spotted me, but he fumbled with something on his nightstand. My lungs screamed for air but I didn't dare breathe with him so close. He would hear the sound. But then he turned and disappeared into the corridor, leaving the door ajar. Sucking in a deep breath, I waited for his steps to move down the staircase before I wiggled out of my hiding place. My legs shook as I straightened.

I touched the rose pendant around my neck.

Devon was leaving. Was he going to kill again? I hurried toward the window, careful to stay pressed against the wall, so nobody could see me from outside. A figure crossed the yard and continued down the street. Soon he'd disappear around the corner.

Not if I was fast enough.

I dashed into Madison's room, grabbed my cell phone and the Taser, and stepped back into the hall. A cough from Linda and Ronald's bedroom made me freeze. Even so, there was no time to spare. I ran down the stairs and was out of the house within seconds, just in time to see Devon turn the corner. My ballet flats made no sound as I jogged over the concrete, following him. Devon wasn't running, but he was walking incredibly fast. I kept as much distance as I could without losing him.

I fumbled with the cell phone and pressed the speed dial key. I needed to tell Alec that Devon was the killer. I tried Alec's cell but it went straight to voice mail. Devon looked over his shoulder, and I pressed myself against the side of a parked SUV. He kept moving. He seemed to know exactly where he was going. I, on the other hand, had no idea.

Keeping an eye on Devon, I shot Alec a quick text.

Following Devon. He's the killer. Is up to something. Update soon.

Alec would want me to wait for backup, but there was no time. I could handle it. I sent off the text, switched my cell to silent, and stuffed it into the pocket of my jeans.

We advanced to a part of town where the street lights were few and far between. Long stretches of our path were cloaked in darkness. My breath and the soft *pad-pad* of my shoes on concrete were the only sounds around us. In the distance I could make out the occasional glow of a window or a street lamp. Devon turned onto a gravel road. I followed, keeping to the roadside so the crunch of pebbles wouldn't give me away. Trees towered on both sides of us, shielding what little light the moon could give.

CHAPTER 21

The road led to an old, abandoned house that could have been the set of a horror movie. Hitchcock would have approved. Frazzled, yellowed curtains fluttered in broken windows. Several of the facade's grayed panels were missing, and the front door was nailed up with boards.

But none of it stopped Devon. As if he'd done it hundreds of times before, he climbed through the window beside the front door.

What was he here to do?

A bang sounded in the house.

I took out the Taser and hurried toward the house. Pressing my back against the facade, I held my breath. The wind whistled in my ears. I inched closer to the window, clutching the Taser against my chest and wishing I'd taken another weapon with me.

I peeked into the house. Light filtered from somewhere deep inside into what looked like a living room. Careful not to touch the jagged remnants of the window, I climbed inside, flinching when mist encircled my feet. It covered the entire floor.

The air in the house was moldy and as cold as it was outside. A moth-eaten couch and a small table with a vase of dust-covered artificial flowers were the only adornments. I took a few steps further into the room, mist swirling around my ankles, and moved toward a half-closed door that led into the hall.

A floorboard creaked under my weight and I froze.

Except for the sound of my breathing, the house was completely silent. Where was Devon?

The mist cleared slightly as if it was trailing somewhere after its master. Keeping an eye on the shaky floorboards beneath me, I cautiously crossed the room.

My heart fluttered in my chest as I risked a glimpse of what lay beyond the door. The only light came from somewhere in the back of the building. My eyes landed on a black shadow on the ground. It looked like a pool of paint had run in a puddle around it. Sickness lurched in my stomach. I inched closer to get a better look, and icy spikes pierced through my spine.

On the ground, in a puddle of his own blood, lay Devon. He was sprawled on his back, his blond hair matted to his head. A few tendrils of fog whirled around him like spidery tentacles. Checking left and right, I hurried toward him and knelt down, shivering as blood seeped through the fabric of my jeans. It still felt warm against my skin.

A dent had flattened the side of Devon's head. It didn't look like it was supposed to. I reached out but stopped when I saw something white poking out of his hair. Brain or skull, I couldn't tell. I had to brace myself to keep from vomiting.

My fingers shook as I pressed them against his throat. Nothing.

I slid my hand along his skin. Up and down. To the left, then to the right. Trying with every finger of my hand to find some sign of life.

Still nothing.

I hovered over his face, then pressed my lips against his blood-smudged mouth, pushing air in. With a hiss, something shot out of his chest and hit me against the arm. I scrambled back. Splatters of blood covered my arm.

I stared down at his chest. Seven holes had oozed blood and his sweatshirt was soaked with it. Someone had stabbed him repeatedly. Shaking, I leaned over and pushed another breath into his mouth. Again something hit me. More blood.

I leaned back on my haunches, a dark realization settling in my mind. His lungs were perforated.

Gasps rattled my body and turned to pathetic hiccups as tears trailed over my cheeks. Devon was dead.

I pressed my face into the crook of his neck, trying to catch his scent one last time. A hint of cinnamon reached my nose, but it was soon clouded by the coppery saltiness of blood.

Gripping the Taser, I staggered to my feet. My nails dug into my skin and the pain gave me the necessary focus to stop my chin from quivering.

A floorboard creaked behind me and I whirled around in time to see something hurtling toward my head but not in time to ward it off. With a crack the thing collided with my skull and blackness consumed me.

I wasn't sure how long I'd been unconscious, but when I came to, my muscles ached. I was on the ground, my feet and hands tied together. With a groan, I forced my eyes open. Through the open window, I could make out the treetops and the black sky littered with stars. It was still night, so not too much time had passed.

I shifted. My cell was gone and so was the Taser. I didn't even know what room I was in. It was much too dark for that.

Across the room, a shadow moved and I froze. Tendrils of haze crawled toward me, emanating from a cloud of denser fog. I twisted until I was sitting upright. It wouldn't protect me but at least I felt safer, more alert. A shadow stirred, slowly becoming distinguishable. The mist dispersed and a person appeared, still hidden by darkness. He moved in front of the door, where a tiny bit of light streamed in, and finally I recognized the illuminated face.

"Ryan?"

"Ryan?" he mocked in a high-pitched voice that immediately raised goose bumps along my arms. Shadows warped his face, giving him an almost diabolical countenance. He took a step toward me and smirked.

"Didn't think I could do it, did you?" Triumph filled his voice.

"I thought it might be you," I whispered.

He crouched in front of me, bringing his face close, far too close. So close that I saw the cold calculation in his eyes. I wished there had been madness there; that would have been easier to deal with.

He sneered. "You think I killed you because you broke up with me and fucked that asshole Yates, don't you?"

I swallowed, stunned into silence. That wasn't the reason?

"That wasn't why I killed you, but it'll make killing Yates much more enjoyable." He smiled widely. "You really don't remember anything, do you? It's been so much fun staring into your unsuspecting little face these last few weeks."

His mouth twisted with glee. He was clutching a long knife in his hand, the blade covered with blood. Red on gleaming silver.

I tried to focus my attention inside, summoning a shift. If I could transform into a man—someone strong like Alec—then I could try to kick Ryan's ass.

He turned the knife absentmindedly, still watching me.

"I want to understand," I said, half pleading. "Why are you doing this?"

I tried to summon my power once more, but the rippling in my skin was faint and stopped almost instantly.

He moved closer, his hot breath spilling onto my cheek. It smelled horrid, like onions and alcohol.

I started working at the rope around my wrists, trying to wiggle my thumb underneath it. It was too tight.

"You," he said like a curse. "I showed you my *gift*, trusted you enough to tell you what I was capable of, and you were scared. You treated me like an abomination."

He'd shown Madison his Variation?

I realized that my own Variation might be my only chance of winning his trust, but telling him about it could rob me of my only advantage.

"You know, Madison, at one point, I thought I loved you. I'd have done anything for you. Anything. I even killed that useless bitch Kristen for you because she wouldn't stop talking shit. I hated her for how she'd been treating you. But *you*, you didn't understand. You were scared and disgusted by me! You would've gone to the police. You would've betrayed me—again and again. So you left me with no choice, Maddy."

I swallowed when he ran his finger over the blade. He pressed the knife lightly against my throat. I stared at him, so scared it was hard to hear him over the pounding of my heart in my ears.

"I'm sorry." The words slipped out without my volition, like the automatic "bless you" when someone sneezes. I wasn't even sure what I was apologizing for.

"You are so clueless." His lips curled.

Something snapped in me. "Maybe that's because you tried to kill me."

He raised the knife to strike, and I focused on my power with all my might. But still, nothing happened. It was as if I'd never had a Variation in the first place.

A crack sounded from somewhere in the house and Ryan froze. The knife was almost at my throat.

He jumped up and crept out of the room, leaving the door ajar. With the light from the corridor streaming inside, I could barely make out my surroundings. There was a bathtub with old-fashioned claw feet and a hole in the ground where the toilet must have been. Over the tub, on a small shelf, rested Devon's hunting knife and my Taser.

I closed my eyes and tried shifting. A rippling started in my toes and slowly traveled up my calves.

A cry crashed through my concentration and the rippling died down. My eyes shot open. Ryan appeared in the doorframe, his hand twisted in blond hair. A streak of fog trailed after him like a lost puppy. He dragged the woman inside and dropped her as far away from me as possible, beside the bathtub. Her face was pressed against the tiles but something about her seemed familiar. Ryan tied her wrists and ankles together with tape. He turned her onto her side, and I saw her face for the first time.

I gasped.

Ryan's eyes darted toward me. "What? Do you know her?"

I shook my head, trying to wipe the shock from my face.

His lips thinned in suspicion. "Are you sure? Why did she follow you here then, Maddy?"

Kate stared at me, one of her eyes already swelling shut and a nasty cut on her temple. Had Major asked her to join the mission without telling me?

"I've never seen her before," I said.

"You're lying," he accused, advancing with the knife.

"I'm not! I don't know her. Maybe she followed Devon here."

Ryan paused, his green eyes contemplating. "Devon." His mouth twisted. "That would be just like the jerk."

"Why did you kill him?"

Kate was trying to bore a hole into my head with her eyes but I didn't look her way. I couldn't risk making Ryan even more suspicious.

"Because he's been prying around too much, sticking his nose where it didn't belong. I had to stop him. I led him here. He thought he was so damn clever but he would've never found me if I hadn't let him follow me. It's a pity that he's dead though. I was planning to blame the murders on him. That's why I killed that bitch Francesca."

Ryan grinned. He advanced on me, slowly, enjoying every moment of his sick little game. I forced my body to relax, even when he knelt down beside me and twirled a strand of my hair around his finger.

"Why did you lead Devon here?" I asked, the words rattling in my throat.

He paused with his finger on my collarbone. "Because this is my spot. Nobody ever comes here. I've been using this place for months to work on my gift."

"The fog," I said before I could stop myself.

He removed his hand, his eyes searching my face. "So you do remember?"

I hesitated. "Some things. You can control fog."

"Not just control. I can create it. It's part of me," he said, pride lighting up his expression.

"But what does that have to do with killing people?"

I could feel Kate's intent gaze on me. Of course, she'd realized by now that we were dealing with a Variant. Maybe she'd known all along.

Ryan leaned back on his haunches, the knife balancing on his thighs. "Why should I tell you?"

"I just want to understand," my voice cracked and it wasn't even pretend. There was little doubt in my mind about the outcome of this night. Kate and I would die.

Fog gathered on the ground, twirling around Ryan, encircling his legs like a cat.

"I've been hiding my talent all my life. I was ashamed. My father always told me I had to keep it a secret, that it was a bad thing, that I was a freak. But there are other people like me. People with *gifts*." He spoke in a reverent tone, his eyes bright with pride.

No kidding, I thought sarcastically. *Two of them are in this room with you.*

If he wasn't a psychopath, I'd have felt sympathy for him. I knew exactly how he felt.

"And I will join them," he continued. "They found me. They told me I needed to break all ties to my former life before I could join them. I had to make sure I got rid of anyone who might be suspicious about me, who might know about my gift."

That didn't sound like the FEA. They would never encourage killing. Maybe it was the group of rogue Variants Holly had mentioned in her e-mail. But how to ask him without giving myself away?

"So the victims all knew about your gift?"

He shrugged. "Nobody else *knew*, but Dr. Hansen was concerned about my blood test results, and that stupid janitor had seen me creating fog. I can't take any risks. Abel's Army is too important for that."

"Abel's Army?" I said. Kate looked like she knew what he was talking about. When she sensed my eyes on her, she lowered her face.

Ryan chuckled. "Enough with the questions, Maddy." He pushed a finger against my lips. I wanted to bite it but he moved his hand downward. His fingers trailed over the scar on my throat, across my breastbone, stopping to rest on the pendant for a moment before he brushed across the *A* over my rib cage. "I love that I left my mark on you, Maddy. I'm kind of sad that it's almost healed." I shuddered at his closeness.

"I doubt Abel's Army will give a shit about your gift, loser.

They have much freakier talents than you could ever imagine. Why would they want a little boy who can play fog machine?"

Kate—she'd come to my aid. I'd never thought I'd see that happen.

"What the hell do you know about Abel's Army?" he demanded, his voice low.

Kate pressed her lips together.

He smiled and walked toward the bathtub. Kate tensed when he stood over her, but he just reached for the faucet and turned the water on, letting it fill the tub. His silence frightened me more than if he'd shouted and raged. My stomach tightened. He moved to the sink and took the Taser from the shelf.

"You will talk," he said. "Because I will make you."

With the Taser in his hand, he knelt in front of Kate. "So you really don't want to tell me how you know about Abel's Army?" Before she could answer or even shake her head, he touched the Taser to her side. Blue sparks flew and Kate screamed.

"Stop it!" I cried.

Electricity crackled again as Kate's screams filled the room. I struggled against my restraints, my eyes burning. Ignoring me, he tased her again. I tried to shape-shift, but nothing happened.

"Leave her alone!" I screamed, and this time he did. He staggered to his feet and lumbered toward me. Miniature lightning bolts crackled between the electrodes of the Taser.

Every breath felt like a jagged flame inside my chest. When he squatted beside me, I shut my eyes, bracing for the pain. Something touched my lips and a scream was on the verge of bursting from my mouth when I realized he'd put tape across my face to shut me up. "I loved you and I killed for you and you didn't care."

He smiled for a moment before my body exploded with pain. Fire shot through my side, into my chest and arms. I gasped against the tape, my throat constricting. Bile crowded in my mouth. Maybe I'd choke on my own vomit, a valiant way to die. He tased me again, and the touch was like flames licking across my skin. I screamed without a sound but he kept on going until my world was fire, blue sparks, and hot tears.

Eventually, he stopped.

"No talking," he said before he walked out.

CHAPTER 22

Taking deep breaths through my nose, I struggled against the pain. Kate was curled up in a fetal position across from me. I tried to speak through the tape over my lips but all that came out were incoherent sounds. At least they managed to draw Kate's attention. She raised her head an inch, her eyes watery and half closed. Slowly she propped herself up on her elbows. I wriggled and shifted until I looked Kate straight in the eyes. For two years I'd avoided that like the plague, determined not to give her access to my head, and now here I was, *inviting* her to read my mind.

If everything went as Ryan wanted, we'd probably be dead soon. There wouldn't be time for regret. Or for Kate to kill me out of anger.

The way her eyes flashed with fury, that was currently on her mind. She struggled into a sitting position, her eyes blazing. Despite the urge to look away, I kept my gaze trained on her. She blinked at me, sweat and blood trickling over her pale skin.

Sorry, Kate. I can't read your mind. What are you doing here anyway?

She licked blood off her lips, coughed, and swallowed thickly like she was trying to find her voice.

Did Major send you?

She shook her head no and closed her eyes for a moment, her face draining of color. She looked sick, and her blouse was drenched in blood; her temple wound had bled a lot. "No," she said finally, her voice raspy. "He doesn't know I'm here."

Kate had disobeyed Major? Wow.

"It's your fault," she continued. "I wanted to keep an eye on you and Alec. I know what happened. Holly's mind is like an open book."

How did you find me?

"I was sitting in a car outside the house. I thought you might go on another midnight stroll to meet Alec. But then I saw you running after that guy."

Why did you follow me inside? You must have known Alec wasn't here. And just a few minutes ago you distracted Ryan from me. Why?

"Not because I like you, if that's what you think. I owe it to Major to do what I can. I've been neglecting my responsibilities enough in the last few days." A coughing fit stopped her from saying anything more.

The tub was full of water. We didn't have much time before Ryan would return.

We need to find a way to escape.

She nodded and ran her eyes slowly over the length of my body before raising one eyebrow.

I can't shift. My Variation isn't working.

"Focus," Kate whispered. Panic flashed on her face.

I closed my eyes. How had I managed to get past my Variation block last time?

Alec. But he wasn't there, at least not physically. I let my favorite memory reclaim me, the memory I'd tried to forget in the last few days. Alec's gray eyes, tender and loving, his lips soft and demanding, his touch like whispered promises on my skin.

The rippling started in my fingers and spread like a wildfire in my body. My skin started quivering and then shrinking; my bones and muscles were next, growing smaller.

I opened my eyes and for the first time I saw admiration, maybe even jealousy on Kate's face, but it was fleeting and quickly replaced with a glower.

The ropes hung loosely around my newly childlike wrists, and slipping out of them was a piece of cake. I stretched, my muscles aching. Letting the rippling sensation wash over me once again, I shifted back into Madison's body.

I made my way over to Kate and tried releasing her from her restraints. But my ropes had been easier to loosen than the tape. It stuck together and was much too strong to rip. Steps sounded in the hall.

Kate's eyes grew panicked. "Hurry! He's coming." My fingers fumbled with the tape, but without a knife or scissors there wasn't a chance to remove it.

The door swung open, almost hitting me in the head. I stumbled back, lost my balance, and collided with the sink. A pang shot through my lower back, making me grimace. Mist crept over the floor, reaching out for me like hungry claws.

Ryan staggered toward me. I'd never realized how tall he was. He held the knife in one hand and lunged at me, but I sidestepped the stab, missing the blade by inches. I punched his arm and the knife clattered to the ground, the sound muffled by the growing mist. He gripped my hair and motioned with his free hand at the fog. Like ropes, it began to slither around my body. I struggled but its hold only tightened. It wound around my throat, cold and wet and constricting. I cried out but its grip was relentless. It strangled me. Strangled by fog. The mysterious way that two of the victims had died. Black dots danced in my vision. I could feel the fog pulsating around me as though it had a heartbeat of its own.

I passed out before I hit the tiled floor.

The taste of blood in my mouth was the first thing I noticed once my senses returned. It took a few more seconds before the whoosh-ing in my ears quieted down enough for me to hear what was going on around me: gasps and screams.

I struggled against the sleepiness.

Another piercing scream raised my hackles. The next scream stopped abruptly and all I heard was the splashing of water. I forced my eyes open. One of them seemed crusted shut with blood and no matter how hard I tried, it wouldn't open more than a gap. Fog floated in the bathroom, a wall of milky white.

I touched my throat and winced. The skin was tender. But there was another spot that ached even more. I glanced down at the hole in my shirt and the A on my skin peeking through. It was glaring red and oozing blood. Ryan had renewed the cut.

Focusing my attention on the mist, I tried to make out what was going on.

Ryan was holding Kate's head under water. She'd stopped struggling, her arms hanging limply at her sides. Summoning my strength, I staggered to my feet. Ryan let go of Kate and the rest of her upper body sank beneath the water's surface. Waves lapped over the edge and flooded the bathroom.

Dots of light danced in and out of my vision.

I willed my body to transform but nothing happened. This couldn't be true. What was wrong with me? Ryan was coming toward me, slashing the air with the knife. Why wasn't he siccing his fog on me? Maybe he too was out of energy.

I tensed my legs the way that Alec had taught me. I struck out into a high kick, but my aim was off and I almost lost my balance. With a deep breath, I tried again. This time I kicked the knife from his hand. It clattered to the ground.

Ryan lunged forward, his hands closing around my throat like the mist had before, tightening until I couldn't breathe. His nails burrowed into my skin. I gripped his arms, trying to pull him off balance, but he was too strong. My fingers dug into him, hurting him as much as I could.

His grip was relentless. My lungs constricted and the blurry black dots returned to my vision. The olive green of his irises disappeared until there was only white. The fog densed, began to hum, snatched at my hair and skin. It would kill me. I didn't have much time.

A faint rippling sensation started in my legs and traveled through my body. I focused all my energy on the shift while more dots danced in my vision. The rippling increased and I felt my bones lengthening, my muscles growing. With a yelp, Ryan let go and the room cleared of mist. Stretching, shifting, reshaping, and then the transformation was over, and I was as tall as Ryan. I'd changed into Alec.

"You're—you're one of us? Did Abel's Army send you?" His irises had returned to their usual green.

"I'm not a killer and I don't care about your army," I said.

He staggered forward again, his arms extended. I blocked him and thrust my knee up, hitting him in the groin. With a groan, he stumbled backward and sank down on one knee, the knife inches from him.

He grabbed it, his knuckles turning white, and advanced on me, weapon brandished. His gait wasn't as steady as it had been before and only a few streaks of haze danced around his legs. He thrust forward like a snake serving its deadly strike. Fire seared my arm where the blade sliced open my skin. Immediately my sleeve soaked up the warm liquid.

The pain triggered the familiar rippling sensation. It was so unfair that my gift abandoned me right when I needed it most. I had to act before that happened. With a battle cry, a mixture of my voice and Alec's, I charged. Ryan froze, his face dumbfounded. The shock lasted only a moment. He slashed the knife in an arc, aiming straight at my head. With a jolt I shifted back to a female body. I didn't even know if it was Madison's or mine. The blade missed me by less than an inch. If I hadn't shifted, Ryan would have scalped me.

He lost his balance, flailed his arms, and stumbled forward, bumping into me with his full force. The impact squeezed the air out of my lungs and made me gasp. We fell backward and my tail-bone slammed into the solid floor, sending a jolt of pain up my spine. Ryan's heavier body landed on top of me, and something hard dug into my stomach.

I grew stiff with fear. Had he stabbed me?

His eyes widened in shock before his mouth went slack. He

sagged against me as something warm and wet soaked my clothes. I pushed him off. He rolled over onto his back, the knife handle sticking out of his midsection. Blood trickled out of his mouth and his eyes lost their focus. Gurgling breaths spurted out of his body. Strands of mist curled around his arms and seeped into his skin.

His chest heaved and then stopped. The last thread of fog disappeared.

Ryan was dead.

CHAPTER 23

I'd wasted too much time.

Every inch of my body ached when I stumbled toward her. My hands shot into the pink water, gripped Kate's shoulders, and pulled her out. She was unnaturally heavy, as if her body had soaked up loads of water. Her head lolled to the side, her face slack as I lowered her to the ground. The gash on her forehead had stopped bleeding.

I pressed my fingertips harder into her skin, trying to find her pulse. There was none. My hands flew over her throat, prodding and touching. Choking fear gripped my chest. Not again.

I wiped the tears from my eyes. Crying over Kate; I'd never thought that day would come. I pressed my palms against her rib cage and started CPR. Three pushes. One, two, three. I leaned over her and released my air into her lungs. Seconds dragged by, maybe minutes. My arms ached, but I couldn't stop. If I stopped, I'd admit defeat. I wouldn't allow it; wouldn't let him take another life. Not when he'd already taken Devon.

"Let me," a male voice said.

A cry ripped from my throat, leaving it raw. I whirled around and my heart must have skipped a beat. Leaning against the door-frame, clothes ripped and bloody, his hair still matted with blood, stood Devon. He couldn't be alive. It was absolutely impossible.

But there he was.

He took a shaky step closer. Struggling with every motion, he dropped to his knees beside me. He was so close that I could see the hole in his head had closed and a thin layer of skin had grown over it.

I blinked. None of this was possible.

He braced himself on his thighs and breathed in as if he had to get used to being alive again. He turned his head to look at me. "You aren't Madison. I should have realized it sooner, but believing the lie was easier."

Without waiting for me to say anything, he placed his hands on Kate. One on her rib cage, one on her cheek. The color of his face turned from white to sickly gray and his eyes narrowed in concentration.

"What are you doing?"

Suddenly I heard the faint intake of breath. At first I thought I'd imagined it, but then Kate's chest heaved under his hand. I cradled her head in my lap.

"How?" I croaked.

Devon sagged against the tub, shuddering. He looked like he was about to pass out. "Healing others and myself . . . that's my gift—just like yours is apparently deceit."

"Why—" I stopped myself.

"I can only heal those that haven't moved on yet. Madison was gone, even though her body was kept alive. I can't explain it but I think it's something about the soul clinging to the body or not. I think it broke Maddy that Ryan was the one who tried to kill her, like somehow it broke her will to live." He trembled, perspiration glistening on his forehead. "That's . . . that's why I couldn't bring her back when I found her at the lake." A tear slid down his cheek. "But I allowed myself to believe that you were her, that by some miracle my gift had brought her back from a place no one returns from."

"But why were you at the lake?"

He stared at his hands, still covered in blood. "I knew that she used to meet there with Yates. I wanted—I don't really know what I wanted to do when I found them. Maybe punch him in the face." He rubbed his hands over his jeans as if to clean them, but the blood stuck to his skin. "Please, at least stop pretending to be her now."

My body shook. I barely felt the rippling, but from the look on Devon's face I knew that I was no longer Madison.

His chest shuddered with a breath. "She still needs medical treatment. I couldn't heal her completely; I'm still too weak from healing myself."

Stroking Kate's hair, I looked over at Ryan's body. His eyes were wide and directed at me.

Devon followed my gaze and shook his head. "I won't bring him back, even if he hasn't moved on yet. I want him gone." I wouldn't have asked him to. Though I wasn't proud of the feeling, I was glad Ryan was dead.

The front door burst open and the sound of thundering foot-steps filled the house.

"We're here!" I called.

Alec and Major stormed in first, a squad of men in black body armor right behind them.

They took in the sight of the dead body on the ground and then of Kate, Devon, and me. I shivered, my arms wrapped around myself. Alec was at our side in a blink. All three of us were covered in blood, but I was mostly uninjured except for what felt like a gaping hole deep within my chest. "I'm okay," I whispered as Alec touched the gash over my eyebrow.

"What happened?" Major asked, his voice controlled.

"It was Ryan. He's a Variant. He could create and control fog."

Major's lips tightened with disappointment, as though he was sad that one precious Variant had slipped through his fingers. Major glanced at Devon, his eyes resting on the dent in his head and the holes in his shirt. But it wasn't my place to decide if Devon wanted his gift to be known.

"Ryan said something about joining Abel's Army."

The room fell silent. Dread flitted across Major's face before he put on his neutral mask. Alec exchanged a look with Major. He knew. They all knew, except for me.

Alec ran his hands over Kate's hair. "Why is she here? She wasn't supposed to be."

"I don't know. But she stopped breathing for a while because she was held under water. She needs to be taken to a hospital."

"What about you?" Alec asked as he lifted Kate into his arms. "Are you sure you're okay?"

"I'm fine." How easily the lie slipped from my lips.

He hesitated, his eyes conflicted.

"Alec, I think you should hurry," Major said.

Alec gave a terse nod, his eyes darting to me once more before he turned. I watched as he walked out. For one last moment, my eyes dropped to Ryan. The other FEA agents were checking him. All except for Major, who only had eyes for Devon and me. He probably knew about Devon already. Major always seemed to know things.

"You should let a doctor check you," he said, looking at my chest.

"I'm fine." I crossed my arms over my body. "What is Abel's Army? And why would Ryan kill to join them?"

Major's dark eyes bored into me, as if he was trying to extract something from my mind. He hesitated. Major never hesitated.

"Abel's Army is a group of Variants."

"Why aren't they part of the FEA?"

"They don't like to play by the rules and they don't want to be under the control of the government. Their leader has his own agenda."

"Abel?" I guessed.

"There's one thing you should never forget: Abel's Army is dangerous. Very dangerous. They're a bunch of criminals, and nothing more. We don't associate with them, under any circumstances." He cleared his throat. "I'll let Stevens take you to headquarters. A helicopter is waiting." Hawk-Face stepped forward when he heard his name.

"Headquarters? But what about Linda and Ronald? They'll be worried."

Devon pushed himself upright, one of his arms wrapped around his chest. "I think it's better if they never see you again," he said softly.

Major gave a nod. "This mission is over, Tessa."

CHAPTER 24

I spent the next two days in bed, recovering; on the third day I couldn't hide anymore.

Holly sank down on the edge of my bed and put a hand on my shoulder. Her hair was fury-red, just the way she'd promised in her e-mail. "Major wants to see you in his office."

I lifted my head from the pillow. "He's back?"

"Alec and Major returned this morning. The entire agency is talking about Abel's Army."

I sat up. "You didn't say anything, did you?" I whispered. I'd told Holly everything last night: in the safety of darkness the words had plummeted from my mouth, and afterward I'd felt as though a weight had been lifted off my shoulders. But Major would be furious if he determined that I was the source of the gossip.

Hurt flickered in her eyes. "Of course not."

"I'm sorry. It's just I don't know what to think anymore. I guess it'll take a while before I'll be back to my old self."

I untangled myself from the blankets and began changing into jeans and a clean T-shirt.

"You didn't tell me," Holly whispered.

I slipped into my jeans before glancing up at her. "Tell you what?"

"That he cut you too."

My hand flew to the *A* over my rib cage. I'd managed to hide it from her until now. "He didn't—he cut me when I was in Madison's body. I thought it would disappear once I changed back. But—" Ryan had left his mark on me. A constant reminder—something, some little part of Madison I'd carry with me until the bitter end. There was only one person who could have removed the mark from my body and he was the one person I couldn't ask. Not after what had happened.

Holly nodded but the sadness in her face was too much.

Outside the room, whispered voices carried through the corridor. The common room was crowded with people, laughing and talking. I walked past them. I'd never felt farther away from life at the FEA. I'd changed during my time as Madison and I didn't think it was something that could be undone.

Tanner fell into step beside me. "Hey Tess, I heard you kicked some serious ass in Livingston. Well done."

I stopped, frozen by his words, and stared at him, unsure if he was pulling my leg. Slowly his grin faded. "That wasn't the right thing to say, huh?" He rubbed his mohawk.

"Sorry, I'm just not in the mood for congratulations. I don't really feel like a winner."

He nodded. "Alec asked for you. It was the first thing he said when he got back."

I forced a smile. "Thanks for telling me. I need to go. Major's waiting."

Major's door was open. Hesitantly I stepped inside. Alec and Major both stood in front of the picture window, looking outward. It seemed like they were arguing about something. Alec shook his head, his expression angrier than I'd ever seen it. I took a step closer, hoping to catch a snippet of their conversation. Suddenly they fell silent and turned to look at me. Without another word from Major, Alec turned and left the room, his hand brushing mine as he passed. The door fell shut and a crushing silence engulfed me.

Major sank down in his chair, and after a moment, I crossed the room and sat across from him. He pointed toward a cup. "I asked Martha to make you tea. She said you like chai."

I reached for the cup and blew on the steaming liquid, breathing in the scent of cinnamon and something spicier. A bit like Alec. I took a sip, knowing that Major was watching me. I cradled the cup against my chest. "Did you talk to Devon?"

Major nodded.

"And?"

"I told him the truth. He's one of us. He'd figured most of it out by himself anyway." He paused for a long moment. "And I invited him to join us."

I jerked. Hot liquid sloshed over the edge of the cup and soaked my shirt, burning the skin beneath. I put the cup down. "What did he say?"

"He said yes."

How would I ever face him again?

"Devon knows that what we did was necessary to catch the killer. He accepts it." Major straightened the cuffs of his shirt. "And there's someone else who'll join ranks with us soon."

"Another Variant?" For a crazy moment I was sure that Major had convinced Devon to bring Ryan back from the dead.

"Phil Faulkner; I know you mentioned him to Alec once."

I gave a nod. So I had been right. Phil was a Variant. "What's his Variation?"

"Venom. His tear ducts and the glands on his palms produce a toxin, a strong sedative."

I thought back to my few encounters with Phil. I'd never paid much attention to him, but something I'd noticed came back to me.

"That's why he sometimes wore those fingerless gloves?"

"Correct. When emotionally challenged, he has some trouble controlling his glands, but we'll be able to help him with that." Excitement lined Major's face. A new Variant was a big deal and now he had two.

"We found letters and documents in the house where Ryan attacked you. Apparently three Variant families moved to Livingston during World War II, worried the government would use them as weapons. They decided to hide and live lives free of their Variations." His lips tightened in obvious disapproval. "Linda Chambers's parents, Ryan's grandparents, and Phil's grandmother."

"And nobody knew?"

"Since Variations often jump a generation, neither Ryan's nor Phil's parents were Variants, and they had no idea. Phil's grandmother told him the truth. Alec and I talked to her and convinced her it was best if Phil joined the FEA. Unfortunately, Linda Chambers's parents died without telling anyone, and so Devon never understood what was happening to him."

"How about Madison; did she have a Variation?"

"Not that we are aware of. Devon claims he's the only Variant in his family and I don't have any reason to doubt him." He paused before adding, "We decided not to burden Mr. and Mrs. Chambers with the knowledge of Variants just yet. Regarding the rest of town, the FEA let Summers and a few others run their magic. According to the local police and the media, Ryan was merely a teen sociopath with a drug problem."

Major drummed his fingers against his desk. He seemed to ponder how much more he should tell me. "Long before you joined us, way before you were even born, Abel's Army was a part of the FEA. But almost two decades ago, they broke things off and now they're recruiting members for their own cause. While we are more than happy to help the government with their larger counter-terrorism efforts, Abel's Army is only too keen to offer their talents to the highest bidder."

"So the agents weren't kidnapped? They joined Abel's Army of their own accord?" It seemed impossible that someone would choose Abel's Army, a group that encouraged killing, over the FEA.

"That's not what I said. We don't know what happened to the agents. What we do know is that Abel's Army is growing. They aren't content with remaining in the background anymore and they are ruthless."

I opened my mouth but Major raised his hands. "That's all I can say."

"So you don't think Abel's Army forced Ryan to kill? Do you think that maybe they brainwashed him?"

"It's a sad fact that some Variants don't need much incentive to go astray. The same Variation that gifts us with extraordinary talents unfortunately sometimes brings with it a predisposition for mental instability. Ryan was one of those volatile Variants. Abel's Army is particularly interested in them."

"But why?"

Major stared down at his hands—breaking eye contact. "Abel has always been of the opinion that the FEA's practice to confine volatile Variants if they're a danger to the public is wrong. He thinks there are other ways to keep them under control, or that their instability can be useful. And it must be said that many Volatiles are gifted with extraordinary Variations and that whoever manages to use them will have a great advantage."

"So what does the FEA do with volatile Variants? Are they always sent to prison?"

"No. There's no certain way to ascertain if someone's volatile, but if there's a history of mental illness in the person's background, that's a red flag. With the right guidance, though, we could have kept Ryan under control. That's why we try to find Variants as young as possible."

"I think Ryan actually loved Madison," I said quietly.

"He might've loved her, and maybe things would have been different if they hadn't broken up. Maybe it was his tipping point and everything spiraled out of control from there. But we will never find out. The fact is, he got drunk on the power his Variation gave him and that was his greatest downfall."

I nodded.

Major gave me a pointed look. "Emotions are a dangerous thing, Tessa. It's best to keep them under your control at all times."

He made a dismissive gesture and I heaved myself out of the chair. I turned before I reached the door. "Sir, as I'm sure you know, Madison's funeral is in a few days. I'd like to go to say good-bye. I think it would help me get over everything that's happened."

"I'm sorry, but I cannot allow that."

"But sir, I wouldn't give myself away. I would be careful not to be seen."

"I'm not trying to be mean, Tessa. I understand your rationale, but I don't think your being there would be wise. It wouldn't accomplish anything and I think you should stay put for a while."

His expression made it clear that no amount of pleading would change his mind.

I bit my lip and turned around, hoping he hadn't seen how much his refusal hurt me.

"You did well, Tessa. Everyone thinks that. I know you're upset and confused and maybe you even feel a bit guilty, but what you did was honorable. The FEA is trying to protect the general public and you did your part. Soon you'll see it that way, too."

I hoped he was right.

CHAPTER 25

_____

It was five A.M. when I finished my first lap in the pool. I was grateful for the solitude. The sound of a door falling shut broke through my concentration and I swam to the edge of the pool, looking for the source. Alec watched me from afar. He was wearing black pajama pants. I doubted he planned on swimming in them. I swam toward the ladder and climbed out of the pool, careful to keep my arms in front of my body and the heinous mark I didn't want him to see. "What are you doing up so early?"

"I couldn't sleep," he said. "And I saw you heading for the pool. I've been wanting to talk to you."

The sound of water lapping over the edge of the pool filled the silence. I couldn't look away from his eyes even though I wanted to, couldn't move even though I wanted to bridge the few steps between us. I dropped my arms and stared at my bare feet, breaking the spell of his gaze.

Alec sucked in a breath. I blinked up at him through my wet lashes, wondering what the matter was until I realized what he was staring at. The red _A_ cut into my skin peeked out from under my swimsuit. I covered it with my palm and turned to walk away, my skin aflame with anger and mortification. His hands on my shoulders stopped me. I closed my eyes, hating how much my body still craved his touch, how it overwhelmed me every time he was close, even though I'd tried so many times to forget him. He spun me around and gently pushed my hand aside.

"You don't know how much I wish he wasn't dead. How much I wish I could kill him myself."

The viciousness of his words mingled with the roughness of his voice washed over me, filling me with a strange sense of relief.

Gently he touched his fingers to the mark. "Does it still hurt?"

The question felt weird coming from Alec. I looked up at him, not caring if he caught the emotion in my eyes. "Nothing ever hurt as much as watching you with Kate."

He stepped back. His eyes wandered over my face, and suddenly it felt like he could see through every layer I'd built to protect myself. "Why do you love her?" I'd asked myself that so often; ever since they returned from their first mission as a couple.

"I don't—I can't—" He exhaled. "It's complicated with me and Kate."

"Complicated," I repeated. "Okay." That was all he had to say about the matter?

He cupped my cheek, and I leaned into the touch. I knew he wanted to kiss me again, knew it from the look in his eyes and the way his fingers traced my cheek, but even more than that, I knew I couldn't let it happen. Not as long as there was Kate. Not as long as every kiss was nothing more than an empty promise. His eyes flickered with hesitation as if he was thinking the same thing.

I was worth more than that.

And though it was almost physically painful, I stepped away. His fingers slipped off my face. "I'm sorry Alec, but I can't do this anymore. Whatever's between us, consider it over." Before I could change my mind, I walked away. He didn't follow me.

The sun was rising. Golden beams caught on the piles of toast and dozens of eggs Martha had laid out for her breakfast preparations. I ate my second plate of French toast. One of the things I'd missed most about the FEA was Martha and her cooking. She took care of me and cooked for me the same way Linda had done. The FEA wasn't a traditional family, but I had come to realize that it was close. Maybe that was enough.

I'd spilled my guts to Martha about my poolside talk with Alec and she'd listened patiently. She'd given me the same advice she always did when I talked to her about Alec: everything will fall into place if I could just be patient. But I'd run out of patience a long time ago. I'd have to find a way to move on without him.

I finished my last bite of raspberries and put my fork down. Even Martha's fabulous food couldn't calm my stomach. What I was about to do was more than just a minor breach of the rules.

"Madison's funeral is today. Tony asked me to talk to you," Martha said suddenly.

"Why?" I whispered. Had Major found out about my plan? Had Kate gotten a glimpse into my head and seen it?

"He's worried about you. He noticed that you haven't put Livingston behind you yet." She wrapped an arm around my shoulder. "You have to learn to let go."

"I know." I nodded solemnly. I'd learned that lesson this morning. I didn't look directly at her, too worried she might see something in my face that would give me away.

"Sometimes a good-bye from afar is enough." She kissed my temple. "You need to release your pain. We want our old Tessa back."

"I want the old Tessa back, too. Minus her Alec obsession," I said with a shaky smile.

Martha put a hand over her heart, her eyes widening ridiculously. "Be still my heart. Did you just make a joke, *mein Mädchen*?"

I pressed my forehead against her shoulder, feeling guilty for not heeding her pleas. But I'd made up my mind and nothing would stop me now.

I hurried back to my room, where the clothes Holly had stolen from Summers were waiting for me. I slipped into them and shifted into the image of Summers. Holly had made sure that I wouldn't run into the real Summers, who was giving Holly a private Variation lesson.

I forced myself to walk through the corridors slowly, despite my fear of running into Major. Some of the tension disappeared from my body once I was finally outside and approaching the airfield. Tanner was polishing his favorite helicopter and straightened when he saw me.

"We need someone to fly Tessa to Livingston. Major and I have decided to let her attend the funeral. Everything should be ready in ten minutes." Summers's voice came out strong and certain.

Tanner frowned but nodded. "Sure thing."

I turned and left before I could give myself away and returned ten minutes later in my own body. My heart didn't stop pounding until we were off the ground, and even then I barely allowed myself to relax. Once Major found out what I'd done, and there was no doubt that he would, I'd be punished. But I'd worry about that later. For now, I knew what I needed to do.

CHAPTER 26

The helicopter dropped me off in a meadow near Livingston before turning to make its way back to headquarters. Nobody had stopped us. Surprisingly Tanner hadn't tried to entertain me during the flight. Maybe he'd sensed that I wasn't in the mood for joking before a funeral. I planned to spend the night in a motel in Manlow and take a train back to the FEA the next morning. I reasoned that maybe Tanner wouldn't get in too much trouble that way.

Instead of going directly to the cemetery and waiting for the funeral to begin, I walked to the Chambers' house. I snuck into the back garden and peered through the living room windows.

Everyone was gathered inside. Linda and Ronald, Madison's aunts and uncles, her grandparents, Ana, and Devon. He was the only one who understood what had happened, the only one who knew his sister hadn't died a week ago but had actually been gone for much longer. Somehow Major had convinced him to keep it from his family, to tell them the lie the FEA had prepared.

Devon looked out into the garden as if he could feel my presence. I ducked. It wasn't right for me to be here. This was their private moment of grief. I had no place in their lives.

A door creaked—the back screen door. I knew the sound by heart. Before I could slink away, Devon stood in front of me, dressed in black from head to toe. There were dark shadows beneath his eyes.

I tried to back away from him but he cornered me at the end of the backyard, bordering on the forest. His hand curled around my arm, preventing me from slipping away. I didn't try to shake him off. Whatever he had to say, I would bear it. I deserved it all. I pulled my coat tighter around my body and looked up. Fatigue crowded at the edges of his eyes and mouth. "You shouldn't have come." His voice was quiet and gentle. A lethal blow served with serenity.

I recoiled and his hand slipped lower, his fingertips tracing the bare skin of my wrist. Sparks shot through my arm at the contact. I jerked, but his touch remained steady. His eyes searched mine. Softly he said, "You're hurting."

I freed my wrist from his fingers and wrapped my arms around myself. "I'm not hurt," I whispered.

"You know what I mean."

I scanned the trees, their withered bark green with moss. The air hung around us, heavy and humid. It had barely stopped raining over the last few days.

"Sometimes anguish can be so strong that it turns into something physical, something I can feel."

"Can you heal it like you do wounds?" My voice was so quiet, I wasn't sure he heard it over the pitter-patter of rain hitting the leaves above us. But then he shook his head. I nodded, blinking back the tears threatening to spill over my eyes. I took a shuddering breath.

"So what did you tell your parents?" For a dangerous moment I'd wanted to say "our parents."

Devon looked back at the house as if he could see them through the walls. "Major Sanchez told them. He said that Madison followed Ryan into the house and he killed her. I tried to save her, but it was too late." His voice was hollow, the words mechanical.

"They believed him?"

Devon let out an empty laugh. "Do you even have to ask?"

I shook my head. Of course not. The story made sense. And Major could be very convincing.

He cleared his throat. "I need to get back inside. We have to leave soon." His eyes held mine but they were guarded. "Tessa, I'm sorry. But I don't think you should come. It'll only make it worse." Without another word he headed for the back door and disappeared inside.

Though Devon didn't want me to attend the funeral, I couldn't bring myself to leave. I'd come all the way from headquarters and risked everything to find closure.

The cemetery was crowded with people. Everyone, it seemed, felt compelled to say good-bye to a girl who'd died too young.

I followed in their wake—like a shadow. Tears rolled down my cheeks but they weren't for Madison alone. I'd said good-bye to her weeks ago. This good-bye was for everyone. Linda and Ronald, Mom and Dad as I'd come to think of them, walked ahead of the crowd, the mourners right behind them like a cloud of sadness. But in front of them all, like a beacon of light, was Madison's white casket. It glowed despite the gloom of the day.

People gathered around the hole in the ground. An ocean of black clothes and pale faces. So many faces I knew. People I'd called friends in recent weeks. People whose laughter was as familiar as my own. People who didn't know the real me, and never would. I stood on a hill, shrouded between trees, with a good view over the gravesite. Nobody would notice me there.

Ana leaned against her stepfather, clutching at his coat. Her face was blotchy and for once she wasn't wearing makeup. I felt a pang when I realized that the friendship I'd felt with her had never existed, our warmth had never been real.

I didn't dare look at Linda and Ronald just yet, afraid of what I would see on their faces and how it would make me feel. I tucked my body behind one of the trees, afraid that if Devon caught sight of me he would come to send me away. Then something else caught my attention. A good distance behind the family stood a man in a black coat and sunglasses. He wasn't paying attention to the funeral; he was staring at me. I didn't recognize him, in fact I was fairly certain I'd never seen him before. Had I drawn attention to myself standing up here alone? Was it really that obvious that I didn't belong here? He probably wondered why I was hiding between trees and gawking at him. I looked away and pulled up the collar of my coat.

The first notes sounded of the song her family had chosen. "The Rose."

I stared at the golden pendant in my hand. When I looked up, my eyes finally sought out Madison's family. Linda clutched the front of Ronald's suit, her tearful, pale face half buried in his chest. I wanted to go over and wrap my arms around them. I wanted to tell them I was sorry—for more things than they'd ever know—and I wanted to tell them how much I'd come to care for them. I wanted to tell them that I'd do anything for parents like them.

Linda and Ronald walked up to the gaping hole in the ground and threw white roses on top of the casket. Devon was next, a few tears trailing slowly over his face. The others followed until an ocean of pure white covered the wood of Madison's final resting place. Linda raised her head and for a moment our eyes met. My body flooded with stolen memories and emotions, and my heart swelled with a love I knew I shouldn't feel. Her face showed no recognition at all. To her I didn't exist and never would.

I clutched the rose pendant against my chest so tightly that the edges of it cut into my palm. It was a gift that wasn't mine and never had been—like the love Madison's parents had showed me. And yet sometimes I'd dared to imagine how it would be if they loved me, if *someone* loved me as unconditionally as they'd loved Madison.

More than two years had passed since I'd left home and not once had my mom tried to contact me, not once had she asked if I was well. She didn't know a thing about my life now. Unconditional love was something my mother didn't understand. My hand clenched until my nails dug into my skin, but no matter how hard I pressed, the ache deep within me overshadowed anything else I could possibly feel.

A gentle touch took hold of my hand and loosened my fist. The hand entwined its fingers with mine and I didn't need to look up to know who it was. I'd recognize that smell of spring and spearmint, and the steely strength behind his careful touch, any time. He'd found me; he always did.

"What are you doing here?" I asked softly.

"Holly told me. I came looking for you. I knew Summers and Major wouldn't have allowed you to attend the funeral, so I took a helicopter and rushed here."

"Major let you take another helicopter? So he knows?"

"I didn't ask him. But he'll notice eventually." His voice had a hard edge to it but softened for his next words. He had defied Major—for me? "My God, Tessa, I was so worried. You shouldn't be here alone. You have no clue how dangerous it is out here."

"Dangerous?"

"I overheard Major talking to Summers. Abel's Army has a spy in town who kept an eye on Ryan and the investigations. They know far more than we realized. And do you think they would pass up the chance to kidnap you?"

"But why would they pay me any attention?"

"Major thinks that Abel's Army realized the FEA sent you to pose as Madison and now they want you for themselves. He's been discussing ways to protect you. They want to keep you on lockdown in headquarters until this whole thing blows over."

I was still in shock. "But why would Abel's Army want me?"

"You are far more valuable than you think." For a moment, he looked like he wanted to take the words back. Was there more? "Your Variation would be very useful to them. You can be whoever you want to be, whoever *they* want you to be. Just imagine the possibilities for someone as ruthless as Abel. Believe me, Abel's Army would be crazy not to target you."

I felt cold all over. My eyes searched the crowd for the spot where the man with the sunglasses had stood but he was gone.

He hadn't worn the glasses to hide his crying—he'd worn them to hide his eyes.

"There was a man with sunglasses. He was watching me."

Alec gripped my shoulders. "Where is he?"

"I don't know. He was there a minute ago, but he's gone."

"Are you sure he was looking at your face? That he saw your eyes?" His grip tightened until it was almost painful.

"I think so. His sunglasses blocked my view. But if they already know about me, it doesn't really matter that he saw my eyes, right?"

He let go. "Right."

That didn't sound convincing.

"Look, we don't know who the man was. Maybe he wasn't even Abel's Army. And I'm safe in headquarters." I didn't feel the certainty my voice conveyed.

"You're right. They won't get you. I won't let them. I'll do anything to keep you safe." He sounded fierce, as if he'd do anything for me.

I didn't look at him because then he'd have seen it all in my eyes.

"You mean too much to me, Tess."

Those words ignited a hope I wanted to trample down with my FEA-assigned boots before someone else could, before *he* could.

"Why?" The choked sound gave it all away, laid me bare to him, made me vulnerable, but I couldn't help it. I'd been strong for so long, and I was tired of it. So tired of it all.

"You know why."

But those three words weren't enough anymore. They would have been enough a month, even a week ago, but today I needed more. No more empty promises, no matter how beautiful they sounded.

"No, I don't know why. Tell me," I whispered.

He squeezed my hand gently, but I didn't dare look, too scared that his eyes would reveal a hurtful truth. But he took my face into his hands and tipped my head back until his lips were inches from mine.

"I broke up with Kate," he said softly. My eyes grew wide and for a moment I couldn't breathe. "I should have done it long ago. We've been doing nothing but argue. Our relationship has always been a matter of reason, never of love. When I stayed in Livingston to clear things up with Major, I couldn't think about anything but you, and every time I visited Kate in the hospital you were on my mind. And when I saw the mark on your rib cage, I can't describe how that made me feel. I realized how close I'd come to losing you, and when I found out that you were at the funeral . . ." He shook his head, as if it scared him just thinking about it. "I've tried to fight my feelings for you because I thought you were too young and because of Major . . . but I just don't care anymore. I'm tired of resisting, tired of fearing the consequences."

His thumb brushed across my cheek and then his lips pressed against me, warm and soft. I melted into the kiss, relaxing against him. After a moment, he pulled back and exhaled. "I want to do this every day."

I smiled against his mouth. "Then do it."

He pulled back and scanned the area. "We should leave now. I want to get you back to headquarters as soon as possible."

Alec led me down the hill toward the entrance of the cemetery and past the mourners. Devon looked up. Our eyes met, and for the briefest moment I felt a twinge of emotion I couldn't explain. Part of me was glad that he would join the FEA soon, before he could be targeted by Abel's Army, but the other part worried how we would act around each other. Would it be awkward? Or would we try to help each other deal with everything that had happened?

"What about Devon? Who will keep him safe?"

"Before Major and I left Livingston, he assigned Agent Stevens to watch out for Devon. I saw his car in front of the graveyard."

Relief settled in me. I didn't want anything to happen to Devon, couldn't bear the thought of never seeing his smile again. Alec wrapped his arm around my waist, and I let the rightness of his touch carry away the doubt and worry.

As we passed through the gates of the cemetery, I glanced over my shoulder one last time. I didn't spot the man with the sunglasses but I was inexplicably sure he was watching—that *Abel's Army* was watching *me*.

Major had made it sound like Abel would stop at nothing to get what he wanted. He had already taken two agents. And if Alec's worries were justified, I was the one he wanted next.

ACKNOWLEDGMENTS

I owe thanks to the following people, who made this book possible:

My fantastic agent, Jill Grinberg, for finding the perfect home for me and my book. Having you at my side during the sub process was the best thing that could have happened to me. Katelyn Detweiler, who's always there to sort things out and answer my e-mails. Cheryl Pientka, who tries to get *Impostor* out into the world and who never seems to grow tired of my questions! I loved meeting the three of you in New York!

My fabulous editor, Caroline Donofrio, for falling in love with Tessa and her story, for swooning over Devon and Alec, and for making this book so much better.

The Razorbill team for wanting me and my book, and for giving it a stunning cover!

My friend Elke, who loved *Impostor* from the start and compared it to Vampire Academy, a series we both love. Little did she know back then that I'd end up sharing a publishing home with VA! You are a prophet, my friend!

My crit partners, Kathy, Shari, and Tracy for helping me through the tough times that followed after writing this book. You know what I'm talking about. I wouldn't have stayed sane without you.

The many beta readers that made this book better: Shveta Thakrar, Trisha Wolfe, Heather Anastasiu, Nikki Loftin, and McCormick Templeman. You rock!

But the absolutely biggest thanks go to my husband, who never lost faith in me, who talked me off the ledge more than once, and who was there for me during the many sleepless nights I spent obsessing over publishing! Danke, dass du immer für mich da bist. Ich liebe dich.